2024

FOS · BOS 12

Fachabitur-Prüfungsaufgaben
mit Lösungen

Bayern

Englisch

STARK

44. ergänzte Auflage
www.stark-verlag.de

Inhaltsverzeichnis

Original-Fachabiturprüfungen

Sobald die Original-Prüfungsaufgaben 2023 freigegeben sind, können sie als PDF auf der Plattform MyStark heruntergeladen werden (Zugangscode vgl. Umschlaginnenseite).

Sollten nach Erscheinen dieses Bandes noch wichtige Änderungen in der Prüfung vom bayerischen Kultusministerium bekannt gegeben werden, finden Sie aktuelle Informationen dazu ebenfalls auf der Plattform MyStark.

Autoren

Hinweise und Tipps, Übungsaufgaben, Lösungen zu den Prüfungsaufgaben:
Günther Albrecht und Michael Albrecht

digitale Kurzgrammatik: Redaktion

Vorwort

Liebe Schülerinnen, liebe Schüler,

dieser Band hilft Ihnen bei der gezielten Vorbereitung auf die **Fachabiturprüfung** in Englisch in der **12. Klasse** an den Beruflichen Oberschulen in Bayern.

Durch die Einführung des **LehrplanPLUS** findet die Fachabiturprüfung seit dem Schuljahr 2018/2019 in etwas anderer Form statt als in den Vorjahren. Mit dem vorliegenden Buch können Sie sich optimal auf die aktuellen Anforderungen vorbereiten:

In einem **umfangreichen Hinweisteil** erhalten Sie detaillierte Informationen darüber, wie die Prüfung genau abläuft, welche Aufgabenstellungen vorkommen können und welche Hilfsmittel Sie benutzen dürfen. **Tipps zur Bearbeitung der Aufgaben** geben Ihnen Sicherheit für die Prüfung. Eine Sammlung von ***useful phrases*** hilft Ihnen, einen umfassenden Wortschatz für die Bearbeitung der *writing*-Aufgabe und die mündliche Prüfung aufzubauen.

Anhand der **Original-Prüfungsaufgaben** der letzten Jahre können Sie dann gezielt für das Fachabitur trainieren. Da der Prüfungsteil *reading* auch nach Einführung des neuen Lehrplans nahezu gleich geblieben ist, eignen sich die Prüfungsaufgaben 2016 bis 2018 weiterhin hervorragend zum Üben. Auch die *writing*-Aufgaben aus diesen Jahren können Sie ideal als Vorübungen zum neuen Aufgabenformat *material-based writing* verwenden. Darüber hinaus enthält der Band **Übungsaufgaben im Stil der Prüfung** zur Vorbereitung auf das *material-based writing* und das aktuelle Format der mündlichen Gruppenprüfung. Mit den Original-Prüfungsaufgaben ab 2019 können Sie schließlich jeweils eine vollständige Prüfung im neuen Format bearbeiten und testen, ob Sie für den „Ernstfall" gut gerüstet sind.

Zu allen Aufgaben finden Sie **Lösungsvorschläge**, mit denen Sie Ihre Lösungen kontrollieren und herausfinden können, wo Sie noch Schwächen haben.

Wir wünschen Ihnen viel Freude bei der Arbeit mit diesem Buch und viel Erfolg in Ihrer Fachabiturprüfung!

Günther Albrecht
Michael Albrecht

Hinweise zu den digitalen Zusätzen

Auf alle digitalen Zusätze können Sie online über die Plattform **MyStark** zugreifen. Ihren persönlichen Zugangscode finden Sie auf der Umschlaginnenseite vorne im Buch.

PDF der Original-Prüfungsaufgaben 2023

Sobald die Original-Prüfungsaufgaben 2023 zur Veröffentlichung freigegeben sind, können sie als PDF auf der Plattform MyStark heruntergeladen werden.

Digitale Kurzgrammatik

Mit der Kurzgrammatik können Sie sich eine knappe und verständliche Übersicht über die wichtigsten Themenfelder der englischen Grammatik herunterladen. Schlagen Sie hier die Grammatikregeln zu Fehlern nach, die Sie noch häufig machen.

Interaktive Aufgaben – *Basic Language Skills*

Anhand zahlreicher **interaktiver Aufgaben** können Sie Grundlagen wie **Hörverstehen**, **Leseverstehen** und **Sprachverwendung im Kontext** trainieren und sich auf diese Weise eine sichere Basis für eine gute Sprachbeherrschung erarbeiten:

- „**Listening**" – authentische Audiodateien mit vielfältigen Aufgaben, die Ihr Hörverstehen testen
- „**Reading**" – abwechslungsreiche Lesetexte und dazugehörige Aufgaben
- „**English in Use**" mit gemischten Aufgaben rund um den Gebrauch der englischen Sprache
- Alle Aufgaben sind interaktiv, d. h., Sie können sie direkt am PC bearbeiten und erhalten sofort eine Rückmeldung zu Ihren Antworten.

Web-App „MindCards“

Mit der Web-App „**MindCards**“ können Sie am Smartphone Vokabeln lernen. Auf diesen interaktiven Karteikarten finden Sie hilfreiche Wendungen, die Sie beim Schreiben von Texten oder im mündlichen Sprachgebrauch einsetzen können.
Scannen Sie einfach die QR-Codes oder verwenden Sie folgende Links, um zu den „MindCards“ zu gelangen:

https://www.stark-verlag.de/mindcards/writing-2
https://www.stark-verlag.de/mindcards/speaking-2

Writing

Speaking

Hinweise und Tipps

Vorbereitung auf die Prüfung

- Arbeiten Sie im Laufe des Schuljahres kontinuierlich mit und beteiligen Sie sich aktiv am Unterricht. Lassen Sie Hausaufgaben und freiwillige Übungen von Ihrem Lehrer oder Ihrer Lehrerin korrigieren. So erhalten Sie eine Rückmeldung über Ihre Stärken und Schwächen.
- Beschäftigen Sie sich auch in Ihrer Freizeit mit Englisch. Lesen Sie englische Bücher oder schauen Sie Filme in der Originalsprache an (die englischen Untertitel können meist bei Bedarf eingeblendet werden). Hören oder sehen Sie regelmäßig Nachrichten oder interessante Sendungen auf Englisch. Im Internet finden Sie eine Vielzahl englischer Seiten, z. B. mit aktuellen Filmkritiken oder Podcasts zu den unterschiedlichsten Themen. Die meisten englischsprachigen Zeitungen, Radio- und Fernsehsender bieten diesen Service auf ihren Internetseiten an. Sie erweitern so Ihren Wortschatz und werden feststellen, wie viel leichter Sie Englisch verstehen, wenn Sie die Sprache regelmäßig hören oder lesen.
- Suchen Sie den Kontakt zu Native Speakern und sprechen Sie möglichst oft Englisch. In vielen Städten gibt es deutsch-amerikanische Institute oder Zentren, die Stammtische und regelmäßige Treffen abhalten, und das Internet bietet weitere Möglichkeiten (per Chat, Lerntandem o. Ä.), um sich mit Muttersprachler*innen auszutauschen. Je mehr Sie aktiv sprechen, desto sicherer werden Sie und desto gelassener können Sie in die Prüfung gehen.
- Nutzen Sie die Übungsaufgaben und Original-Prüfungen in diesem Buch, um sich gezielt auf die Prüfungssituation vorzubereiten. Notieren Sie beim Bearbeiten der Aufgaben, wie lange Sie jeweils brauchen, und machen Sie sich anhand Ihrer Erfahrungen einen Zeitplan, an dem Sie sich auch in der Prüfung orientieren. Üben Sie besonders die Aufgabenformate, die Ihnen noch Schwierigkeiten bereiten.
- Die Prüfungsteile *material-based writing* und die mündliche Gruppenprüfung lassen sich leichter bewältigen, wenn Sie auf hilfreiche Wendungen zurückgreifen können. Eine Liste solcher *useful phrases* finden Sie in diesem Kapitel.

Aufbau der Prüfung und Bewertung

Die Prüfung besteht in Englisch aus einem schriftlichem Teil und einer mündlichen Gruppenprüfung.

Schriftliche Fachabiturprüfung

Die schriftliche Prüfung setzt sich aus den Bereichen ***reading*** und ***material-based writing*** zusammen. Für den *reading*-Teil haben Sie 90 Minuten Zeit und für das *material-based writing* 60 Minuten. Zwischen den beiden Teilen findet eine Pause von 30 Minuten statt. Als Hilfsmittel dürfen Sie ein einsprachiges Wörterbuch benutzen. Klären Sie aber in jedem Fall vorab mit Ihrer Englischlehrkraft, ob Ihr Exemplar zur Prüfung zugelassen ist.
Sowohl beim *reading* als auch beim *material-based writing* können Sie maximal 24 BE erzielen, insgesamt also 48 BE. Ihre Note für den schriftlichen Teil der Prüfung wird nach folgendem Notenschlüssel ermittelt:

Notentendenz	Punkteschema	BE
+	15	48–46
1	14	45–44
–	13	43–41
+	12	40–39
2	11	38–36
–	10	35–34
+	9	33–32
3	8	31
–	7	30–29

Notentendenz	Punkteschema	BE
+	6	28–27
4	5	26
–	4	25–24
+	3	23–22
5	2	21–19
–	1	18–17
6	0	16–0

Mündliche Gruppenprüfung

Die mündliche Gruppenprüfung dauert ca. 20 bis 25 Minuten; dazu kommen 20 Minuten Vorbereitungszeit. Es werden jeweils 4–5 Personen gleichzeitig geprüft.

Berechnung der Gesamtnote

Die schriftliche Prüfung wird im Vergleich zur mündlichen Gruppenprüfung doppelt gewichtet. Wenn Sie also beispielsweise im schriftlichen Teil 10 Notenpunkte erreicht haben und in der mündlichen Gruppenprüfung 8 Punkte, ergibt sich folgende Gesamtnote: (2 x 10 Punkte + 8 Punkte) : 3 = 9,33 Punkte (Note 3+)

Im Folgenden werden die einzelnen Prüfungsbereiche genauer dargestellt.

Der *reading*-Teil umfasst mehrere Aufgaben zum Leseverstehen, die sich auf zwei oder drei Originaltexte beziehen (Gesamtumfang ca. 2400 Wörter). Neben Sachtexten (z. B. Zeitungsberichten, Interviews oder Reportagen) kann auch ein literarischer Text verwendet werden (siehe z. B. 2019-7 f.). Lesen Sie den Text und die daran anschließenden Aufgaben zuerst genau und konzentriert durch. Schlagen Sie unbekannte Wörter erst nach, wenn Sie feststellen, dass sie für die Beantwortung einer Aufgabe wichtig sind.
Der Prüfungsteil *reading* hat sich auch durch die Einführung des LehrplanPLUS kaum geändert, sodass Sie sich mit allen Original-Prüfungen aus diesem Band optimal vorbereiten können.

Aufgabentypen

- *multiple choice questions*
  Zu jeder *multiple-choice*-Aufgabe gibt es in der Regel vier Wahlmöglichkeiten, von denen genau eine zutrifft. Die Aufgaben können sich z. B. auf den Textinhalt beziehen, aber auch auf die Haltung des Autors/der Autorin abzielen oder Wortbedeutungen erfragen. Häufig ist angegeben, welche Textabschnitte für die Aufgabe relevant sind, sodass Sie nicht jedes Mal den gesamten Text durchsuchen müssen.
  Die Antwortmöglichkeiten scheinen auf den ersten Blick oft recht ähnlich. Daher ist es wichtig, dass Sie die Optionen sehr sorgfältig lesen und sich die Bedeutung klar machen. Denken Sie daran, dass die „most suitable option", also die am besten passende Möglichkeit, gesucht ist. Vergleichen Sie die Antworten noch einmal genau mit der Frage und wählen Sie die passendste aus.
- *multiple matching*
  Beim *multiple matching* geht es darum, richtige Zuordnungen zu treffen. Sie erhalten z. B. eine Liste von Personen und eine Liste von Aussagen und müssen die Aussagen den richtigen Personen zuordnen. Am besten markieren Sie sich im Text mit verschiedenen Farben die entsprechenden Bezugspunkte (Namen, Institutionen etc.). So können Sie die einzelnen Aussagen leichter zuordnen.
  Manchmal müssen Sie auch entscheiden, welche Überschriften zu welchem Textabschnitt passen oder Sie sollen Sätze, die aus dem Text entnommen wurden, der richtigen „Lücke" im Text zuordnen.
  In der Regel sind beim *multiple matching* mehr Antwortmöglichkeiten vorgegeben als für die Zuordnung nötig wären – lassen Sie sich also nicht durch falsche Auswahlmöglichkeiten in die Irre führen.
- *gapped summary*
  Bei diesem Aufgabenformat wird Ihnen eine Zusammenfassung *(summary)* des Textes oder von Teilen des Textes vorgelegt. Ihre Aufgabe ist es, Lücken *(gaps)* in der Zusammenfassung mit passenden Wörtern aus dem Text zu füllen. Beachten Sie, dass die einzusetzenden Wörter nicht verändert werden dürfen! Zudem müssen die Wörter im *summary* dieselbe Wortart aufweisen wie im Lesetext. Wird etwa das

Wort „challenge" im Lesetext als Verb gebraucht, so muss es auch im *summary* als Verb verwendet werden (und nicht etwa als Nomen). Pro Wort ist genau eine Lücke vorgesehen – wenn Sie also eine Phrase einsetzen sollen, die aus zwei Wörtern besteht (z. B. „on purpose"), sind entsprechend zwei Lücken vorgegeben. Bei Wörtern, die durch einen Bindestrich miteinander verbunden sind (z. B. „long-term"), gibt es nur eine Lücke. Das *summary* folgt nicht unbedingt der Reihenfolge des Textes – die gesuchten Wörter kommen aber im selben Sinnzusammenhang vor wie im Lesetext.

- *short-answer questions*
  Bei diesem Aufgabentyp müssen Sie Fragen zum Inhalt oder zur Sprache des Textes beantworten oder eine Tabelle/Mindmap o. Ä. mit den passenden Informationen ergänzen. Sie können die Antworten wörtlich aus dem Text übernehmen oder eine eigenständige Formulierung wählen. Rechtschreibfehler führen nur dann zu einem Punktabzug, wenn dadurch der Sinn Ihrer Antwort nicht mehr erkennbar ist.
- *mediation*
  Bei der Sprachmittlungsaufgabe müssen Sie Fragen zum (englischen) Lesetext auf Deutsch beantworten. Eine Mediation ist aber keine wörtliche Übersetzung. Vielmehr sollen Sie zeigen, dass Sie die wesentlichen Aussagen des Textes bzw. einzelner Textpassagen richtig erfasst haben und auf Deutsch wiedergeben können.

Prüfungsteil *Material-Based Writing*

Für das *material-based writing* wird Ihnen eine bestimmte Situation mit einer konkreten **Frage- und Problemstellung** vorgegeben – beispielsweise, dass Sie für eine Zeitschrift einen Artikel über das Thema „Plastikmüll" schreiben sollen. Zusätzlich werden Ihnen **drei Materialien** zu diesem Thema vorgelegt. Dabei kann es sich um Cartoons, Statistiken, Zitate o. Ä. handeln. Mindestens eine der Quellen muss auf Deutsch und mindestens eine auf Englisch sein. Ausgehend von der Aufgabenstellung sollen Sie einen englischen Text verfassen, in dem Sie alle drei Materialien sinnvoll in Ihre Argumentation einbinden, ohne sie jedoch wörtlich zu zitieren oder detailliert zu beschreiben. Ihr Text soll mindestens **300 Wörter** umfassen.
Sie haben für diese Aufgabe **60 Minuten** Zeit und können zwischen **zwei Themen** wählen.

Gehen Sie bei der Bearbeitung folgendermaßen vor:

- Sehen Sie sich zunächst **beide Themenstellungen** inklusive Materialien an und entscheiden Sie sich für das Thema, das Ihnen besser liegt und zu dem Sie mehr Hintergrundwissen mitbringen.
- Lesen Sie sich die **Aufgabenstellung** sehr genau durch. Meist sind darin bereits konkrete Vorgaben enthalten, wie Ihr Text aufgebaut sein soll (z. B. dass Sie zunächst ein Problem beschreiben und anschließend Lösungsvorschläge machen sollen).

- Überlegen Sie sich außerdem, welche **Textsorte** von Ihnen verlangt wird und an wen sich der Text richtet (**Zielgruppe**). Abhängig davon sind u. U. bestimmte formale Kriterien zu beachten (beispielsweise ist für einen Artikel eine Überschrift nötig und der Sprachstil sollte in der Regel eher sachlich sein).
- Sehen Sie sich die **Materialien** genau an. Überlegen Sie, welche Aspekte Sie daraus in Ihre Argumentation einbeziehen können und in welcher Reihenfolge Sie sie anführen möchten. Sie müssen die Materialien nicht im Detail beschreiben, es muss jedoch deutlich werden, dass Sie auf alle drei Materialien Bezug nehmen.
- Fertigen Sie (ausgehend von Ihrer Analyse der Aufgabenstellung und der Materialien) eine **Grobgliederung** an, die Ihnen als Leitfaden beim Schreiben dient.
- Beginnen Sie nun mit dem **Ausformulieren** des Textes. Führen Sie Ihre Leserschaft mit einem einleitenden Gedanken an die Thematik heran. Achten Sie darauf, dass Ihr Text sprachlich korrekt und inhaltlich schlüssig ist. Nutzen Sie Konnektoren und andere *useful phrases* (z. B. „On the one hand, … On the other hand, …", „Summing up, …"), um Ihre Argumentationsschritte nachvollziehbar zu machen. Im Schlussteil sollten Sie Ihren Text mit einem Resümee oder Ausblick abrunden.

Insgesamt können Sie beim *material-based writing* bis zu 24 BE erzielen. Bei der Bewertung Ihres Textes spielen folgende Kriterien eine Rolle:

- **Inhalt (8 BE):** Wurde die Aufgabenstellung richtig erfasst? Wurden alle Materialien sinnvoll verwendet? Ist Ihre Argumentation logisch schlüssig?
- **Verständlichkeit der sprachlichen Ausgestaltung (8 BE):** Ist Ihr Text zügig lesbar oder beeinträchtigen Fehler das Verständnis? Werden die Sätze sinnvoll miteinander verknüpft?
- **Natürlichkeit der sprachlichen Ausgestaltung (8 BE):** Ist Ihr Text in einem weitgehend idiomatischen und abwechslungsreichen Sprachstil verfasst?

Anhand der **Übungsaufgaben 1 bis 4** und der **Original-Prüfungen ab 2019** können Sie sich einen konkreten Eindruck verschaffen, was in der Prüfung auf Sie zukommt, und das *material-based writing* gezielt trainieren.
Die in diesem Buch enthaltenen Original-Prüfungen bis einschließlich 2018 folgen noch einem etwas anderen Muster. Bis dahin bestand der Prüfungsteil *writing* aus zwei Teilen: Im ersten Teil musste ein Cartoon oder eine Statistik beschrieben werden *(descriptive writing)*, im zweiten Teil wurde eine *composition* verlangt *(argumentative writing)*. Diese Aufgaben eignen sich ideal als Vorübungen für die neue Prüfung, da Kompetenzen wie der richtige Umgang mit Cartoons und Statistiken und das argumentative Schreiben auch beim *material-based writing* vorausgesetzt werden. Tipp: Trainieren Sie diese Kompetenzen zunächst „einzeln" anhand der Original-Prüfungen bis 2018 und bearbeiten Sie dann die komplexeren Aufgaben zum *material-based writing* (Übungsaufgaben und Original-Prüfungen ab 2019).
Auf den nächsten Seiten finden Sie zudem einige ***useful phrases***, die Ihnen für das *material-based writing* nützlich sein können. Prägen Sie sich diese Wendungen gut ein und versuchen Sie, sie bereits beim Üben regelmäßig anzuwenden.

Useful phrases

■ Texte strukturieren

eine Argumentation einleiten	*First of all, ...* *To begin with, ...*
Aspekte ergänzen	*First(ly), ... Second(ly), ... Finally, ...* *In addition, ... / Additionally, ...* *Moreover, ...* *Furthermore, ...* *Besides, ...* *Apart from ...*
Aspekte betonen	*Above all, ...* *Most importantly, ...*
Ähnlichkeiten aufzeigen	*Similarly, ...* *In the same way, ...* *Likewise, ...*
Gegensätze ausdrücken	*However, ...* *Yet ...* *While ...* *... whereas ...* *Although ... / Even though ...* *By contrast, ... / In contrast to ...* *Despite ... / In spite of ...* *Nevertheless, ...* *On the one hand, ... On the other hand, ...*
Beispiele nennen	*For example, ... / ..., for example.* *For instance, ... / ..., for instance.* *..., such as ...* *..., e. g. ...* *Take the case of ...*
Gründe angeben	*Due to ...* *Owing to ...* *That is why ...* *For this reason ...* *... because (of) ...* *As ...* *Since ...*
auf die Folgen von etwas hinweisen	*As a result, ...* *Consequently, ...* *Thus, ...* *Therefore, ...* *Hence, ...*

Bedingungen anführen

If …
Unless …
Provided that …

Schlussfolgerungen ziehen

In conclusion, … / To conclude, …
Summing up, … / To sum up, …
Taking all this into account, …
In brief, …
In a nutshell, …

■ Materialien einbinden

Quellen zitieren

According to (a newspaper report/current research/ recent statistics/a study conducted by …/a poll/ a survey among …), …
Research shows that …
As we can see from …
… once said/wrote that …

Kernaussagen wiedergeben

(The image/poster/cartoon/report/quote/…) shows/represents/illustrates/draws attention to/ hints at/reveals/is meant to criticise …

Statistiken und Diagramme auswerten

to rise/go up/increase (slightly/dramatically/ continually/…)
to rise/go up/increase by …
to rise/go up/increase from … to …
an increase/a rise of …
to double/treble (= sich verdoppeln/verdreifachen)
to surge (= dramatisch zunehmen)
to peak at … (= einen Höchststand erreichen bei)

to drop/go down/decrease/fall (slightly/dramatically/ continually/…)
to drop/go down/decrease/fall by …
to drop/go down/decrease/fall from … to …
to plummet (= stark zurückgehen)
to bottom out at … (= einen Tiefstand erreichen bei)

to stand at …
to stay/remain at …
to level out at … (= sich einpendeln bei)
to amount to … (= sich belaufen auf)

Viele weitere hilfreiche Wendungen zum Bereich „Writing“ enthalten übrigens unsere MindCards, auf die Sie u. a. über nebenstehenden QR-Code Zugriff haben.

Die mündliche Gruppenprüfung findet getrennt von der schriftliche Fachabiturprüfung statt. Der genaue Termin wird Ihnen sieben Wochentage vor dem Prüfungstag bekannt gegeben.
In der mündlichen Prüfung werden **4 bis 5 Personen** in einer Gruppe geprüft. Das Los entscheidet, wer mit wem in der Gruppe ist. Die Aufgabenstellung wird Ihnen schriftlich ausgehändigt und Sie haben **20 Minuten Zeit**, um sich auf das Prüfungsgespräch vorzubereiten. Während dieser Zeit dürfen Sie sich innerhalb der Gruppe nicht austauschen (Aufsicht vorhanden). Es stehen Ihnen aber ein- und zweisprachige Wörterbücher zur Verfügung und Sie können sich Notizen machen.
Als Aufgabenstellung werden Sie mit einer **konkreten Situation** konfrontiert und erhalten ggf. zusätzliches Material (z. B. Bilder). Sie sollen sich beispielsweise vorstellen, Sie seien Mitglied der Redaktion eines Magazins und suchen ein passendes Titelbild für die aktuelle Ausgabe, oder Sie sollen sich mögliche Themen für einen Fernsehbeitrag über „the most urgent global issues“ überlegen.

Das Prüfungsgespräch verläuft dann folgendermaßen:

- Zunächst gibt jeder und jede von Ihnen ein kurzes Statement ab (ca. 1 Minute), in dem Sie Ihr Bild oder Ihre Idee vorstellen (**Präsentationsphase**).
- Anschließend wird in der Gruppe über die in der Aufgabenstellung genannte Frage oder Problematik diskutiert (**Diskussionsphase**). Dabei sollte jede/jeder von Ihnen auf ca. 5 Minuten Gesprächszeit kommen. Insgesamt dauert das Prüfungsgespräch also **20 bis 25 Minuten**.

Konzentrieren Sie sich während der Vorbereitungszeit vor allem darauf, Ihren Beitrag für die Präsentationsphase zu erarbeiten. Nutzen Sie diesen monologisch angelegten Prüfungsteil, um von Anfang an einen positiven Eindruck zu hinterlassen. Der Verlauf der Gruppendiskussion lässt sich zwar nicht genau planen – dennoch sollten Sie sich auch hierzu in der Vorbereitungszeit Gedanken machen und ggf. wichtige Aspekte oder nützliche Formulierungen notieren. Achten Sie während der Gruppendiskussion darauf, dass ein echtes Gespräch zustande kommt und dass Sie alle Gruppenmitglieder in die Diskussion miteinbeziehen.
Auf der nächsten Seite finden Sie einige ***useful phrases***, die Sie im Prüfungsgespräch verwenden können. Zudem enthält dieser Band zwei **Übungsaufgaben zur mündlichen Gruppenprüfung**, mit denen Sie die Prüfungssituation simulieren können.

Useful phrases

ein Bild beschreiben	*My picture/photo shows …* *It was taken in/at …* *In the foreground/background one can see …* *On the right/left there is/are …* *The picture reveals/draws attention to/…* *Its overall message is …* *In my opinion, it is ideal/perfect for the purpose because …*
die eigene Meinung ausdrücken	*(Personally,) I think …* *In my opinion/view …* *The way I see it, …* *To be honest, …* *I guess/suppose …*
andere nach ihrer Meinung fragen	*What do you think (about …)?* *What's your view/opinion (on …)?*
zustimmen	*You're (absolutely) right.* *I (quite/totally) agree.* *Exactly!/Absolutely!* *That's a good point.* *I think so too.* *You may have a point there.*
widersprechen	*I don't think so.* *I'm afraid I don't agree with you.* *I'm not quite sure whether …* *I see your point, but …*
Vorschläge machen	*Why don't we …?* *How about …?* *Maybe we could …* *My idea/suggestion would be to …*
eine Reihenfolge festlegen	*My first choice would be …* *I like … the best/most because …* *I'd go for …* *… would be my number one/two/three/…*
zu einem Ergebnis kommen	*I suppose it's time to come to an end …* *So, to summarise/round off our discussion, …* *So, as a conclusion, we can probably agree …* *So, if I got you right, we agree on …*

Eine Vielzahl von weiteren hilfreichen Wendungen zum Bereich „Speaking“ enthalten übrigens unsere MindCards, auf die Sie u. a. über nebenstehenden QR-Code Zugriff haben.

ÜBUNGSAUFGABEN

Berufliche Oberschulen Bayern ▪ Englisch 12. Klasse

Übungsaufgabe 1 *(Material-Based Writing)*: *Plastic Pollution*

Talking about the problem of plastic pollution, your class has decided to take action. That is why you write an article entitled "Plastic Waste in Our Oceans: Facts and Solutions" for an international student magazine. Elaborate on the present situation and make a suggestion which is helpful to tackle the problem effectively.

Write at least **300 words** using the material provided.

Source 1

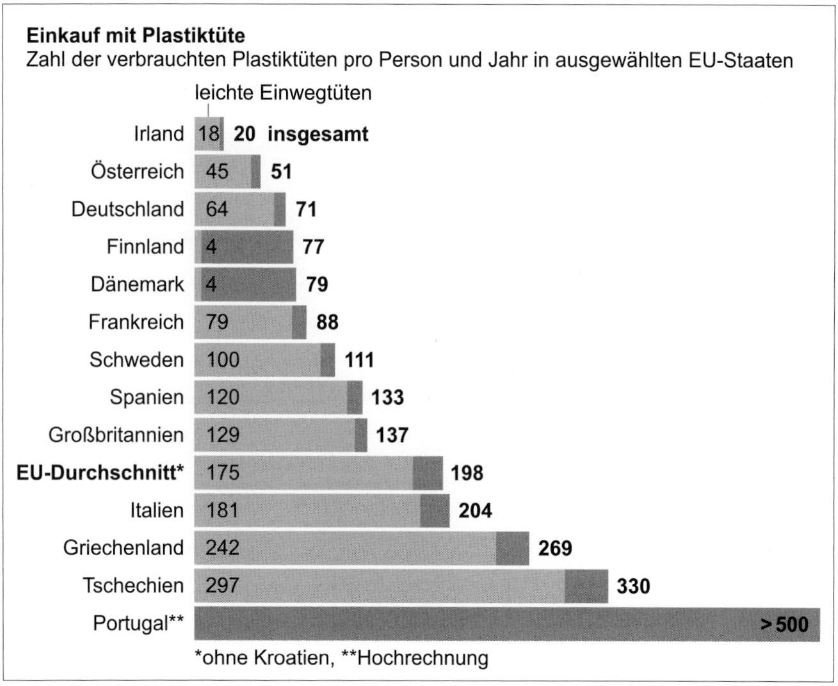

Daten nach: EU-Kommission

Source 2

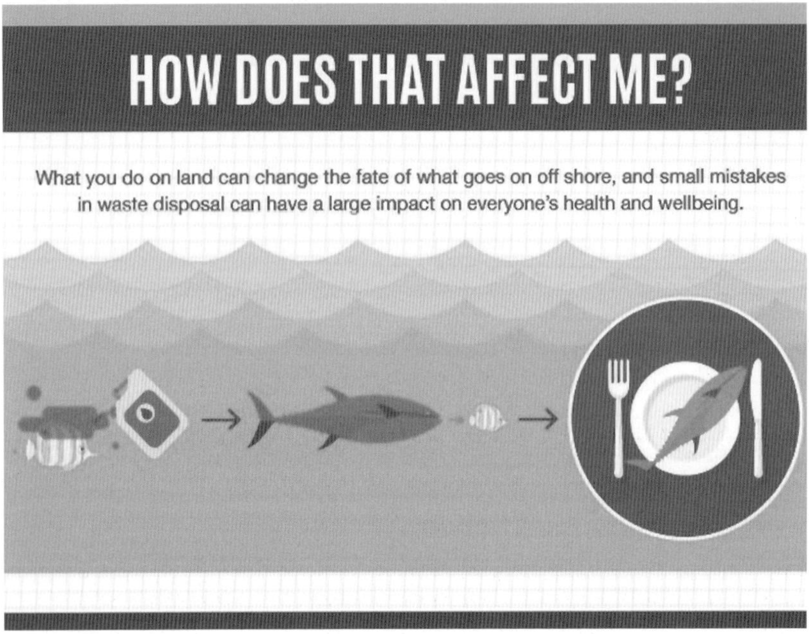

Marine Savers/www.marinesavers.com/2016/02/pollution-in-our-oceans/, CC BY-SA 4.0

Source 3

„Jede Minute gelangt ein Müllwagen voller Plastik in die Ozeane. [...] Im Jahr 2050 könnte in den Meeren die Menge an Plastik die Menge der Fische übersteigen."

ZEIT ONLINE/nsc, 19. 01. 2016, http://www.zeit.de/wissen/umwelt/2016-01/plastik-umweltverschmutzung-meer-studie-weltwirtschaftsforum

Lösungsvorschlag

TIPP

Beim *material-based writing* sollten Sie zunächst die **Aufgabenstellung** genau analysieren:

- Welche Textsorte wird von Ihnen verlangt und wer ist die Zielgruppe?
- Wie lautet die Frage- bzw. Problemstellung?
- Legt diese bereits einen bestimmten Aufbau für Ihren Text nahe?

Sehen Sie sich als nächstes die vorgegebenen **Materialien** an:

- Welche Information(en) sind im Hinblick auf die Aufgabenstellung besonders relevant?
- Sie sollen die Quellen nicht wörtlich zitieren oder im Detail beschreiben, es muss aber erkennbar sein, an welchen Stellen Sie sich auf welches Material beziehen.
- Achten Sie darauf, wirklich alle drei Quellen in Ihre Argumentation mit einzubeziehen.
- Zusätzlich zu den Quellen können Sie für Ihre Argumentation auch auf **eigenes Hintergrundwissen** über das Thema zurückgreifen.

In der vorliegenden Aufgabenstellung sollen Sie einen **Artikel** für ein internationales Schülermagazin schreiben. Für einen Artikel ist eine **Überschrift** nötig – diese ist hier bereits durch die Aufgabenstellung vorgegeben. Der **Sprachstil** sollte sachlich sein, muss aber bei einem Schülermagazin nicht ganz so nüchtern ausfallen wie etwa bei einem Wissenschaftsmagazin.
Thematisch geht es um die **Verschmutzung der Weltmeere durch Plastik**. Sie sollen auf die gegenwärtige Situation eingehen und einen Vorschlag unterbreiten, wie das Problem gelöst werden könnte. Der Hauptteil Ihres Texts ist also zweigeteilt (Fakten zur aktuellen Lage – Lösungsvorschlag). Er sollte von einer Einleitung (mit einer kurzen Hinführung zum Thema) und einem Schluss (in dem Sie z. B. ein Fazit ziehen oder einen Ausblick geben) eingerahmt werden.

In der Beispiellösung wird **Source 3** verwendet, um zunächst das Ausmaß des Problems zu verdeutlichen. Anschließend werden einzelne, besonders aussagekräftige Zahlen aus **Source 1** aufgeführt als Beispiele, wie wir alle zur Verschmutzung beitragen. Anhand von **Source 2** wird schließlich erklärt, wie das Plastik in die Meere gelangt und letztlich wieder zu einer Gefahr für uns Menschen werden kann. Für den Lösungsvorschlag und Schlussgedanken wird auf eigene Ideen zurückgegriffen.

Plastic Waste in Our Oceans: Facts and Solutions

Have you ever been to the seaside? Have you thought about what's with you in the water apart from other people, animals and plants? Probably not. And yet, our oceans are increasingly filled with one thing – plastic waste.

Einleitung: Hinführung zum Thema

According to a newspaper report, by 2050 there could be more plastic in the oceans than fish. We all contribute to this pollution every day: Take, for example, the use of plastic shopping bags. Each EU citizen uses 198 of them on average per year. In Portugal the number is even more than twice as high – a shocking amount of waste.

Problembeschreibung: Source 3 Source 1

But how does all the plastic end up in our oceans? Environmental researchers have shown that microplastics (contained in packaging material and cosmetics, for instance) are washed away and finally get into the sewage system. As the sewage tanks can't hold these small particles, they find their way into rivers and from there into the oceans. Microorganisms like plankton filter these particles from the water. They themselves are then eaten by fish that end up on our plates – with the consequence that plastic material fills our stomachs, too.

Source 2

This vicious cycle must be stopped. It is the responsibility of every one of us to take care of the environment. Therefore, we should use sustainable packaging like tote bags, baskets or glass bottles and reuse them as often as possible. And, of course, we should not throw away rubbish carelessly. Even more efficient measures could be brought about by researchers and industry, by redesigning plastics in such a way that it decomposes more quickly and by developing new, biodegradable materials.

Lösungsvorschlag: eigene Ideen

To sum up, I believe we all have to think differently, in a more cyclical way. At the moment our economy is predominantly linear, profit-oriented and heedless of the environment – with the result that we risk endangering not just the ocean's ecosystem but also our own health. *(315 words)*

Schluss: Fazit

You would like to participate in an international youth congress on "The Future of Work". You are requested to hand in a paper on the consequences of automation. Elaborate on the impact of machines and robots on the world of work and explain how you evaluate this phenomenon.

Write at least **300 words** using the material provided.

Source 1

Percentage of work activities with potential for automation, select industries

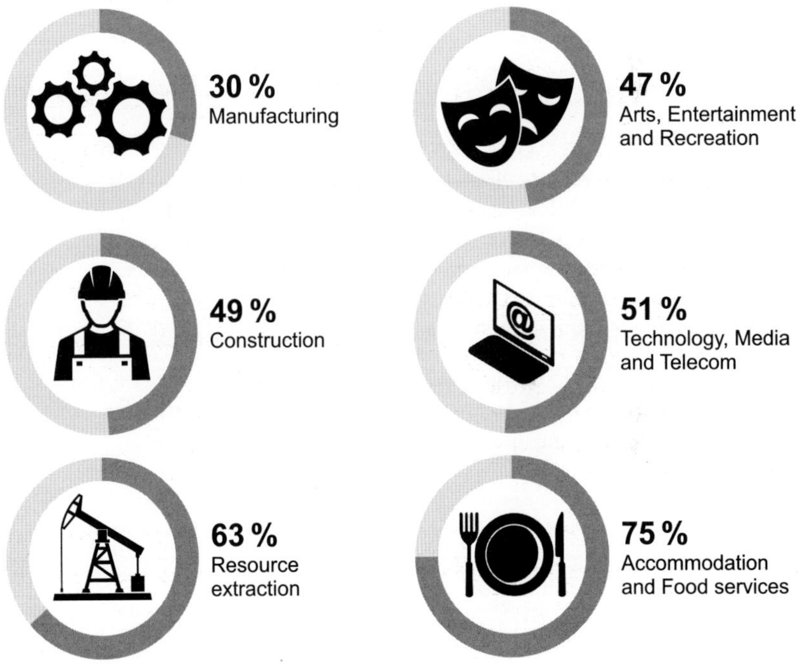

McKinsey analyzed 800 occupations to assess the percentage of work activities that could already be automated using existing technology

Daten nach: Four fundamentals of workplace automation, McKinsey Quarterly *2015*
Illustrationen: Zahnräder © StudioIcon. Shutterstock; Bauarbeiter, Ölförderung © VoodooDot. Shutterstock; Theatermasken © Panptys. Shutterstock; Laptop, Teller mit Besteck © Kheng Guan Toh. Shutterstock

Source 2

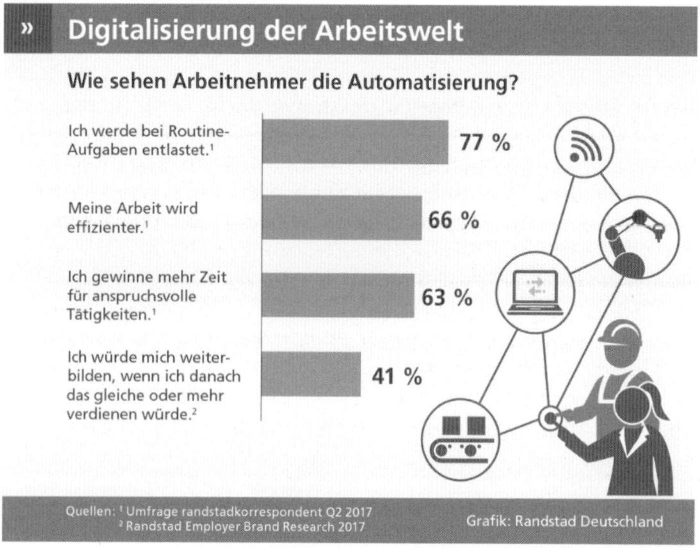

© obs/Randstad Deutschland GmbH & Co. KG

Source 3

© Jon Carter/Cartoonstock.com

Lösungsvorschlag

TIPP

Bei dieser Aufgabe müssen Sie ein **Paper** (eine Art Aufsatz) für einen Jugendkongress erstellen. Darin sollen Sie auf die **Auswirkungen der Automatisierung** auf die Arbeitswelt eingehen und darlegen, wie Sie dieses Phänomen bewerten. Überlegen Sie, wie Sie die vorgegebenen **Materialien** sinnvoll in Ihre Argumentation integrieren können. In der Beispiellösung werden – nach der Überschrift und einer kurzen Hinführung zum Thema – zunächst die negativen Auswirkungen der Automatisierung thematisiert. Zwei Beispiele aus **Source 1** belegen, dass viele Tätigkeiten bereits jetzt automatisiert werden können. Anhand des Cartoons in **Source 3** wird dann aufgezeigt, dass dies zu erheblichen Arbeitsplatzverlusten führt. Dass die Automatisierung trotz allem auch positive Folgen haben kann, wird am Beispiel der Aussagen aus **Source 2** deutlich gemacht. Der Schluss bringt noch einmal die Ambivalenz des Phänomens auf den Punkt und bietet einen kurzen Ausblick.

The Consequences of Automation

Einleitung: Hinführung zum Thema

Automation has increased at an astonishing pace in the last decade and is generally regarded as part of the "fourth industrial revolution". As the previous "industrial revolutions" had dramatic consequences on society, especially on the labour market, it is well worth looking into the potential impacts of machines and robots on the world of work today.

Negative Auswirkungen:

Source 1

On the one hand, the growing importance of robotics has been observed with suspicion, especially in those sectors of the economy where the potential for automation is high. According to a McKinsey report, three quarters of all work activities in the food and tourism sector, for example, could be automated. Even in areas where creativity is required, such as the arts and entertainment, nearly half of all activities could also be done by machines. It is little wonder, then, that many employees worry that they might become redundant and be replaced by a robot. Hence, the cartoon showing a boss telling an obviously older employee that he is too "analogue" to meet the demands of the company, is not satire – it is bitter reality.

Source 3

Positive Auswirkungen: Source 2

On the other hand, automation can also be met with optimism. According to a survey, more than three quarters of the labour force sees automation as a possibility to be relieved from routine work. Almost two thirds answered that they gained time for more demanding, i. e. satisfying, activities. Of people interviewed in another poll, 41 % said they would be willing to do further training to meet the changing requirements in the workplace given they earned at least as much as before.

As these examples show, automation seems to be a double-edged sword: On the one hand, it threatens jobs in nearly all branches of the economy. On the other hand, it can free us from repetitive chores to dedicate ourselves to more interesting tasks and to pursue further training. And perhaps, thanks to automation, social skills like empathy will also play a more important role in the workplace in future – as a distinctly "human" quality with a clear advantage over technology. *(343 words)*

Schluss: Zusammenfassung und Ausblick

Berufliche Oberschulen Bayern ▪ Englisch 12. Klasse

Übungsaufgabe 3 *(Material-Based Writing): Biofuels*

While talking about global challenges such as climate change and hunger, your class has decided to take action. That is why you want to write an article entitled "Biofuels – Blessing or Curse?" for an international student magazine. Elaborate on the global impact of biofuels and explain why you would or would not recommend them.

Write at least **300 words** using the material provided.

Source 1

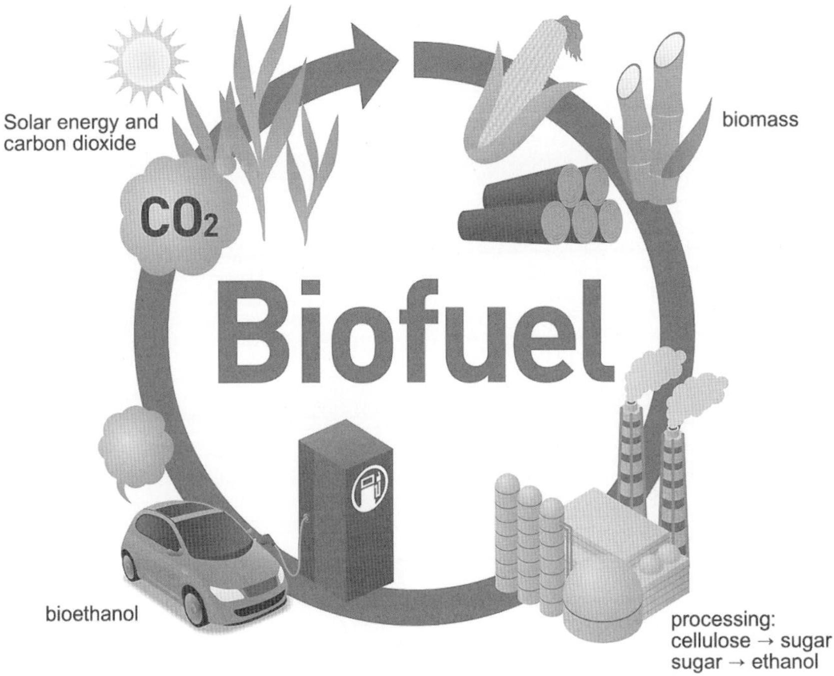

© chombosan/shutterstuck.com

Source 2

© *Resource Media*

Source 3

© *Orlando Eisenmann*

Lösungsvorschlag

TIPP

Bei dieser Aufgabe müssen Sie einen **Artikel** über das Thema „**Biosprit**" für ein internationales Schülermagazin schreiben. Darin sollen Sie auf die globalen Auswirkungen von Biokraftstoffen eingehen und darlegen, ob Sie deren Verwendung empfehlen würden oder nicht. Der Titel Ihres Artikels ist bereits durch die Aufgabenstellung vorgegeben. Führen Sie zunächst in einer kurzen Einleitung auf das Thema hin. Im Hauptteil sollten Sie auf die Vor- und Nachteile von Biosprit eingehen: In der Beispiellösung wird dazu zunächst anhand des Kreislaufs in **Source 1** erklärt, warum Biosprit aus Pflanzen eine umweltfreundliche Energiequelle darstellt. Anschließend wird ausgeführt, inwiefern die Biospritproduktion – andererseits – das Problem des Welthungers verschärft. Die Zahlen aus **Source 2** und der schockierende Cartoon (**Source 3**) untermauern dieses Argument. Der Text mündet in einer persönlichen Empfehlung, Biosprit besser nicht zu verwenden, und zeigt mögliche Alternativen auf.

Biofuels – Blessing or Curse?

Biofuels have long been promoted as a green source of energy and an important contribution in the fight against global warming. However, it is becoming increasingly obvious that they also have negative effects which need to be taken into account.

Einleitung: Hinführung zum Thema

At first sight, the production of biofuels appears to be a particularly sustainable way of producing energy. Plants use the energy from the sun and carbon dioxide from the atmosphere to grow. Crops such as maize or sugar cane multiply very quickly and produce large amounts of biomass that can be harvested. With the help of chemical processes, the cellulose contained in these plants is transformed into ethanol, which can be used as biofuels by cars. The carbon dioxide released by these vehicles is eventually consumed by plants so that the cycle continues – a climate-neutral form of generating energy.

Vorteile von „Biosprit": Source 1

However, there is also a flipside to this process. As more and more crops are being used for biofuel production, the prices for wheat, maize etc. are going up – with fatal consequences: While rich, industrialised countries can afford to "waste" food plants on biofuel production, poor and developing countries often do not even have enough crops to feed their own population. Research shows that eight bushels of maize could be used either to generate 21.6 gallons of biofuels or to feed one person for a whole year. Hence, while drivers in the West fill the tanks of luxury cars with fuel made from crops, people in other parts of the world are starving. Biofuels thus turn from a blessing into a curse.

Nachteile von „Biosprit": eigenes Hintergrundwissen

Source 2

Source 3

To sum up, although biofuels are a relatively clean source of energy, I would not recommend using them as they worsen the problem of world hunger. In my opinion, only (remains of) plants and other biomass that are not suitable for food should be used for biofuel production. In addition, we should combine our efforts to fight global warming by saving fuels and using only those forms of energy and transport that are both environmentally and ethically sound. *(339 words)*

Schluss: persönliche Einschätzung

You have become interested in the criminal justice system in the USA after talking about this topic in class. That is why you write an article entitled "Law Enforcement in the USA – A Just System?" for an international student magazine. Elaborate on the issues of law and social justice and make a suggestion as to what could be done to improve the system.

Write at least **300 words** using the material provided.

Source 1

© Janine Wiedel Photolibrary/Alamy Stock Photo

Source 2

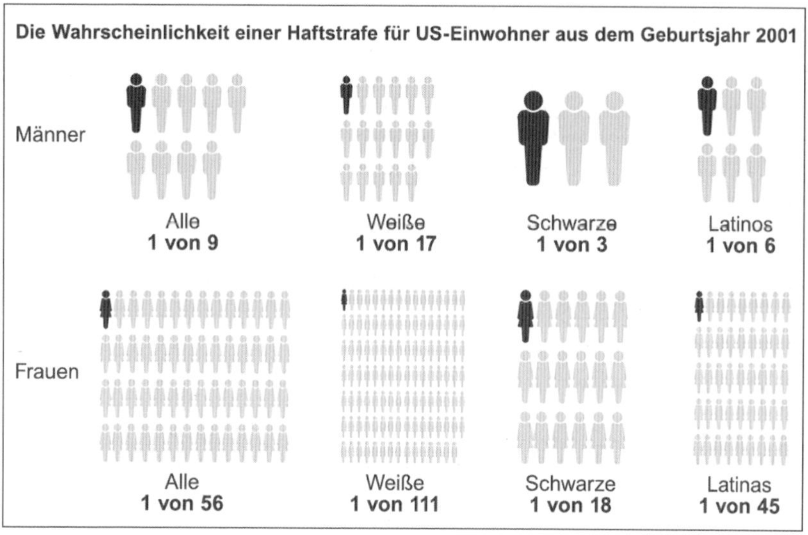

Daten nach: Bureau of Justice Statistics

Source 3

© Jerry King, www.jerryking.com

Lösungsvorschlag

TIPP

Bei dieser Aufgabe sollen Sie einen **Artikel** für ein internationales Schülermagazin schreiben, in dem Sie der Frage nachgehen, ob Gesetze in den USA gerecht umgesetzt werden. Dass Ihre Antwort darauf kein eindeutiges „Ja“ sein kann, wird bereits durch den zweiten Teil der Aufgabenstellung deutlich („... and make a suggestion on what could be done to improve the system.“). Sie sollten also in erster Linie auf Probleme innerhalb des Justizvollzugs eingehen.
In der Beispiellösung wird – ausgehend von **Source 1** – zunächst auf die „Black Lives Matter“-Bewegung eingegangen. Diese Protestbewegung hatte sich als Reaktion auf Fälle von Polizeigewalt gegen Afroamerikaner gebildet, was aus dem Foto allein allerdings nicht eindeutig abzuleiten ist. An diesem Beispiel wird deutlich, dass Sie immer auch das Zeitgeschehen verfolgen sollten, um über die nötigen Hintergrundinformationen zu den dargestellten Fotos, Cartoons etc. zu verfügen. Um zu belegen, dass das Rechtssystem nicht „farbenblind“ ist, sondern nicht-weiße Menschen benachteiligt, werden als weitere Beispiele Statistiken aus **Source 2** aufgeführt. Anhand des Cartoons in **Source 3** wird schließlich aufgezeigt, dass das Rechtssystem auch Menschen aus verschiedenen sozialen Schichten ungleich behandelt bzw. es deutliche Unterschiede gibt, wie welche Delikte geahndet werden. Zum Schluss werden verschiedene Lösungsvorschläge gemacht, wie der Rechtsvollzug in den USA verbessert (d. h. gerechter gestaltet) werden könnte.

Law Enforcement in the USA – A Just System?

In class we have recently been talking about the criminal justice system in the USA. A central question that arose was whether this system is just or whether some groups of people are treated differently from others. Our research into this matter has revealed some appalling evidence.

Einleitung: Hinführung zum Thema

Over the past few years, for example, several unarmed black men have been killed while being arrested by white police officers. As a result, a protest movement under the name of “Black Lives Matter” emerged, bewailing the racism within the police and the legal system.

Beispiele für Probleme: Source 1 und eigenes Hintergrundwissen

A look at some statistics showing the chances of being imprisoned in the USA supports these accusations of racial prejudice. While only one white man in seventeen runs the risk of being taken into custody, it is every third black man that does so. Moreover, one in six Latino men may end up getting arrested.

Source 2

Apart from racial bias, the US judicial system obviously also has different approaches to the various legal offences and to people from different social classes. To give you an example: In the recent financial crisis, bank managers filling their pockets by illegal actions on Wall Street got away with minor sentences, whereas in some states a consumer of marijuana, a minor offender by comparison, might go to prison for years.

Source 3

To draw a conclusion, law enforcement in the USA needs to be improved. A first step would be to recruit more people from different ethnic and social backgrounds as police officers, lawyers and judges, etc. As studies have shown, a diverse workforce leads to greater sensitivity towards issues of discrimination and helps to reduce bias. Yet, this alone is not enough. Society as a whole must change, which is a huge challenge. At school, children should be taught to overcome prejudice and embrace difference. Furthermore, the media should be careful not to spread stereotypes, such as by presenting African Americans or poor people as "gangsters". In this way, both law enforcement and society as a whole will hopefully become more just and discrimination might soon be a thing of the past. *(348 words)*

Lösungs-vorschläge: eigene Ideen

Preparation:	20 minutes
Notes:	You are allowed to take notes and to take them with you.
Presentation:	Briefly state your personal point of view according to the situation for approximately one minute before the actual discussion starts.
Timing:	You should talk for about 5 minutes during the whole discussion.
Topic:	Cover picture for an international magazine's special issue on social media

Situation

As editors of an international student magazine you have decided to publish a special issue on social media. The articles contained in it will deal with some of the advantages of social media, but also highlight the many problematic aspects and discuss what is characteristic of the "smartphone generation". Now you are looking for a suitable cover picture for that special issue.

Discussion

1 Present your picture and briefly give the others an idea why it is perfect for the cover of the special issue.

2 Weigh up the strengths and weaknesses of each picture and rank the pictures according to which picture you find best for the cover.

Optional aspect for discussion

Find a suitable headline for the cover which gives your readers a good impression of the content in the special issue.

Picture 1

© Syda Productions. Shutterstock

Picture 2

© upschuette / www.fotolia.com

Picture 3

© *zadorozhna/www.fotolia.com*

Picture 4

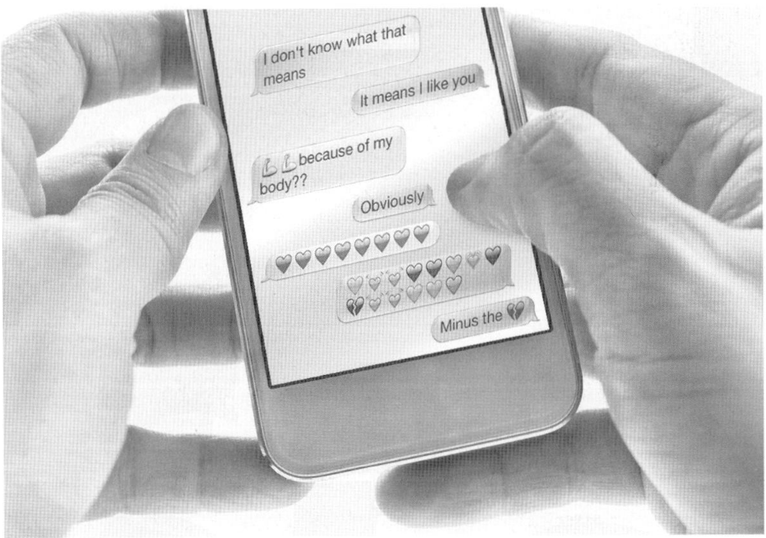

© *Can Stock Photo/weedezign (nur Hände mit Smartphone, ohne Text)*

Picture 5

© Wordley Calvo Stock/www.fotolia.com

Lösungsvorschlag

TIPP

Lesen Sie sich zunächst die Aufgabenstellung genau durch und versuchen Sie, sich in die vorgegebene **Situation** hineinzuversetzen: Sie sind Redakteur*in einer internationalen Schülerzeitung und sollen ein Bild für die Sonderausgabe zum Thema „Social Media" auswählen. Alle Redaktionsmitglieder sollen zunächst ca. 1 Minute lang ihr Bild vorstellen (**Präsentationsphase**) und begründen, warum es sich ideal als Titelbild eignet. Anschließend soll in der Gruppe diskutiert werden, wo die Stärken und Schwächen der einzelnen Bilder liegen, und Sie sollen sich auf eine Reihenfolge der Bilder einigen (**Diskussionsphase**).
Machen Sie sich zunächst einige **Notizen**, wie Sie Ihr Bild beschreiben würden und welche Gründe Sie anführen könnten, warum es sich als Titelbild eignet. In den untenstehenden Beispiellösungen werden zu jedem Bild einige mögliche Aspekte genannt – selbstverständlich sind hier auch andere Lösungen denkbar. Auf den zweiten Prüfungsteil, die Gruppendiskussion, können Sie sich nicht ganz so konkret vorbereiten. Dennoch sollten Sie sich bereits vorab überlegen, welche Kriterien für die Festlegung der Reihenfolge eine Rolle spielen könnten. Vielleicht fallen Ihnen auch nützliche Formulierungen ein, die Sie in der Diskussion verwenden könnten. Überlegen Sie sich außerdem bereits einen möglichen Titel für die Sonderausgabe („**Optional Task**").

Discussion: Task 1

Picture 1

- The picture shows five young people sitting next to each other, each holding a mobile device (either a smartphone or a tablet).
- They are all staring at the screen rather than talking or interacting with the others.
- The picture would be ideal for the cover because it shows how common it is to use modern technology – people use it almost all the time and nearly everywhere.
- What is more, it illustrates that some of the advantages of social media have actually become disadvantages:
  - Social media can be an ideal way to keep in touch with friends and to find out about certain subjects.
  - However, some people now tend to interact more online than face-to-face. They don't really pay attention to what is happening around them or the people they are with. Some even get addicted to their smartphones or other gadgets.

Picture 2

- The picture shows the audience at a live concert.
- People in the audience are holding their smartphones over their heads in order to film the stage or take pictures.
- The picture would be ideal for the cover because it illustrates the ambivalence of social media:
  - On the one hand, modern technology allows us to keep memories of special events, to relive special moments later and also share them with others.
  - On the other hand, people often don't really enjoy the show because they are too busy recording. They miss the special atmosphere of the moment in order to have something to upload or watch later. In addition, the filming can be annoying for other people in the audience, as it blocks their view and distracts them too.

Picture 3

- The picture shows a young woman taking a selfie.
- She is wearing trendy clothing, cool sunglasses, and is posing for the picture.
- The picture would be perfect for the cover because it illustrates the role of social media platforms where people present themselves, and the advantages and disadvantages connected with this:
  - On the one hand, social media is a great possibility to communicate with others and create a certain self-image.
  - On the other hand, there is increasing social pressure to present yourself as trendy/happy/fit etc. Often, the projected image does not correspond to the "real" person. Moreover, people sometimes upload pictures which they later regret.

Picture 4

- The picture shows someone holding a smartphone chatting to another person via a messaging service (such as WhatsApp).
- The message contains only a few words but a lot of emoticons.
- The picture would be ideal for the cover because it shows how communication has changed over the past years:
  - A lot of young people now prefer chatting to phoning or writing texts. The messages are often rather short and people are expected to answer quickly. Thanks to emojis and emoticons, communication has also become more visual and creative.
  - However, this "shortened" style of communication can come across as impolite (especially for older people). Moreover, the visual elements can easily lead to misunderstandings (as can also be seen in the picture).

Picture 5

- The picture shows a young woman with a smartphone in her hands.
- She is staring at the screen, looking rather tired or sad.
- The colours in this photo are all rather dark, which creates a gloomy atmosphere.
- The picture would be perfect because it allows for different interpretations:
  - Maybe the woman is sad or shocked because of a bad message she got.
  - Perhaps she is even being bullied online.
  - It could also be that she is tired because she has been looking at her smartphone all day or she is fed up with constantly getting messages.

Discussion: Task 2

individual solutions

Optional Task

The smartphone generation – examining the truth behind the cliché

Preparation:	20 minutes
Notes:	You are allowed to take notes and to take them with you.
Presentation:	Briefly state your personal point of view according to the situation for approximately one minute before the actual discussion starts.
Timing:	You should talk for about 5 minutes during the whole discussion.
Topic:	Little things that make a big difference

Situation

Radio Youth FM intends to produce a series of podcasts focusing on "**Little things that make a big difference**". Each podcast will last 30 minutes and you and your friends have been invited to support the editing team by collecting ideas on how each of us can change little things in their everyday lives to make the world a better place, be it in social or environmental terms.

The first task you are involved in is to figure out the best ideas to be presented in the first podcast. This is why each of you has come up with **two** examples which you think are particularly inspiring. To prepare for the first meeting with the editing team you first discuss your suggestions with your friends.

Discussion

1 Present your ideas. Tell your friends why you think your ideas need to be part of the podcast and how exactly they will make a difference.

2 Discuss your ideas and agree on the **three** best ideas that you would recommend to **Radio Youth FM** for the first podcast. Also decide on the order the ideas should be broadcast in.

Optional aspect for discussion

If there is still time left, make suggestions about how you could further spread your ideas in addition to the podcast. Which forms of communication would you (not) use, how would you present your ideas, etc.?

Lösungsvorschlag

TIPP

Wie Sie an dieser Übungsaufgabe sehen, müssen in der mündlichen Gruppenprüfung nicht immer Zusatzmaterialien (z. B. Bilder) vorgeben werden. Bei dieser Aufgabe sollen Sie sich beispielsweise Ideen überlegen, mit welchen kleinen, alltäglichen Dingen man die Welt zum Besseren verändern könnte. Nach der 20-minütigen Vorbereitungszeit soll dazu zunächst jeder Prüfling zwei Ideen präsentieren. In der anschließenden Gruppendiskussion müssen Sie sich auf drei Vorschläge einigen, die im Rahmen eines Podcasts vorgestellt werden. Außerdem sollen Sie sich darauf verständigen, in welcher Reihenfolge die drei Beiträge im Podcast vorkommen sollen.
Der folgende Lösungsvorschlag stellt exemplarisch zwei Ideen vor.

Discussion: Task 1

Call someone you didn't treat nicely and apologise

- Sometimes, we say things (either on purpose or unintentionally) that hurt other people.
- Afterwards, we feel bad for it, and the other person feels angry, sad or disappointed. In the worst case, they may even want to break off the friendship.
- Unfortunately, we are often too proud or too ashamed to apologise, yet the tiny word "sorry" would make a huge difference:
  - The other person would realise that they are important for us and that we care about their feelings. We would feel better too because we wouldn't have such a bad conscience.
  - Our relationship with that person would be better than without an apology.
  - Moreover, by saying sorry, we might encourage others to follow our example and do the same in similar situations. This would create an atmosphere where it is okay to admit to having made a mistake.

→ This idea is a perfect example of how small things (one word!) can make a big difference. Thus, it would be ideal for the podcast.

Buying local

- All of us should try to buy more at local shops or markets rather than online.
- For example, you can go food shopping at the local farmers' market or in the organic shop around the corner, buy books at the bookstore in your town etc.
- This would make a big difference, both socially and environmentally:
  - You support the local economy and help to create or preserve jobs in the area.
  - You get in touch with the people who produce or sell the things, and they can give you first-hand information about their products.
  - You are likely to meet other people from your neighbourhood.
  - Usually, buying local is more environmentally friendly too, as it involves less CO_2 emission for transporting, storing or delivering and less packaging etc.

→ This suggestion shows how small, everyday actions can have a large impact, and how each of us can contribute to making the world a better place. This is why it would be ideal for the podcast.

Discussion: Task 2
individual solutions

Optional Task

- We could initiate a "Day to Say Sorry" and announce it via Facebook and other social media: People should be encouraged to say sorry to the people they have hurt and to whom they have never really apologised. Perhaps some may want to share their stories of reconciliation online.
- We could start Facebook groups called "Support your local shop / farmer" for different towns or areas. There could be special events (e. g. food tasting, open days allowing people to look behind the scenes, readings at the local bookshop etc.) as well as cool buttons and reusable bags with the slogan "buy local" printed on them.

PRÜFUNGSAUFGABEN

READING

Text I Hitchhiking Robot, Safe in Several Countries, Meets Its End in Philadelphia

(A) After an adventure that included spending a week with a heavy metal band, cruising through the canals of Amsterdam and participating in a wave at a Boston Red Sox game, a hitchhiking robot met a brutal demise in a Philadelphia alley on Saturday. It was 1 year old. With yellow boots, blue limbs and "San Francisco or Bust" written around its chin, the robot, a.k.a. hitchBOT, was left by its creators near a highway in Salem, Massachusetts, on July 17, hoping the kindness of strangers would see it safely to its West Coast destination. The creators, David Harris Smith and Frauke Zeller, two Canadian professors, said they had built the robot as "an artwork and social robotics experiment" and had successfully sent it across Canada, Germany and the Netherlands. Short and stocky, with a bucket for a body and the red LED lights of its face enclosed in plastic, the brightly colored robot would be difficult to miss.

(B) Over its two weeks in the United States, hitchBOT made its way from Boston to New York – stopping to take photos in Times Square – and to Philadelphia. It made light, automated conversation and took photos of its surroundings about every 20 minutes, documenting its travels on its popular Twitter, Facebook and Instagram accounts. It had brief instructions written on its back for the supporters who would guide it through its American bucket list, which included listening to jazz in New Orleans and being the fifth face in a photo of Mount Rushmore.

(C) But its creators said the robot's journey was cut short by vandals – it was found early Saturday dismembered in Philadelphia's historic Old City neighborhood. A video blogger, Jesse Wellens, found the robot on the steps of Philadelphia's art museum and posted a video of their brief night together on YouTube. "HitchBOT, do you need a seatbelt?" Mr. Wellens asked as he loaded it into a car. "Yes," hitchBOT responded, to Mr. Wellens's surprise. Mr. Wellens considered paying a taxi $ 350 to bring the robot to Washington, D.C., before leaving it on a bench, as the robot's instructions suggested. It was the last known time someone would interact with it. Mr. Wellens said he had obtained a surveillance video that appeared to show someone in a football jersey throwing the robot's arms on the ground before kicking something on the bench. The video's contents could not be independently confirmed.

(D) The creators were sent a photo of the vandalized robot but said they did not know who destroyed it or why, according to The Associated Press. They said they would not press charges or attempt to find the vandal. "We know that many of hitchBOT's fans regret what happened, but we want them to be assured that this experiment is not over," the professors said in a statement. "For now, we will focus on the question: 'What can be learned from this?' and explore adventures for robots and humans in the future." The vandalism sparked disappointment on social media. Several people in the local tech community offered to fix the battered robot. Philadelphians were wary that the episode would reflect badly on the city, and others had the same fears with regards to all Americans. But the bot itself carried a more positive tone on Twitter: Its creators said more information on its future could come soon. *(559 words)*

Task I: Mixed Reading Tasks (Hitchhiking Robot …) **(10)**

1 Gapped Summary (paragraphs A to C) **(7)**

Fill the gaps in the summary with appropriate words or expressions (<u>one</u> word per line) from the <u>corresponding sections</u> of the text. Do not make any changes or adjustments. Please also provide the number of the line in which you have found the word/expression.

A robot called hitchBOT was sent on a journey through Europe and North America. The small but ______________ ______________ (l.) machine could easily be spotted by passers-by, who the designers hoped would take hitchBOT to its final stop in California. HitchBOT also had the ability to talk to people, and ______________ (l.) were provided by the designers so that volunteers could help the robot tick off all stops on its ______________ ______________ (l.) while in the US. However, the little robot did not make it to California: A man in Philadelphia had the final chance to ______________ (l.) with hitchBOT before it was detected ______________ (l.) the next day. Allegedly, a ______________ ______________ (l.) documented the robot's last moments, although the evidence it contained was not ______________ (l.) by neutral sources.

2 Sentence Completion **(3)**

Complete the following sentences with words/expressions from paragraph D. <u>Up to three words for each answer</u>.

2.1 Which legal action will the person who destroyed hitchBOT <u>not</u> have to expect?

The inventors do not intend to ______________________________.

2.2 Which expression shows that hitchBOT's fate made people feel sad?
The destruction of the robot ______________________________.

2.3 What happened to the robot may ______________________________ the nation as a whole.

Text II Finding Takers for Lonely Leftovers

(A) BERLIN – Fresh from a bracing workout at the gym, Anton Kaiser gazed hungrily into a refrigerator, considering arugula, pineapple jam, salted butter and two bags of green grapes before reaching for a white bread roll, baked that morning. "I haven't eaten all day," he said, "so it's great." Perhaps best of all, it was free, available in the middle of a graffitied courtyard in the Kreuzberg district of Berlin. Like the rest of the offerings in this so-called food sharing refrigerator, Mr. Kaiser's bread roll would, under normal circumstances, have gone straight into the trash.

(B) But in Germany, where concern about discarded groceries has mounted in recent years, such refrigerators – stocked with leftovers from private parties and restaurants, and open to the public – are just one of several initiatives aimed at keeping edibles out of the garbage. There are roughly 100 of these food sharing sites in Germany. About 50 have refrigerators, and the rest are just shelves. They are a small, offline branch of Foodsharing.de, a two-year-old Internet platform that gives members a chance to connect with other food sharers online, should they find themselves in possession of an extra cabbage or, as one Foodsharing post put it, "too many delicious organic potatoes for one person to eat."

(C) A filmmaker and journalist, Mr. Thurn had not planned to start a food revolution, or even a sharing website. But while shooting a segment about dumpster-diving[1], he was shocked by what he encountered. "The feeling I had, when I saw the great amount of edible food in the bins, was anger," he said.

(D) His documentary, "Taste the Waste," which was released in 2010, struck a chord in Germany. With its images of discarded lettuce, bins of bright, red tomatoes and entire warehouses of old bread, as well as emotional interviews with German farmers about potatoes that – whether too big, too small or too strangely shaped for supermarket shelves – simply rot in fields, the film became a touchstone for the burgeoning movement to reduce the wasting of edibles. The idea to share food online came up soon after. "I'm a filmmaker," Mr. Thurn said. "But people on our team said to me: 'They are sharing everything on the Internet. Why don't we share food?'"

(E) For safety, Mr. Thurn and his team established a few basic rules. Nothing with a sell-by date can be shared; no fresh meat or fish is allowed; prepared food is fine, but salads that have been left out all day in the sun are not. As a rule of thumb, people should share food that they would want to eat themselves.

(F) Under German laws regulating food distribution, sharing food between individuals is allowed. But the food sharing refrigerators and shelves operate for the most part under the radar. While there have been problems with members being rude or greedy, Mr. Thurn said, so far no one has complained of getting sick. City officials in Berlin, which has 12 such sites, did shut one down last year because no group or person was overseeing it and documenting where the food came from, to ensure that it was safe, as required by law.

(G) Working directly with organic grocers, bakeries and other stores, food savers head out in teams to pick up food, whether slightly wilted parsnips, blemished grapefruit or overripe avocados, just before the rejects end up in the trash. "It really gives you a sense of the value of food," said Lilo Brisslinger of Berlin, one of an estimated 9,000 food savers in Germany, Austria and Switzerland. To qualify as a food saver, Ms. Brisslinger, 26, who holds a master's degree in Islamic studies, had to take a quiz. Punctuality is one of the main requirements, so prospective savers are tested on what to do in case of vacations or forgetting a pickup appointment. "Our goal is 100 percent reliability," Mr. Fellmer said. "Otherwise store managers feel like, 'Aha, those hippies again.'"

(H) In the past year, food savers and sharers kept about 1,000 tons of food from the trash, organizers said. "Of course, if you look nationwide, this is nothing," Mr. Thurn said. "I wouldn't consider food sharing the solution. What's more important than the rescued kilos is to make more people change the way they think."

(I) Sandra Teitge, one of the founders of Dinner Exchange Berlin, a project that caters meals using produce left over at shops or farmers markets at the end of a day, said she believed that overabundance had led not just to waste, but also to a lack of creativity and flexibility. "We are used to eating and buying what we want, exactly when we want it," she said. "I grew up in East Berlin, and in East Germany, you didn't really have much. But we still managed to eat nice things."

(K) Culinary Misfits, a cafe that opened in Berlin four months ago, hopes to address the problem of food waste from another angle. Working directly with farmers to procure three-legged carrots and knobby potatoes that supermarkets reject, the two designers behind Culinary Misfits hope to show that a beet the size of a soccer ball is just as delicious as a standard one. "<u>All of these supermarket carrots, they're like soldiers in their plastic bags</u>," said Lea Brumsack, one of the cafe's owners. "What people buy, it's not natural. You can buy a perfectly shaped apple from New Zealand at the store, but just outside of Berlin, the trees are weighed down with apples nobody is picking."

(927 words)

Sally McGrane: Finding Takers for Lonely Leftovers in a Culinary Nook of the Sharing Economy. From The New York Times, *Nov 26, 2014*

Annotation

1 dumpster-diving = searching garbage containers for food

Task II: Mixed Reading Tasks (Finding Takers for Lonely Leftovers) (10)

1 Multiple Choice (paragraphs A to H) (7)

Mark the most suitable option by crossing the appropriate letter.

1.1 Anton Kaiser …

- **A** ☐ shares the contents of his fridge with others.
- **B** ☐ gets free food at his local gym.
- **C** ☐ eats food others would have thrown away.
- **D** ☐ prefers to eat fresh produce.

1.2 Which statement about Germany is made in paragraph B?

- **A** ☐ There are already about 100 websites to exchange food.
- **B** ☐ Wasted food has led to more and more unease lately.
- **C** ☐ The amount of food wasted has increased recently.
- **D** ☐ The food-sharing sites are only accessible to registered members.

1.3 Mr. Thurn's film …

- **A** ☐ reflects growing awareness of the food waste problem.
- **B** ☐ criticizes the food industry for polluting the environment.
- **C** ☐ shows disapproval of people living on food which has been thrown away.
- **D** ☐ states that a whole industry has developed around people's leftovers.

1.4 Which of the following food would <u>not</u> be acceptable at food sharing sites?

- **A** ☐ Home-made lasagna
- **B** ☐ Fried chicken wings
- **C** ☐ Raw salmon
- **D** ☐ Dried apricots

1.5 If you want to run a food sharing site in Germany, you need …

- **A** ☐ a strategy against some members' improper behaviour.
- **B** ☐ supervisors to guarantee that the food is still edible.
- **C** ☐ enough financial support from local food stores.
- **D** ☐ the permission of the state authorities.

1.6 Which of the following is <u>not</u> mentioned about food savers in paragraph G?
They …

- **A** ☐ must have certain personal qualities.
- **B** ☐ work in groups when collecting the leftovers.
- **C** ☐ gain a higher appreciation for food through their work.
- **D** ☐ are respected by local business people.

1.7 Which statement is true according to paragraph H?

- **A** ☐ Food sharing has brought about a widespread shift in mindsets.
- **B** ☐ Germany's waste has been reduced drastically.
- **C** ☐ The German government has failed to participate in food sharing.
- **D** ☐ The food sharers' efforts are just a drop in the ocean.

2 Mediation Englisch – Deutsch **(3)**

Beantworten Sie die folgenden Fragen <u>auf Deutsch</u>.

2.1 Welche Gesellschaftskritik übt Sandra Teitge in Absatz I? (2)

____

____

____

2.2 Erläutern Sie die nachstehende Aussage von Lea Brumsack im Textzusammenhang: (1)

"All of these supermarket carrots, they're like soldiers in their plastic bags." (Zeile 64/65)

____

____

____

Text III From Parties on a Budget to Helicopter Arrivals: Britain's School Proms Boom

Extravagant graduation dos take cues from the Kardashians – but not everyone is willing to splash out

(A) "Helicopters? It's absolutely ridiculous! What's that about?" says Gary Chinery, head of year 11 at Blackburn central high school (BCHS). Chinery is supervising arrangements for the school prom. There will be no helicopters. Tickets are £ 10 and everyone is welcome. Extravagant US-style proms have become a multimillion-pound business in the UK, with some parents spending hundreds of pounds on a dress or suit, hair, makeup and luxury vehicle hire for their 16-year-old, and even more on the pre- and post-prom parties. Chinery, however, has done it on a tight budget – calling on friends, contacts and local businesses for donations – with the aim of making the post-GCSE party available to all. The PE teacher and his friends have loaned dresses, the local Co-op has laid on the limousines and the evening promises to be a brilliant success.

(B) BCHS serves a community that includes areas of deprivation. "It's a fantastic family school," says Chinery, who has been with the same group of youngsters since they started aged 11. "I've got really attached to these students. I wanted everybody to come and celebrate at the end of the year if possible." On Tuesday night, 120 16-year-olds will dress up in their finest for a three-course dinner at a local hotel. There will be 150 cupcakes with the school logo, one photographer, two limousines and goodie bags. Looking on will be 60 proud members of staff – none more so than Chinery.

(C) Sarah Burns runs Prom Fayres UK, which stages events to bring together the burgeoning number of businesses providing prom services and school prom organisers. She claims the industry – from the venue and car hire to the designer dresses, chocolate fountains, fun casinos and spray tan – is worth £ 80m. "Some of the mothers look at it as a mini-wedding. They get really giddy," she says. "The girls love it because it's their first red carpet event – they're watching what goes on in America, they're into the Kardashians[1]."

(D) There are, however, prom refuseniks. One UK headteacher estimated that 30 % of his year-11s would not turn up for one reason or another. In the US, high school students boycott official proms and organise "morps" – prom backwards – as an alternative.

(E) Nevertheless the UK prom business is booming. Orsett Hall in Essex is a veteran venue in the school prom business. The hotel has been hosting them for the last 15 years, and this season it has 35 bookings over the next few weeks – even squeezing two in on one night to fit them all in. Scott Carey of the hotel's events team outlines the different prom packages: "For £ 39.95 – the most expensive package – you get a three-course meal, limitless soft drinks, a DJ, one bouncer and the services of a prom coordinator. Extras include a photo booth (£ 350 for three hours and 200 prints), thrones for the prom king and queen (£ 30), a red carpet (£ 25) and the hire of the bridal suite to get ready for the evening (£ 150). Hair and makeup packages include two 'hair ups' for £ 50, a spray tan, gelish nails with 'hair up' for £ 70, or full makeup plus 'hair up' for £ 80." Orsett Hall has seen teenagers arrive in helicopters (£ 800 + VAT), fire engines, Hummer limos and US-style big-rig trucks. Elsewhere, they've turned up for proms on mobility scooters, in a horse and carriage and a US police car. "I've seen them for 15 years, so I've seen it all," says Scott Carey. "We've had quite a few come back years later when they get married or to have their engagement parties, or birthday parties."

(F) Patsy Kane, executive headteacher of two girls' schools in Manchester, has students whose families originate from many different parts of the world and the prom has become a celebration of diversity, reflected in the dresses and jewellery. Tickets this year cost £ 27, but a student organising committee has been working for months on raising money through tombolas and cake sales to keep costs down. There are prizes for the best hair and the best dress, as well as to the overall prom queen. Mrs Kane says: "The girls really go to town – they wear beautiful outfits. The hair's beautiful, the makeup is beautiful, and they really enjoy making an effort. There aren't any boys because we're schools for girls, and every year someone says: 'Can we invite boys?' And we don't, because it's a wonderful celebration of friendship. It's very special. It goes beyond the commercial. I don't think it's a big thing how much your dress cost – that's not something that gets asked. It's just a wonderful, wonderful atmosphere. They've been together for five years. It's hard for them to realise they are not going to see each other every day any more. They all say they're going to keep in touch, but they won't be able to. It's the end of an era."

(G) Things have changed a bit since Chinery left school. "There was no prom back in the day," he says. "We had it in the staff room – we had some biscuits, some crisps and some bottles of pop, and we sat round talking to the teachers. And that was it."

(865 words)

Slightly adapted from Weale, Sally: From Parties on a Budget to Helicopter Arrivals. Britain's School Proms Boom, The Guardian, *June 14, 2015, Copyright Guardian News & Media Ltd 2018*

Annotation

1 The Kardashians = Rich American family who have their lives portrayed in a reality television series

Task III: Mixed Reading Tasks (From Parties on a Budget ...) (10)

1 Multiple Matching (8)

Who could have said what? Match the statements below (1–12) with the four people. Please note: For each person there are two statements. There are four more statements than you need.

Person	Statement 1	Statement 2
Gary Chinery		
Sarah Burns		
Scott Carey		
Patsy Kane		

	Statements for Multiple Matching
1	Some return because their prom was such a brilliant event.
2	We organise meetings between companies and those responsible for the parties.
3	My girls really like to show off their dresses in the city centre.
4	The party is about the students cherishing the strong bond between them.
5	The turnover of my company amounts to £ 80m.
6	These young people have become so important to me over the years.
7	Some family members are as euphoric about the prom as if someone was getting married.
8	With all the various ethnic backgrounds it is hard to agree on a prom dress code.
9	My mates have contributed so that everybody can afford the prom.
10	We give an award for the nicest gown.
11	I can understand that some pupils dislike such events.
12	I have witnessed students getting to their prom in all kinds of unusual ways.

2 Mediation Englisch – Deutsch (2)

Beantworten Sie die folgende Frage auf Deutsch.

"Extravagant graduation dos take cues from the Kardashians – but not everyone is willing to splash out". Welche unterschiedlichen Einstellungen zeigt dieser Textuntertitel auf?

____

____

____

____

WRITING

Task IV: Descriptive Writing (9)

Choose one of the following tasks (1 or 2) and write about 100 words.

1 Describing a cartoon

Describe the situation and state what point the cartoonist is making about the police in the United States.

Slightly adapted; © Nate Beeler/politicalcartoons.com

Annotation

Kitty = a typical way of referring to a cat

2 Describing statistics

Describe and interpret the following chart.

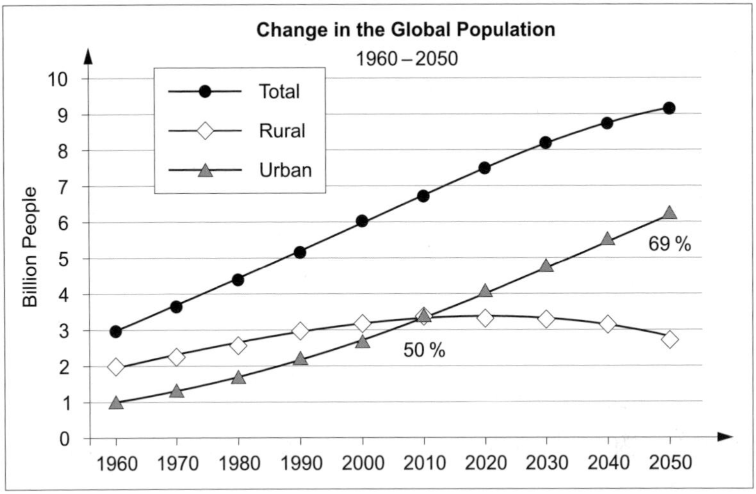

Source: United Nations, Department of Economic and Social Affairs, Population Division (2014). World Urbanization Prospects: The 2014 Revision.

Task V: Argumentative Writing (21)

Choose one of the following topics. Write at least 200 words.

1 Composition Topic 1

A considerable number of young people choose to keep on living with their parents even after they have graduated and taken up a job.
Comment on the consequences of staying at "Hotel Mum" for both parents and children.

2 Composition Topic 2

"There is too much money in professional sport these days."
Do you agree that professional sport, for example football, is just about business?

Lösungsvorschläge

READING

Task I: Mixed Reading Tasks (Hitchhiking Robot …)

1 **TIPP**

Für diese Aufgabe 1 kommen nur die Absätze A bis C in Frage. Wie in den Arbeitsanweisungen angegeben, sollen die Antworten wörtlich übernommen werden, wobei jedem Zeilenstrich ein Wort entspricht. Sie sollen auch die jeweilige Zeile angeben, in der die entsprechende Wendung zu finden ist. Lesen Sie die Absätze zum Verständnis gründlich durch. Ferner folgt die Zusammenfassung nicht immer der gleichen Reihenfolge wie im Text.

Worterklärungen zum Ausgangstext:

- Überschrift: „Meets Its End in Philadelphia" entspricht Z. 3: „met a brutal demise in a Philadelphia alley".
- Z. 10: *bucket* – Kübel (hier: Körper des Roboters)
- Z. 17: *bucket list* – hier: Liste der Dinge, die der Roboter erledigt, bzw. der Orte, die er besucht haben sollte
- Z. 20: *dismembered* – verstümmelt, zerstückelt
- Z. 27: *surveillance* – Überwachung
- Z. 29: *to confirm* – bestätigen, bezeugen

Worterklärung zum Lückentext:

- letzter Satz: *allegedly* – angeblich

A robot called hitchBOT was sent on a journey through Europe and North America. The small but **brightly colo(u)red (l. 11)** machine could easily be spotted by passers-by, who the designers hoped would take hitchBOT to its final stop in California. HitchBOT also had the ability to talk to people, and **instructions (l. 16)** were provided by the designers so that volunteers could help the robot tick off all stops on its **bucket list (l. 17)** while in the US. However, the little robot did not make it to California: A man in Philadelphia had the final chance to **interact (l. 26)** with hitchBOT before it was detected **dismembered (l. 20)** the next day. Allegedly, a **surveillance video (l. 27)** documented the robot's last moments, although the evidence it contained was not **confirmed (l. 29)** by neutral sources.

2 **TIPP**

Für diese Aufgaben ist Absatz D heranzuziehen. Die Lösungen sind wörtlich aus dem Text zu übernehmen, müssen aber den Satz grammatikalisch und/bzw. idiomatisch korrekt zu Ende führen. Zeilenangaben sind nicht verlangt, werden hier aber gemacht, um Ihnen einen rascheren Überblick zu verschaffen.

Zu 2.1:
Z. 32: *to press charges* – Anklage erheben, auf eine Entschädigung/Vergütung dringen

Zu 2.2:
Z. 36: *sparked* – hier: rief hervor (eigentlich: entzündete; *a spark* – ein Funke); *disappointment* – Enttäuschung

2.1 The inventors do not intend to **press charges** (l. 32)

2.2 The destruction of the robot **sparked disappointment** (l. 36).

2.3 What happened to the robot may **reflect badly on** (l. 38) the nation as a whole.

Task II: Mixed Reading Tasks (Finding Takers for Lonely Leftovers)

1 **TIPP**

Für diese Aufgabe kommen nur die Absätze A bis H infrage. Beachten Sie, dass Ihnen in manchen Fragen eindeutige Anhaltspunkte gegeben werden (siehe Fragen 2, 6 und 7) und vor allem Personen (siehe Fragen 1 und 3) die Suche nach Textstellen erleichtern können.

1.1 Siehe Z. 6/7: "Mr. Kaiser's bread roll would […] have gone straight into the trash."

1.2 Siehe Z. 8/9: „in Germany, where concern about discarded groceries has mounted in recent years"

1.3 Siehe Z. 25/26: "the film became a touchstone for the burgeoning movement to reduce the wasting of edibles."

1.4 Siehe Z. 30: "no fresh meat or fish is allowed"

1.5 Siehe Z. 36–39: "City officials in Berlin, which has 12 such sites, did shut one down last year because no group or person was overseeing it and documenting where the food came from, to ensure that it was safe, as required by law."

1.6 Hier sind die Textstellen angegeben, die den falschen Optionen entsprechen:
- Zu Option A siehe Z. 44–46: "To qualify as a food saver, Ms. Brisslinger […] had to take a quiz. Punctuality is one of the main requirements"

- Zu B siehe Z. 40/41: “food savers head out in teams to pick up food”
- Zu C siehe Z. 42/43: “It really gives you a sense of the value of food”
- Zu Option D findet man keinen Textbeleg, sie ist somit die richtige Lösung.

1.7 Siehe Z. 51: “if you look nationwide, this is nothing”

1.1 Anton Kaiser …

C ☒ eats food others would have thrown away.

1.2 Which statement about Germany is made in paragraph B?

B ☒ Wasted food has led to more and more unease lately.

1.3 Mr. Thurn’s film …

A ☒ reflects growing awareness of the food waste problem.

1.4 Which of the following food would not be acceptable at food sharing sites?

C ☒ Raw salmon

1.5 If you want to run a food sharing site in Germany, you need …

B ☒ supervisors to guarantee that the food is still edible.

1.6 Which of the following is not mentioned about food savers in paragraph G? They …

D ☒ are respected by local business people.

1.7 Which statement is true according to paragraph H?

D ☒ The food sharers’ efforts are just a drop in the ocean.

2 **TIPP**

Die Fragen beziehen sich auf die Absätze I und K. Eine wörtliche Übersetzung ist hier nicht verlangt, vielmehr genügen kurze Stichpunkte.

Zu 2.1:
Siehe Z. 55–57: “she believed that overabundance had led not just to waste, but also to a lack of creativity and flexibility.”

Zu 2.2:
Siehe Z. 61–64: “Working directly with farmers to procure three-legged carrots and knobby potatoes that supermarkets reject, the two designers behind Culinary Misfits hope to show that a beet the size of a soccer ball is just as delicious as a standard one.”

2.1 Sie kritisiert, dass der Überfluss in unserer Gesellschaft dazu geführt hat, dass nicht nur viel Essen weggeworfen wird, sondern dass viele Menschen auch nicht mehr kreativ und flexibel im Umgang mit Lebensmitteln sind.

2.2 Gemüse, das in Supermärkten erhältlich ist, muss immer gleich aussehen / darf keine Schönheitsfehler haben / muss stets makellos sein.

Task III: Mixed Reading Tasks (From Parties on a Budget …)

1 TIPP

Jeder der vier genannten Personen sind jeweils zwei Aussagen zuzuordnen. Gehen Sie so vor, dass Sie die Namen im Text markieren und dann die Aussagen mit den vorliegenden Sätzen abgleichen. Vier der zwölf vorliegenden Sätze bleiben unberücksichtigt.

- **Gary Chinery: Statements 6 + 9**
  - Siehe Z. 14: "I've got really attached to these students." (statement 6)
  - Siehe Z. 7–9: "calling on friends, contacts and local businesses for donations – with the aim of making the post-GCSE party available to all." (statement 9)
- **Sarah Burns: Statements 2 + 7**
  - Siehe Z. 19/20: „to bring together the burgeoning number of businesses providing prom services and school prom organisers." (statement 2)
  - Siehe Z. 22/23: "Some of the mothers look at it as a mini-wedding." (statement 7)
- **Scott Carey: Statements 1 + 12**
  - Siehe Z. 43/44: "We've had quite a few come back years later" (statement 1)
  - Siehe Z. 40–43: "teenagers arrive in helicopters […] fire engines […] big-rig trucks. […] 'I've seen them for 15 years, so I've seen it all'" (statement 12)
- **Patsy Kane: Statements 4 + 10**
  - Siehe Z. 55: "it's a wonderful celebration of friendship." (statement 4)
  - Siehe Z. 50/51: "There are prizes for the best hair and the best dress." (statement 10)

Person	Statement 1	Statement 2
Gary Chinery	**6**	**9**
Sarah Burns	**2**	**7**
Scott Carey	**1**	**12**
Patsy Kane	**4**	**10**

2 **TIPP**

Für diese Aufgaben ist der Textuntertitel heranzuziehen. Eine wörtliche Übersetzung ist natürlich nicht verlangt. Sie sollen im Textzusammenhang interpretierend auf Deutsch erläutern.
Worterklärungen:
- *(a) do* – eine Fete/Feier/Party
- *to take one's cue from sb* – jemandes Beispiel folgen
- *to splash out* – viel Geld ausgeben

Viele/Manche holen sich Anregungen/lassen sich inspirieren von reichen Leuten/den Kardashians, um etwas Außergewöhnliches/Extravagantes bei der Schulabschlussfeier zu machen – aber nicht jeder ist bereit, mit Geld um sich zu werfen.

WRITING

Task IV: Descriptive Writing

1 **TIPP**

Bei dieser Aufgabe sollten Sie thematisch erkennen, dass es um polizeiliche Übergriffe in den USA geht.
- **Inhaltlich:** Ein Polizist versucht eine Katze vom Baum zu retten, während hinter ihm eine ältere Frau die Szene auf ihrem Smartphone festhält. Die Sprechblase verrät, dass die Frau der Katze versichert, sie sammle Beweise für den Fall, dass der Polizist von seiner Schusswaffe Gebrauch mache.
- **Kernaussage:** Kritik an der Brutalität der Polizei in den USA, die bei der amerikanischen Bevölkerung immer mehr Besorgnis auslöst.

The topic of the cartoon is police violence in the US.
A police officer is trying to rescue a cat from a large tree. Behind the officer there is an elderly woman with a walking stick documenting the scene on her smartphone. She is assuring her cat "Kitty", in a loud voice, that she is collecting proof in case the police officer uses violence or even his gun.
The cartoonist's point of criticism is the brutality of the police in the US, which has led to increasing worries among the population, who no longer entirely trust their police force. *(99 words)*

2 **TIPP**

Thematisch zeigen die drei Graphen die Entwicklung der gesamten Weltbevölkerung und die Anzahl der Menschen in ländlichen und städtischen Gebieten in der Zeit zwischen 1960 und 2050 auf.

- **Inhaltlich:** Während 1960 doppelt so viele Menschen auf dem Land wie in den Städten lebten (zwei Milliarden vs. eine Milliarde), lebten 2010 ebenso viele Menschen in den Städten wie auf dem Land, wobei die Weltbevölkerung insgesamt zunahm. Im Jahr 2050 hingegen wird der Anteil der städtischen Bevölkerung voraussichtlich auf 69 % steigen, und man erwartet, dass sich die Weltbevölkerung auf mehr als neun Milliarden Menschen im Vergleich zu 1960 verdreifacht hat.
- **Kernaussage:** Sowohl die Welt- als auch der Anteil der städtischen Bevölkerung hat zugenommen und wird auch weiterhin beträchtlich steigen.

The three lines in the graph depict the growth of the global population and the number of people in rural and urban areas between 1960 and 2050.
There is a big contrast between 1960, where the percentage of people living in the country was twice the percentage of those living in cities, and 2010, where the percentages of people living in urban and rural areas were equal. In 2050 urban citizens will make up 69 %, and the world population in total is expected to have tripled to more than nine billion people.
The message is that both the world population and the percentage of urban dwellers have increased and will continue to increase significantly. *(114 words)*

Task V: Argumentative Writing

1 **TIPP**

Topic 1 fragt nach den Folgen sowohl für die Eltern als auch für die Kinder, wenn die Kinder selbst nach Studium oder Berufsausbildung noch bei den Eltern wohnen bleiben, und wie Sie dazu stehen. Das ist eine eher komplizierte Aufgabenstellung, weil zum Argument eine Bewertung erfolgen sollte. Es handelt sich somit um eine Verschränkung von steigernder und dialektischer Aufsatzform. Zum Schluss sollten Sie zu einer zusammenfasenden Lösung kommen.

More and more young people continue living with their parents even after they have completed their education or started a career. What are the consequences for both parents and children?
To begin with, although children will have pecuniary benefits as they usually won't have to meet costs for food and lodging, "Hotel Mum" might postpone their process of maturing or they will not take on responsibility for their own life or a partnership on equal terms.

Being forced to organize your meals, your laundry or paying your bills might be tedious and uninspiring, but it certainly helps you to become independent as much as to complete your studies or an apprenticeship successfully.
In addition, this situation may become very ambiguous for parents – not only with regard to financial matters. Raising children can be very fulfilling and make life meaningful, but it also demands great self-discipline and requires the willingness to sacrifice individual interests for the sake of the children. Parents often experience a kind of relief when children move out to be on their own. Neglected interests can be revived and new areas in life can be discovered.
Ultimately, if, on the one hand, both parents and children can share the rent and their expenditures equally, and, on the other hand, can manage to maintain their privacy and independence, it would no longer be "Hotel Mum". *(226 words)*

2 **TIPP**

Topic 2 ist dialektisch anzugehen mit mindestens einem Argument dafür und einem dagegen. Den Standpunkt, dem Sie eher zuneigen, sollten Sie ans Ende setzen. Als Schlussgedanke bietet sich die Synthese (Lösung) unter einem neuen Gesichtspunkt an.

When talking about professional sport, you have to differentiate between national and international perspectives, as baseball in Germany would be of only minor importance, whereas in the US it is one of the most popular sports.
Let me begin with football. In Germany, as well as in other European countries, it is predominantly popular, which can be seen by observing viewing rates of clubs in both national and international leagues.
The enthusiasm of the respective fans causes fierce competition between clubs and associations, thus creating a market where enormous sums of money are paid for stars like Messi, Müller or Lewandowski. Here it can be seen that sport is largely about business. Moreover, organisations such as FIFA or UEFA are believed to be mainly concerned with business and there is a tendency towards corruption and the illegal transfer of money.
On the other hand, excellent sport and sportsmanship can be experienced, and it often sets an example for the entire younger generation, who go in for sports and follow the positive role models created by players. Additionally, the example of football can be transferred to other kinds of sport like basketball, handball, hockey or cycling.
Summing up, professional sport is about business, but not only, as long as responsible managers and representatives on national and international bodies and committees stick to "fair play" and maintain control of democratically achieved guidelines.
(230 words)

Berufliche Oberschulen Bayern ▪ Englisch 12. Klasse
Fachabiturprüfung 2017

READING

Text I The American Teenager in 2015 – On the Fringe of Something New

In this article, TIME looks at the American teenager in 2015 and compares its findings with a similar study done in 1965.

From the pages of TIME

(A) It's harder to be a teen now than it was in 1965 – at least according to teenagers. That's not in spite of the Internet and the iPhone. It's *because* of all the technology that surrounds us. "We have more responsibilities because of all the technology that we have," says Sharon Bayantemur, a 17-year-old student. "People expect more from you because they know you have a cell phone and they can contact you and you have to pick up. Back then you didn't really have that obligation."

(B) Teens say finding romance during high school is still important, but they're not expecting to find lifelong love. The median age for marriage jumped from 22 to 28 between 1965 and 2013, according to the U.S. Census Bureau. "Back in the day you were very worried about finding a husband so they could take care of you," says Emma Baker, an 18-year-old. "Nowadays women can make a living on their own and be very independent. The pressure is a whole lot less."

(C) Same-sex relationships are greeted with indifference in some circles, too. Even the oldest teens were in elementary school when Massachusetts became the first state to legalize same-sex marriage in 2004. Though gay teenagers can still face discrimination, David Sides, a 17-year-old, says the antagonism is lessening. "Like, nobody cares. That's your thing. I'm not gonna tell you you can't do it, but I'm not going to give you a high five for it."

(D) At the same time, sexual activity among teens has been on a steady decline in recent decades. The number of partners per sexually active student is down too. Young folks have some theories for explaining the drop. "We have so many things nowadays to keep us busy, whereas back then they had nothing to do," 16-year-old Caitlyn Ascencio says laughing. (These facts, however, haven't done much to assuage the long-held notion in high school that everyone else is having sex.)

(E) Today's youngest teens barely remember a time before the U.S. had a black president, but ongoing racial tensions are still evident to many of them. Though the Segregation described in 1965 is considered to be a thing of the past, some teens say their perception of racial progress changed following the lack of indictments for police officers involved in the killings of two black men, Michael Brown and Eric Garner, in 2014. There's a sense among many, especially at schools largely populated by minorities, that racial issues will persist in the future. "There's always going to be a race problem all around the world," says Ibrahim Diallo, the 18-year-old captain of East Side's basketball team. "You're just going to have to find a way to deal with it."

(F) But teens are also searching for nuance in what's become a heated social debate. "My uncle is a captain in the police force and I respect him as a person," says Luz Robles, a 17-year-old at East Side who serves as student council president. "I don't think it's the police in general. I think it's just certain people who are spoiling it for all of them."

(G) Teens are still experimenting with new substances, but their preferences have changed. Alcohol use by teens has declined since the 1970s. Marijuana use plummeted in the '80s, when Nancy Reagan was teaching students to "Just Say No" to drugs, but today usage is right about where it was in 1975. Forty percent of 12th graders say they've smoked weed in the past year. With marijuana legalized in a growing number of states, the drug is no longer viewed as particularly dangerous or rebellious. "You would speak about it in a hushed tone maybe, like, ten years ago," says Lonny Hancock, a 16-year-old at East Side. "Now you could be screaming across the room to a friend, 'Hey! Want to go smoke?'"

(H) Today's teens are coming of age in the shadow of the largest financial calamity since the Great Depression. College tuition, room and board has increased more than tenfold since 1965 and the income gap between the wealthiest 1 % of Americans and everyone else has been growing for three decades. For many teens, these realities mean choosing a college is more about pragmatism than pursuing a dream. There's also an anxiety about the world that will be waiting after college. "It's going to be a lot more difficult," says Jacob Lamb, a 17-year-old senior at Briarwood. "I feel like a college degree is worth a lot less than it was. There's a lot more people competing for the same jobs."

(I) But the changes of recent decades have also created new opportunities. Beth Rodriguez, a 13-year-old from Denver, believes she'll have an easier time reaching college than her parents. "They were undocumented when they came here, so they didn't really get the chance to go to college," she says. "I think I'll have it a lot easier."

(J) None of these kids know what will come ahead – but that's part of being a teenager. They'll assume jobs that don't yet exist. They'll carry gadgets we haven't even dreamed up and deal with social problems that haven't yet broken into the mainstream. They're going to figure out the future because they have no other choice. *(870 words)*

Victor Luckerson: The American Teenager in 2015 – On the Fringe of Something New.
In: time.com, *November 12th, 2016.*

Task I: Multiple Matching (The American Teenager in 2015 …) (9)

Who could have said what? Match the statements below (1–12) with the nine people given. Please note: For each person there is one statement. There are three more statements than you need.

	Statements for Multiple Matching
1	It doesn't guarantee success any longer.
2	We are never out of reach.
3	Sad, but true: it will remain a global challenge.
4	Today women have to make money.
5	It's done more openly.
6	Fortunately we can always be reached.
7	My own educational prospects are way better.
8	We have more freedom of choice nowadays.
9	Don't give in to stereotyping.
10	Your way of life is not my business.
11	There are lots of other interesting activities we can engage in.
12	Don't do drugs!

Person	Statement
Sharon Bayantemur	
Emma Baker	
David Sides	
Caitlyn Ascencio	
Ibrahim Diallo	

Person	Statement
Luz Robles	
Lonny Hancock	
Jacob Lamb	
Beth Rodriguez	

Text II I Have a Black Son in Baltimore

(A) BALTIMORE – He assembled the crib and mounted the bookshelves. She unpacked the bedding and filled the closet. Then husband and wife stood in the nursery and worried. Bill Janu, a police officer, is white. Shanna Janu, a lawyer, is black. As they eagerly awaited their baby's birth this spring, they felt increasingly anxious, since their two years of marriage had been punctuated by the killings of African-American men and boys in Ferguson, Brooklyn, Cleveland, North Charleston and Baltimore, all at the hands of the police. Mr. Janu, who longed for a son, tried to reassure his wife. Mrs. Janu emailed him one article after another, warning of the perils that face black boys.

(B) As the due date approached, Mr. Janu found himself praying for a girl. In the delivery room at St. Agnes Hospital, after more than 20 hours of labor, the infant finally arrived, red-faced and wailing with Mr. Janu's blue eyes and Mrs. Janu's full lips and nose. The new father exulted. Then he felt the weight of his new reality. "Now, I have a black son in Baltimore," the white police detective remembered thinking as he cradled his baby boy. Wesley William Janu, born on May 23, 2016, smiled for the first time during a summer bloodied by the worst confrontations between African-Americans and the police in decades.

(C) They know their son is taking his place in the world at a time of unease. Wesley will learn to sit up on his own during the final term of the nation's first African-American president. By the time he is 28, more than half of the population in the United States will very likely be members of ethnic or racial minority groups or mixed race, according to the Census Bureau.

(D) Mrs. Janu, born in Louisiana, grew up in a predominantly white suburb in upstate New York, and married a white detective. Yet these days, she fears that racism and bias might be "hard-wired" into society and wonders how that might affect her family. She worries as her husband holsters his firearm, kisses her goodbye and heads out the door to pursue violent criminals in this predominantly black city. Will he be a target now on the street?

(E) Sometimes, the Janus manage to put aside their worries, losing themselves in the cocoon of their two-story home. They focus on Wesley – Mr. Janu calls him "Little Man" – on the grip of his fingers, the pout of his lower lip, the way he scales tall buildings with his eyes. But this summer, the ugliness of the outside world has always seemed to intrude.

(F) One day, Mr. Janu called to tell her that his squad was bracing for protests. "There's going to be rioting – is that what you're saying?" asked Mrs. Janu, her phone tight to her ear, as she bounced Wesley on her hip. The city remained calm. But this month, the fires were burning in Milwaukee. And the Justice Department released a scathing report, accusing the Baltimore police of systematically stopping, searching and arresting black residents for minor offenses, or even without any cause at all.

(G) Wesley is blithely unaware of the tumult. But his parents have already begun preparing what to tell him, when the time comes. Don't do things that bring too much attention to yourself, even if your white friends are doing it. You can't go running around in a hoodie. Don't run into someone's yard and grab a ball. If a police officer tells you to do something, just do it. Mrs. Janu considers herself the practical parent, but the list fills her with sadness. "Black boys aren't allowed to be innocent or young," she said.

(H) Mr. Janu felt bewildered at first by such talk. He had never imagined such a discussion with his son. "You wouldn't have to explain that to a white child," he said. He said he had lived most of his life "with blinders on." His conversations with his wife have opened his eyes. In the past, Mr. Janu said, he often assumed that the black boys he saw on impoverished street corners were criminals-to-be, youngsters destined for handcuffs. Now, he looks for the exuberance in the faces of the wisecracking, jostling boys still savoring the waning days of summer. He hopes that other police officers will see that, too, someday, in his son. *(721 words)*

Adapted and abridged from Rachel L. Swarns: Black Mother, White Father, a Baby and a Badge. From The New York Times, *2016-08-24*

Task II: Mixed Reading Tasks (I Have a Black Son in Baltimore) (12)

1 Gapped Summary (paragraphs A–C, G–H) (8)

Fill the gaps in the summary with appropriate words or expressions (one word per line) from the corresponding sections of the text. Do not make any changes. Please also provide the number of the line in which you have found the word/expression.

When Mr. Janu ________________ (l.   ) his new-born son Wesley in the delivery room of St. Agnes Hospital, he had mixed feelings. Of course, he ________________ (l.   ) because of the happy event. At the same time, though, he felt extremely scared to have a black son in an era marked by an atmosphere of ________________ (l.   ).
Already during Mrs. Janu's pregnancy, the couple had become more and more ________________ (l.   ) because the past two years had been ________________ (l.   ) by deadly confrontations between US policemen and African-American males. In the face of these incidents, Mrs. Janu had repeatedly tried to make her husband aware of the ________________ (l.   ) involved in being a male black youngster.

In the meantime, Wesley's parents have started thinking about rules for him to follow once he is older. Mrs. Janu thinks she is a __________ __________ (l.). However, the fact that black youths are deprived of their childhood depresses her. And Mr. Janu, who used to have quite a negative picture of young African-American males, has come to realize that he had spent most of his days wearing ________________ (l.).

2 Mediation Englisch – Deutsch (Paragraphen D–F) **(4)**

Beantworten Sie die folgenden Fragen auf Deutsch.

2.1 "[...] racism and bias might be 'hard-wired' into society." (Z. 23 f.)
Welche Befürchtung wird hier zum Ausdruck gebracht? (1,5)

Die Befürchtung, dass …

____

____

2.2 Was wirft das Justizministerium der Polizei von Baltimore vor? (2,5)

____

____

____

Text III Pokémon Go Brings Augmented Reality to a Mass Audience

(A) There are video games that go viral overnight, causing people to coop themselves up in their homes for days to play. But the opposite has happened with Pokémon Go, a free smartphone game that has soared to the top of the download charts: It has sent people into streets and parks, onto beaches and even out to sea in a kayak in the week since it was released. The game – in which players try to capture exotic monsters from Pokémon, the Japanese cartoon franchise – uses a combination of ordinary technologies built into smartphones, including location tracking and cameras, to encourage people to visit public landmarks, seeking virtual loot and collectible characters that they try to nab.

(B) Boon Sheridan, a resident of Holyoke, Massachusetts, has seen the activity first-hand. His home, a converted gable-roofed church that once attracted worshipers, had without his knowledge been designated a Pokémon "gym," a place where players who reach Level 5 in the game must go to train their Pokémon characters. In the last week, as the game became the most downloaded app, he has been wondering how to explain to neighbors all the people who congregated on the sidewalk and pulled up at odd hours. "I want to make sure I tell them, 'Hey, I'm not a drug dealer,'" Mr. Sheridan said. "I know there are people pulling up in front of the house all the time, but trust me I have no say in this."

(C) On Sunday, San Francisco's parks and downtown were crawling with Pokémon Go players while in Washington, the White House and the Pentagon have been designated official Pokémon gyms. A bar in Harrisonburg, Virginia, was offering a 10 percent discount to Pokémon Go players on a specific team, while a tea shop in Japantown in San Francisco offered a "buy one tea, get one free" deal to Pokémon Go players. The number of daily active users on Android devices in the United States alone was closing in on the usage of Twitter, the data analytics firm SimilarWeb estimated. Pokémon Go represents one of those moments when a new technology – in this case, augmented reality or A. R., which fuses digital technology with the physical world – breaks through from a niche toy for early adopters to something much bigger. The idea behind the technology is to overlay digital imagery on a person's view of the real world, using a smartphone screen or a headset.

(D) But Pokémon Go's public nature is also causing unforeseen side effects, attracting crowds that disturb homeowners and creating opportunities for criminals to lure players to remote areas where they can be targeted for theft. In Australia, police have issued tips for how roving Pokémon Go players can safely play the game.

(E) Many technology companies thought A. R. might first take off through specialized business applications that, for example, allow architects to visualize finished building projects in situ. Instead, it took a game based on a beloved entertainment franchise from the mid-1990s in Japan to help the technology go mainstream.

(F) Pokémon, a hybrid of the words "pocket" and "monsters," belongs to the Pokémon Company, which is partly owned by Nintendo, the Japanese game pioneer, which has struggled to adapt to the era of gaming on mobile devices like smartphones and tablets. The uptake of Pokémon Go, which is so far available only in the United States, Australia and New Zealand, has been so furious that it sent Nintendo's market capitalization soaring, adding $ 9 billion. [...]

(G) Pokémon Go, though, is actually the work of a start-up, Niantic Inc., which was created inside Google and spun out of the company last year. Niantic partnered with the Pokémon Company to make Pokémon Go. Like the most successful mobile games, while Pokémon Go is free to play, it gives players opportunities to buy virtual items for a few dollars to speed up their progress. The game's real-world nature also gives Niantic another intriguing moneymaking possibility, by charging fast-food restaurants, coffee shops and other retail establishments to become locations where people are motivated to go to pick up virtual loot. [...]

(H) Jan Dawson, a technology analyst at Jackdaw Research, said Pokémon Go's success was an important moment for augmented reality, mainly because it doesn't require expensive extra equipment like a headset, which virtual reality (V. R.) games often need. "This clearly demonstrates that A. R. can cross over into the mainstream on the devices people already have in at least some cases," he said. "But it doesn't necessarily do anything for the kind of A. R. and V. R. experiences big companies are piling so much money into."

(I) For players, Pokémon Go has been a health booster and a social cementer. Kay Collins, a 22-year-old health care worker in San Francisco, played the game for half a day straight on Sunday, including while waiting in line at a tattoo parlor. "My pedometer says whenever I play the game I take more steps than I used to before I started playing this game," she said. Brad Ensworth, a San Francisco State University student who played the game over the weekend, said he had never been a fan of augmented reality gaming before Pokémon Go, but was drawn in by the game's surprisingly social aspect. "You'll just run into people and spark up conversations immediately," he said while playing the game in Golden Gate Park. "We met this one guy who drove up from San Jose to collect Pokémon in the park, and he had more knowledge about this game than anyone else we've met so far. We called him the Guru." *(921 words)*

Adapted and abridged from Nick Wingfield/Mike Isaac: Pokémon Go Brings Augmented Reality to a Mass Audience. From The New York Times, *2016-07-12*

Task III: Mixed Reading Tasks (Pokémon Go Brings Augmented Reality …) **(9)**

1 Multiple Choice (paragraphs A–G) **(6)**

Mark the most suitable option by crossing the appropriate letter.

1.1 Pokémon Go players …

- **A** ☐ loot public landmarks.
- **B** ☐ seem to be ubiquitous.
- **C** ☐ dominate global game culture.
- **D** ☐ coop themselves up.

1.2 Boon Sheridan is worried because …

- **A** ☐ his church cannot accommodate all the worshipers.
- **B** ☐ Pokémon players schedule their meetings at his house.
- **C** ☐ he is in danger of being charged with drug dealing.
- **D** ☐ his reputation in the neighborhood is put at risk.

1.3 The expression "niche toy" in paragraph C (l. 28) refers to …

- **A** ☐ augmented reality.
- **B** ☐ Android devices.
- **C** ☐ Pokémon Go.
- **D** ☐ digital technology.

1.4 According to paragraphs D–E, Pokémon Go does not …

A ☐ encourage crime.
B ☐ promote mainstream technology.
C ☐ annoy local residents.
D ☐ prompt police reactions.

1.5 Nintendo …

A ☐ struggled to produce innovative mobile devices.
B ☐ sold Pokémon Go for $ 9 billion.
C ☐ was not a pioneer in mobile gaming.
D ☐ is a specialist in hybrid technology.

1.6 Niantic …

A ☐ deliberately disregards retail stores.
B ☐ frequently puts its virtual prey where it pays off.
C ☐ generously sponsors fast-food restaurants.
D ☐ successfully partnered with Google.

2 Sentence Completion (paragraphs H–I) (3)

Complete the following sentences with words/expressions from paragraphs H–I.

2.1 Pokémon Go shows that augmented reality (A. R.) has the potential to ________________________________ without people having to buy any extra equipment. (1)

2.2 As far as the players are concerned, Pokémon Go works as a "health booster and social cementer" (l. 60):

That means it motivates people to ______________________________ (1)

and creates situations in which they ______________________________ (1)
with the people they meet.

WRITING

Task IV: Descriptive Writing (9)

Choose one of the following tasks (1 or 2) and write about 100 words.

1 **Describing a picture: Travelling in Asia**

Describe and interpret the picture.

Source: http://kaskus.co.id

2 Describing statistics

Describe and interpret the following chart.

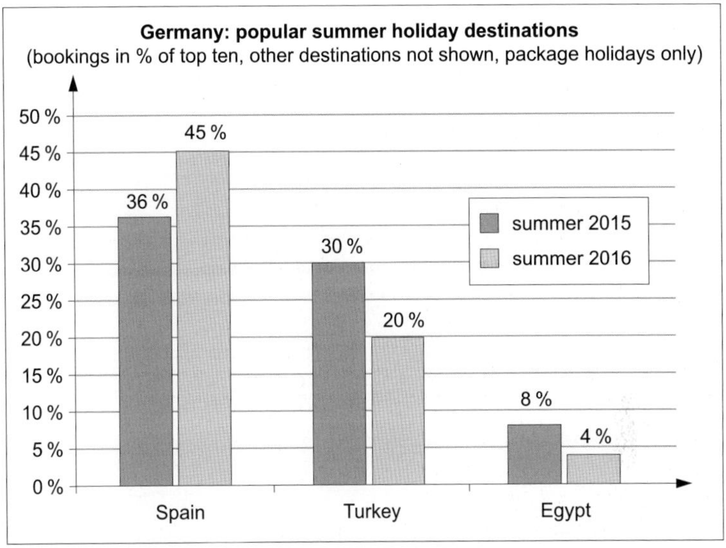

Adapted from www.worksitenews.de

Task V: Argumentative Writing (21)

Choose one of the following topics. Write at least 200 words.

1 Composition Topic 1

In some schools in Canada the curriculum requires students to participate in community work such as helping the elderly or disabled.
Discuss whether community work should be part of your school's curriculum as well.

2 Composition Topic 2

Money is the key to job satisfaction. Do you agree?

Lösungsvorschläge

READING

Task I: Multiple Matching (The American Teenager in 2015 …)

TIPP

Markieren Sie die neun namentlich genannten Personen im Text und lesen Sie der Reihe nach deren Aussagen, die jeweils in wörtlicher Rede vorliegen. Nun studieren Sie die zwölf „Statements" und kreuzen die Zahl an, die am besten den Inhalt der Aussage der betreffenden Person paraphrasiert.

- **Sharon Bayantemur: Statement 2**
  Siehe Z. 6/7: "they know you have a cell phone and they can contact you and you have to pick up."
- **Emma Baker: Statement 8**
  Siehe Z. 13/14: "Nowadays women can make a living on their own and be very independent."
- **David Sides: Statement 10**
  Siehe Z. 18/19: "nobody cares. That's your thing. I'm not gonna tell you you can't do it"
- **Caitlyn Ascencio: Statement 11**
  Siehe Z. 23/24: "We have so many things nowadays to keep us busy"
- **Ibrahim Diallo: Statement 3**
  Siehe Z. 33/34: "There's always going to be a race problem all around the world"
- **Luz Robles: Statement 9**
  Siehe Z. 38–40: "I don't think it's the police in general. I think it's just certain people who are spoiling it for all of them."
- **Lonny Hancock: Statement 5**
  Siehe Z. 46–49: "You would speak about it in a hushed tone maybe, like, ten years ago […]. Now you could be screaming across the room to a friend, 'Hey! Want to go smoke?'"
- **Jacob Lamb: Statement 1**
  Siehe Z. 56/57: "I feel like a college degree is worth a lot less than it was."
- **Beth Rodriguez: Statement 7**
  Siehe Z. 61/62: "when they [her parents] came here […] they didn't really get the chance to go to college, […] I think I'll have it a lot easier."
- Die **Statements 4, 6, 12** treffen also nicht zu.

Person	Statement
Sharon Bayantemur	**2**
Emma Baker	**8**
David Sides	**10**
Caitlyn Ascencio	**11**
Ibrahim Diallo	**3**

Person	Statement
Luz Robles	**9**
Lonny Hancock	**5**
Jacob Lamb	**1**
Beth Rodriguez	**7**

Task II: Mixed Reading Tasks (I Have a Black Son in Baltimore)

1 **TIPP**

Für Aufgabe 1, das *Gapped Summary*, kommen nur die Absätze A, B, C, G und H in Frage. Markieren Sie diese daher am besten und lesen Sie sie zum Verständnis sehr gewissenhaft.
Wie in den Arbeitsanweisungen angegeben, sollen die Antworten wörtlich übernommen werden. Achten Sie auch darauf, dass die Anzahl der Schreiblinien pro Lücke die Anzahl der einzusetzenden Wörter anzeigt. Ferner folgt die Zusammenfassung nicht immer derselben Reihenfolge im Text. Sie sollen zudem die Zeile (in Klammern) mit angeben, in der der entsprechende Ausdruck im Ausgangstext zu finden ist.
In der fünften Lücke könnte man aufgrund des Ausdrucks „deadly confrontations" auf „bloodied" (Z. 15) als mögliche Lösung schließen. Allerdings funktioniert diese Formulierung hier nicht. Es wird nur „punctuated" als richtig akzeptiert.

- Worterklärungen zum Ausgangstext:
  - Z. 4: *anxious (= troubled, concerned)* – besorgt, rastlos;
    since (= as, because) – hier: da, weil, zumal
  - Z. 5: *to punctuate (= perforate, interrupt)* – hier: durchsetzen, durchziehen
  - Z. 8: *perils (= dangers, risks, hazards)* – Gefahren
  - Z. 12: *to exult (= triumph, rejoice)* – jubeln, überglücklich sein
  - Z. 14: *to cradle* (*cradle* = Wiege) – hier: im Arm halten, an sich drücken
  - Z. 17: *unease (= disquiet, anxiety, unrest)* – Unsicherheit, Unruhe
  - Z. 48: *blinders* – Scheuklappen
- Worterklärungen zum Lückentext:
  - *delivery room* – Entbindungsraum, Kreißsaal
  - *pregnancy* – Schwangerschaft
  - *to be deprived of (= robbed of)* – etw. beraubt sein

When Mr. Janu **cradled (l. 14)** his new born son Wesley in the delivery room of St. Agnes Hospital, he had mixed feelings. Of course, he **exulted (l. 12)** because of the happy event. At the same time, though, he felt extremely scared to have a black son in an era marked by an atmosphere of **unease (l. 17)**.
Already during Mrs. Janu's pregnancy, the couple had become more and more **anxious (l. 4)** because the past two years had been **punctuated (l. 5)** by deadly confrontations between US policemen and African-American males. In the face of these incidents, Mrs. Janu had repeatedly tried to make her husband aware of the **perils (l. 8)** involved in being a male black youngster.
In the meantime, Wesley's parents have started thinking about rules for him to follow once he is older. Mrs. Janu thinks she is a **practical parent (l. 43)**. However, the fact that black youths are deprived of their childhood depresses her. And Mr. Janu, who used to have quite a negative picture of young African-American males, has come to realize that he had spent most of his days wearing **blinders (l. 48)**.

2 **TIPP**

Für diese Aufgabe sind die Absätze D–F heranzuziehen. Da eine wörtliche Übersetzung nicht verlangt ist, genügt es, die Hauptaussage wiederzugeben.

Zu 2.1:
- Siehe Zeile 23/24: "racism and bias might be 'hard-wired' into society"
- Worterklärungen:
  - *bias (= prejudice, stereotype)* – Vorurteil, Voreingenommenheit
  - *hard-wired* (*wire* = Draht) – fest verdrahtet, hier: verknüpft, fest verankert

Zu 2.2:
- Die relevante Passage finden Sie in Absatz F in den Zeilen 36 bis 39:
  "And the Justice Department released a scathing report, accusing the Baltimore police of systematically stopping, searching and arresting black residents for minor offenses, or even without any cause at all."
- Worterklärungen:
  - *Justice Department* – Justizministerium
  - *scathing* – hier: vernichtend, scharf kritisierend
  - *to accuse* – beschuldigen
  - *systematically* – hier: planmäßig, gezielt
  - *to search* – hier: durchsuchen
  - *offenses* – Gesetzesübertretungen, Verstöße
  - *cause (= reason)* – Grund, Ursache

2.1 Die Befürchtung, **dass Rassismus und Vorurteile fest in der Gesellschaft verankert sein könnten/fester Bestandteil der Gesellschaft sein könnten.**

2.2 Es werden gezielt afroamerikanische (schwarze) Bürger durchsucht und festgenommen, oft wegen geringer Verstöße oder sogar grundlos.

Task III: Mixed Reading Tasks (Pokémon Go Brings Augmented Reality …)

1 **TIPP**

Die relevanten Textabschnitte sind hier die Absätze A bis G. Lesen Sie zuerst alle Aufgabenstellungen gründlich und suchen Sie in den relevanten Textabschnitten gezielt nach Schlüsselwörtern aus den Teilaufgaben (z. B. Aufgabe 1.2 „Boon Sheridan" findet sich auch im Text, Z. 10).

1.1 Das Wort „ubiquitous" (= allgegenwärtig) in Antwortoption B weist darauf hin, dass die Spieler an vielen Orten auftauchen; in Z. 3/4 sind einige Orte angegeben: "It has sent people into streets and parks, onto beaches and even out to sea in a kayak"

1.2 Siehe Z. 14–16: "he has been wondering how to explain to neighbors […]. 'Hey, I'm not a drug dealer'"

1.3 Siehe Z. 26/27: „a new technology – in this case, augmented reality or A. R., which fuses digital technology with the physical world"

1.4 Beachten Sie, dass danach gefragt ist, was keine Eigenschaft des Spiels ist! Relevant sind hier die Abschnitte D und E (Z. 31–38).
Siehe Z. 37/38: "Instead, it took a game […] from the mid-1990s in Japan to help the technology go mainstream."

1.5 Siehe Z. 40/41: "Nintendo, […], which has struggled to adapt to the era of gaming on mobile devices like smartphones and tablets."

1.6 Siehe Z. 49–51: "The game's real-world nature also gives Niantic another intriguing moneymaking possibility, by charging fast-food restaurants, coffee shops and other retail establishments"

1.1 Pokémon Go players …

B ☒ seem to be ubiquitous.

1.2 Boon Sheridan is worried because …

D ☒ his reputation in the neighborhood is put at risk.

1.3 The expression "niche toy" in paragraph C (l. 28) refers to …

A ☒ augmented reality.

1.4 According to paragraphs D–E, Pokémon Go does not …
B [X] promote mainstream technology.

1.5 Nintendo …
C [X] was not a pioneer in mobile gaming.

1.6 Niantic …
B [X] frequently puts its virtual prey where it pays off.

2 **TIPP**

Zur Ergänzung der Sätze sollen Wörter oder Ausdrücke aus den Absätzen H und I verwendet werden. Verzichten Sie auf eigene Formulierungen und passen Sie die relevanten Ausdrücke an die gegebene Satzstruktur an.

2.1 Pokémon Go shows that augmented reality (A. R.) has the potential to **cross over into the mainstream** (l. 56) without people having to buy any extra equipment.

2.2 That means it motivates people to **take more steps** (l. 63) and creates situations in which they **spark up conversations** (l. 67) with the people they meet.

WRITING

Task IV: Descriptive Writing

1 **TIPP**

Bei dieser Aufgabe sollten Sie erkennen, dass es um das Thema Tourismus in armen Regionen oder Entwicklungsländern geht.

- **Beschreibung:**
  - Zwei junge Touristinnen (vermutlich aus einem westlichen Land) machen gerade Nahaufnahmen …
  - von zwei Kindern irgendwo in Asien, die vor einer ärmlichen Hütte sitzen.
  - Die Kinder schauen entweder ziemlich verwirrt in die Kamera, weil sie nicht wissen, was sie von der Sache halten sollen oder …
  - sie posieren für die Touristen gegen ein Trinkgeld/eine Spende.
- **Kernaussage:** Kritik an der schamlosen Ausnützung von Armut, am Voyeurismus und/oder an der Gedankenlosigkeit westlicher Touristen in armen Ländern.

The topic of this picture is tourism in poor countries.
You can see two young female western tourists smiling and taking close-up photos of two Asian children sitting in front of a shabby house. The children are looking into the camera. They seem either perplexed, not knowing what to make of the situation, or they are posing for the tourists for a small amount of money.
This picture can be seen either as a fierce criticism of the thoughtlessness of western tourists on a "photo-safari" through Asian slums, or as a sharp accusation of the wealthy "western world" exploiting the plight of poor countries. *(104 words)*

2 **TIPP**

Thematisch zeigt die Statistik die drei beliebtesten Urlaubsziele deutscher Urlauber und die Veränderung im Buchungsverhalten in den Jahren 2015 und 2016.

- **Beschreibung:** Vorab muss klar sein, dass lediglich die „Top Drei" der beliebtesten Urlaubsländer in der Statistik gezeigt werden und es sich ausschließlich um Pauschalreisen („package holidays") handelt. Am Vergleich der Prozentangaben für die Buchungen nach Spanien, in die Türkei und nach Ägypten kann man erkennen, dass Reisen in die letzteren Länder sehr (im Falle von Ägypten sogar um die Hälfte) zurückgegangen sind, während Spanien an Beliebtheit zugelegt hat. Buchungen nach Spanien machten 2016 fast die Hälfte aller Pauschalreisen aus (45 %).
- **Kernaussage:** Der Rückgang der Buchungen in die Türkei und nach Ägypten hängt vermutlich mit der unsicheren politischen Lage in diesen Regionen zusammen. Spanien, als subjektiv sichereres Land, wird hingegen als Urlaubsziel bevorzugt.

The given chart shows the popularity of the top three summer holiday destinations of German tourists in the years 2015 and 2016.
In both years Spain and Turkey were very popular destinations. Spain, however, experienced an increased share of bookings of package holidays by nine percent in 2016. Those of Spain rose up to 45 percent, whereas those of Turkey dropped by a third, down to twenty percent overall. A similar development can be seen in package tourism to Egypt, where it halved to four percent.
All this could be interpreted with more Germans opting for safer holiday destinations avoiding places troubled by political instability and/or terrorism. *(108 words)*

1 **TIPP**

Topic 1 stellt die Frage, ob gemeinnützige Arbeit verpflichtend an Schulen eingeführt werden soll oder nicht. Es sollte also dialektisch (d. h. pro oder kontra) behandelt werden, wobei man in der Regel das Argument am Schluss bringt, das die eigene Meinung widerspiegelt.

Community work is an important factor in society. Without its many voluntary workers, our country would be less social and less effective. Should we add more people to this pool of helpers by making community work an obligatory part of our schools' curricula?

On the one hand, one must disagree, because community work would not be "voluntary" any more if you declared it mandatory. Additionally, when you have unqualified personnel in the health or social sector, for example, who might not be able to give the elderly or disabled people the proper care and attention they need, new problems could arise.

On the other hand, there is a disproportion between the younger and the elder generation, as both the average life-span of people continues to increase and not enough children are born. This means that more young people are desperately needed to attend to the elderly – and to all people who need assistance in their daily lives, too. Schools could provide special training here.

Another issue is that younger people should be made more sensitive to the needs of the elderly and the disabled. They should be taught how important it is for their own benefit regarding their own future and how rewarding it is to assist and help people in need.

In conclusion, I strongly recommend that community work should be implemented into the curricula of our schools and colleges. *(231 words)*

2 **TIPP**

Bei **Topic 2** wird gefragt, ob man der Ansicht ist, dass Geld allein ausreicht, um im Beruf Erfüllung zu finden. Das Thema kann dialektisch abgehandelt werden, es ist aber auch möglich, dass nur die Vor- oder Nachteile angeführt werden. Vergessen Sie nicht, einen Schlussgedanken zu formulieren, der abrundet oder einen Kompromissvorschlag bzw. eine begründete Entscheidung dafür oder dagegen vorsieht.

A job must provide not only your livelihood, but also a decent standard of living with the chance of securing your financial situation in retirement. However, job satisfaction definitely means more than this.

Sometimes people find themselves in a dilemma when they have to choose between different job offers. Young people are especially tempted to give priority to money to be able to afford the same things as their peer groups, like a car, the latest smartphone, a stylish piece of clothing etc. Later they might come to realize that money doesn't buy job satisfaction, which, of course, contributes greatly to one's happiness.

To me, job satisfaction is a crucial part of my personal happiness. It includes having a good relationship with my colleagues, and a job requiring all my abilities, so that I can gain expertise in my field of work. As we spend a large part of our lives doing our jobs or practising our professions, it is essential that we spend this time in a meaningful way. If possible, our jobs should provide fulfilment.

Money can contribute towards making job satisfaction and fulfilment a lot more attainable, of course. However, if money gave us the ability to buy happiness, all rich people would be happy, which obviously is not the case.

Summarizing, my personal happiness – regarding my job and my life as a whole – does not depend solely on how much money I earn and have. *(239 words)*

Berufliche Oberschulen Bayern ▪ Englisch 12. Klasse
Fachabiturprüfung 2018

READING

Hinweis: Für die Fachabiturprüfung wurde der folgende Lesetext etwas abgeändert – aus lizenzrechtlichen Gründen muss der Text hier jedoch in der ursprünglichen Fassung des *Christian Science Monitor* abgedruckt werden. Die zu Prüfungszwecken geänderten Passagen sind durch eine kleinere Schriftgröße und hochgestellte Zahlen gekennzeichnet. In den Fußnoten zu den entsprechenden Ziffern finden Sie jeweils den Wortlaut aus der Fachabiturprüfung. Bitte orientieren Sie sich bei der Bearbeitung der Aufgabe an dieser Fassung.

Text I Why It's Becoming Cool to Live in Your Car

– or a 150-Sq. Ft. Apartment[1]

(A) When Shawna Nelson leaves her office in Seattle's suburbs, she does what 28-year-olds often do: dines with friends, goes out dancing, or sees a show. […] But at the end of the night Ms. Nelson always returns to Dora, the dusty Ford Explorer she calls home. In the back, where a row of seats should be, lies a foam mattress […]. Nelson keeps a headlamp handy for when she wants to read before bed. Then, once she's sure she won't get ticketed or towed, she turns in for the night. "I still strive to have some sort of routine," says Nelson, who started living in her car about a year ago. […]

(B) For her, it was an easy choice. She's not alone. As housing costs soar, US communities have faced ballooning homelessness, declining homeownership, and tensions over gentrification. But the rising expense of homes, when combined with the demographic, cultural, and technological trends of the past decade, has also prompted a more positive phenomenon: smaller, leaner living. This conscious shift, mainly among portions of the middle and upper classes, springs from a desire to live more fully with less.

(C) For some it means choosing tiny homes and "micro-apartments" – typically less than 350 square feet – for the chance to live affordably in vibrant neighborhoods. For others, […] it means hitting the road in a truck or van, communing with nature and like-minded people along the way. Proponents range in ages and backgrounds, but they all share a renewed thirst for alternatives to traditional lifestyles like single-family homes, long cherished as a symbol of the American dream.

(D) John Infranca, a law professor at Boston's Suffolk University who specializes in urban law and policy, says the phenomenon is driven largely by Millennials, who have been the faces of both the affordable housing crisis and the shift to minimalism. […] "There is some cultural demand for simpler living," says Professor Infranca. "And by virtue of technology, we are able to live with a lot less." […]

(E) "I think the recession changed the playing field for a lot of people," notes Sofia Borges, an architect, trend consultant […]. "Job security, homeownership – a lot of that went out the window and never really returned. When a change like that happens, you have to change your ideas a little bit too."

(F) That was certainly the case for Kim Henderson, who was a marketing manager making more than $ 80,000 a year before the recession. "I never again found a job like I had (before 2008)." says Ms. Henderson, now in her 50s. "When they were available, they went to younger people."

(G) Today Henderson makes about $ 37,000 a year as an executive assistant to a bar owner and lives in the Bristol Hotel, a mixed-use apartment building in the heart of downtown Los Angeles. Her studio […] is 175 square feet – the equivalent of about four king-size beds. […]

(H) Henderson pays $ 685 a month including electricity – a bargain for Los Angeles, where studios average $ 1,500. She can save money and still have enough disposable income to eat out and travel, she says. But at least as important is the sense of liberation. "There's an energy you get from purging," Henderson says. "You don't need six towels. You don't need a ton of dishes. You pick the things out that you really want to keep in the 'useful' category." […]

(I) "It's a value proposition," says David Neiman, whose Seattle design firm focuses on small-efficiency dwelling units, which start at 150 square feet. "I could live for the same price in a central location in housing that's clean, has internet, and I can walk to work and exciting things. Or I can live farther away, have more space, and it's in a secondary neighborhood and I have to drive."

(J) Instead of renting a micro-unit in an urban center, filmmakers Alexis Stephens and Christian Parsons decided two years ago to build their own 130-square foot house and load it onto the bed of a U-Haul […]. They then set off across the country in a bid to live more simply and sustainably, travel, and invest in their own place – all while documenting the experience.

(K) The Tiny House Expedition has since become a thriving enterprise. Ms. Stephens and Mr. Parsons have interviewed tiny house advocates and dwellers across 30,000 miles and 29 states.[2] […] "People are empowering themselves to build housing options that work for them that are not available in the market," Stephens says.

(L) Tiny homes can range from about 100 to 300 square feet and cost between $ 25,000 to $ 100,000 […]. Stephens and Parsons built theirs using reclaimed material for about $ 20,000 […]. For those with more lavish tastes, vendors like Seattle Tiny Homes offer customizable houses – complete with a shower and a washer and dryer – for about $ 85,000. […]

(M) Still, the movement to live smaller may not be as extensive as social media makes it seem, some housing analysts say.[3] Zoning regulations – especially in dense urban areas – often restrict the number and size of buildable units, slowing growth among micro-apartments and tiny homes. […]

(N) Living mobile isn't all grand adventures and scenic views, either. Van dwellers say they've had to contend with engine trouble, the cold and the heat, and unpleasant public restrooms. And Henderson in Los Angeles says she once lived in an affordable micro-housing development that had a pervasive drug-dealing problem.[4]

(O) Still, those who have embraced leaner living say what they might lose in creature comforts, they gain in perspective and experience. In crisscrossing the country, Stephens and Parsons opened themselves up to the kindness of strangers. "It's a nice reminder that as Americans we have so much more in common than we realize," Stephens says. They also spend more time connecting with others, instead of closeting themselves at home.[5]

(P) "Whether you're choosing a van, a school bus, a tiny house, or a micro-apartment, you get a lot of the same benefits," Ms. Stephens says. "We need more housing options in America, period [...]. We've boxed ourselves in a very monolithic housing culture. We're showing it's OK to venture outside of that." *(992 words)*

From the Christian Science Monitor, *August 21, 2017*

Wortlaut der Fachabiturprüfung

1 [Der zweite Teil des Titels war in der Textversion der Fachabiturprüfung nicht enthalten.]

2 Ms. Stephens has interviewed tiny house advocates and dwellers across 30,000 miles and 29 states.

3 Still, the movement to live smaller may not be as extensive as social media makes it seem, the housing analyst Bratt McLean says.

4 Van dweller Rita Sanchez says she had to contend with engine trouble, the cold and the heat, and unpleasant public restrooms. She once lived in an affordable micro-housing development that had a pervasive drug-dealing problem.

5 In crisscrossing the country, Parsons and his partner opened themselves up to the kindness of strangers. "It's a nice reminder that as Americans we have so much more in common than we realize," Parsons says. "We also spend more time connecting with others, instead of closeting ourselves at home."

Task I: Multiple Matching (Why It's Becoming Cool to Live in Your Car …) (9)

Who could have said what? Match the statements below (1–12) with the nine people given. Please note: For each person there is one statement. There are three more statements than you need.

	Statements for Multiple Matching
1	Downgrading has a cleansing effect.
2	Economic crises force people to think differently.
3	Home is where you park your van.
4	I try hard to make my day as "normal" as possible.
5	Leaner living is not as widespread as you might think.
6	I'm addicted to being in new places and meeting new people.
7	People are creative and find very individual solutions.
8	Travelling around we had more social contact than before.
9	You have to consider different options carefully.
10	The idea of downsizing is such a hard concept for me.
11	Innovation makes it possible to cut back.
12	You have to cope with all sorts of problems.

Person	Statement
Shawna Nelson	
John Infranca	
Sofia Borges	
Kim Henderson	
David Neiman	

Person	Statement
Alexis Stephens	
Bratt McLean	
Rita Sanchez	
Christian Parsons	

Text II Mo' Money, Mo' Problems: Woman Who Won Record $ 758 Million Jackpot under Policed Protection

(A) You already know that the Powerball jackpot Mavis Wanczyk won this week was the largest single lottery prize ever in North America. (A Powerball jackpot last year was bigger, but three winners split it.) You already know it was $ 758 million. But do you really know how big it was? Put it this way: It's more than the combined net worth of Ivanka Trump and Jared Kushner.

(B) Of course, Ms. Wanczyk, a 54-year-old health care worker, won't see most of that money. She chose a lump-sum payment over an annuity, which lowers the total to $ 480.5 million. Then there are taxes: 25 percent to the federal government and 5 percent to her state, Massachusetts. That leaves her with about $ 336 million to take home. Who cares? She's almost as rich as Katy Perry and Matthew Perry combined.

(C) She immediately gave up her job of 32 years. "I've called and told them I won't be coming back," she told reporters, to raucous laughter. Her first order of business is to "sit back and relax."

(D) Granted, the history of lotteries is littered with cautionary tales. Murder. Alcoholism. Lost friends. Huge spending sprees, then bankruptcy. Well-known research in the 1970s and 1980s, by the sociologist H. Roy Kaplan, found that the lucky winners weren't that much happier than their unlucky neighbors.

(E) Winning the lottery certainly comes with its perks – Wanczyk has said in a press conference that she can now retire early from her job as a hospital worker in Massachusetts – but there are some downsides, too. According to The Associated Press (AP), police have installed patrols around Wanczyk's home to protect her from press, gawkers, and potential criminals. "This is a great thing," Officer Michael Wilk, a spokesman for Chicopee police, told the AP. "But we want her to know we're there if she needs us."

(F) Members of the media and curious bystanders have reportedly descended on Wanczyk's house since she was announced as the lottery winner. Police have asked her neighbors to report any suspicious activity. "Besides media, there have been people knocking on doors, asking where she lives," Wilk said. "We're not going to tolerate her being harassed."

(G) There is good reason to take safety measures. In 2015, Craigory Burch Jr. was shot and killed by masked men who broke into his home – just two months after Burch won a $ 434,272 Georgia lottery prize.

(H) During her press conference, Wanczyk said that she wants to use her winnings to relax. But with excitement still palpable in the wake of her history-making win, she might have to wait for another few weeks. *(429 words)*

Adapted from Astor, Maggie: Mo' Money, Mo' Problems. Woman Who Won Record $ 758 Million Jackpot under Policed Protection, The New York Times, *August 24, 2017.*

Task II: Gapped Summary (Mo' Money, Mo' Problems ...) **(7)**

Fill the gaps in the summary with appropriate words or expressions (one word per line) from the corresponding sections of the text. Do not make any changes or adjustments. Please also provide the number of the line in which you have found the word.

For Mavis Wanczyk, becoming a lottery multi-millionaire definitely has its ______________ (l.   ), above all the chance to ______________________ (l.   ) in her mid-fifties as well as the millions of dollars that will turn her into one of the wealthiest women in the US. Of course, the sum will not be paid out entirely, and public authorities are going to impose high ______________________ (l.   ), too.
In addition, there are many ________________________ (l.   ) stories of lottery winners that have been unable to cope with their sudden wealth. According to ________________________ (l.   ) done in the past, winning the lottery does not necessarily lead to more happiness.
In some cases, lottery winners even have to be put under police protection to ensure that they are not ______________________ (l.   ) by nosy people. In the case of Ms. Wanczyk, the authorities have also called on local residents to watch out for __________________ (l.   ) occurrences.

Text III From Gang Life to College, One Paycheck at a Time

Hinweis: Für die Fachabiturprüfung wurde der folgende Lesetext leicht geändert – aus lizenzrechtlichen Gründen muss der Text hier jedoch in der ursprünglichen Fassung des *Christian Science Monitor* abgedruckt werden. Die zu Prüfungszwecken geänderte Passage ist durch eine kleinere Schriftgröße und ein Sternchen gekennzeichnet. In der zugehörigen Fußnote finden Sie den Wortlaut aus der Prüfung.

(A) Tony Franklin was fresh off a 10-year prison sentence for assaulting a police officer. As he walked into court to see his probation officer he was "down and out," he says. As a former gang member from Boston's Dorchester neighborhood, Mr. Franklin was standing at what experts identify as a crossroads: He could resort to his former means of making money on the streets, or he could walk in a new direction.

(B) With a son on the way and bills to pay, Franklin says there were times he would break down, not knowing what to do. But prison had been an eye-opener for Franklin, he says, and he wanted to do good. He needed a circuit breaker.

(C) It came in the form of Ismail Abdurrashid, a charismatic community figure and teacher at College Bound Dorchester (CBD), an organization designed to give at-risk youth the wraparound supports and education needed to go to college. "He just came out of nowhere like, 'oh, excuse me, this college program is willing to help you with everything you need right now,'" Franklin says.

(D) Specifically, that program was CBD's flagship, Boston Uncornered, which, after a brief pilot, recently had its hard launch. Over the next three years, it aims to serve 600 of Boston's 2,600 gang members and to have 250 enroll in college. The program recruits the most influential gang members, gives them a $ 400 per week stipend to renounce gang life and focus exclusively on their education, and then mentors and assists them, guiding them through the maze of financial aid applications, and teaching them life lessons like how to shop and pay their bills – whatever it takes to get them into and through college.

(E) Given the long-running debate in the United States over the merits of prison education, Boston Uncornered's approach is potentially controversial. CBD's chief executive officer Mark Culliton says it's a first-in-the-nation program because it demands a major shift in thinking: moving from seeing the most disruptive gang members – "core influencers" – as the central problem, to seeing them as part of the solution. […]

(F) "The Boston Uncornered Program is cutting edge; a fresh, welcomed approach to resolving the issue of gangs, poverty, crime, and hopelessness," says Lisa Taylor-Austin, a national and international gang expert. Ms. Taylor-Austin says that of the myriad different intervention and suppression programs, she has not seen a program as comprehensive as Boston Uncornered since the founding of Homeboy Industries in the 1980s.* Homeboy offers mentoring, pays participants a stipend or hourly rate, and includes apprentice programs in silk screening, baking, and solar panel installation. But she says Uncornered is unique because it gets students to a college-level education, which allows them to build careers, not just get jobs. This, she says, should have a ripple effect as successful former gang members reach out to their communities, especially gang involved and at-risk youth. […]

(G) CBD has been building the concept over the last four years. A pilot program with 40 students, says CBD, has shown enough promise over the last six months for the organization to believe it's worth expanding. Of the 40 students in the program, 85 percent have not been reincarcerated for a criminal sentence, 78 percent have persisted in the program, and 21 students – more than half – are currently enrolled in college. [...]

(H) The vital ingredient in the success of this program, Taylor-Austin says, is a gang member's desire to change. "In my work with gang involved youth I never met a gang member who didn't want a job, a paycheck and legitimate career," Taylor-Austin says. "This program is unique in that it offers all of these options." In Franklin's case, at 31 years old, he says, he was raring to go. He says he had reached the point where he was no longer blaming all his bad actions on his childhood with his caring, but often neglectful, drug-addicted mother and grandmother.

(J) During his decade in prison he completed his GED[1], read books, and wrote poetry. If he can pass one remedial math class, he will be ready to begin studies in sociology at Bunker Hill Community College in the fall. Eventually, he says, he'd like to work as a motivational speaker for kids. "We're not supposed to make it, we're going against all odds, but a lot of us, given the right opportunity we'll grow," he says, likening himself and his colleagues to Tupac Shakur's song about the rose that grew from the concrete. [...]

(K) But while the $ 12–$ 15 an hour these former gang members are getting paid might sound steep, the economic rationale stacks up, according to Culliton. CBD figures suggest a "core influencer" costs Massachusetts around $ 53,000 per year, (the national average is $ 100,000 per year) for things like incarceration and probation, compared to roughly $ 30,000 a year for the program. CBD estimates the program will cost $ 18 million over three years, funded mostly by private philanthropy [...]. So far program officials have raised about $ 4.8 million

(L) Calculating costs can be "tricky," according to Ben Struhl, a policy analyst from MIT's Poverty Action Lab, which, along with a team from Northeastern University, will gather and analyze data to measure the effectiveness of the program. But Mr. Struhl says he's excited because the research could be essential in proving the approach works.

(M) "We know in general things like these can work, but we don't have a great sort of mapping of what specific types of programs are most impactful, and which ones are the most cost effective," Struhl says. "If we can do that better, by looking at programs like College Bound Dorchester, we might actually be able to really establish a better way forward with some of these criminal justice debates." [...] *(963 words)*

From the Christian Science Monitor, *May 24, 2017*

Annotation

1 GED: General Educational Development Test

* **Wortlaut der Fachabiturprüfung:** "Of the myriad different intervention and suppression programs, I have not seen a program as comprehensive as Boston Uncornered since the founding of Homeboy Industries in the 1980s."

Task III: Mixed Reading Tasks (From Gang Life to College …) **(14)**

1 Multiple Choice **(7)**

Mark the most suitable option by crossing the appropriate letter.

1.1 When Tony Franklin was released from jail he was …

- **A** ☐ relieved.
- **B** ☐ broke.
- **C** ☐ confident.
- **D** ☐ depressive.

1.2 What is <u>not</u> true for the Boston Uncornered program? (paragraph D)

- **A** ☐ It concentrates on leading figures in gang culture.
- **B** ☐ It helps participants to do paper work.
- **C** ☐ It offers the former gang members scholarships.
- **D** ☐ It pays all the participants' living expenses.

1.3 According to paragraph E, the main idea of the Boston Uncornered program is that …

- **A** ☐ prison education is the key to success.
- **B** ☐ personal problems of the gang members should be addressed.
- **C** ☐ prominent gang members are treated as a force for good.
- **D** ☐ gang members should give up their former way of life.

1.4 Ms. Taylor-Austin regards Boston Uncornered as …

- **A** ☐ an all-embracing approach.
- **B** ☐ very ambitious.
- **C** ☐ not far-reaching enough.
- **D** ☐ a copy of a former program.

1.5 According to paragraphs H and J, Franklin …

- **A** ☐ has failed an important math test.
- **B** ☐ has not forgiven family members.
- **C** ☐ is unsure about his future career.
- **D** ☐ was ready to make a U-turn in his life.

1.6 Which problem is mentioned in paragraph K?

A ☐ The program still lacks over two thirds of the funds needed.
B ☐ The program is more expensive than the traditional approach.
C ☐ The state has to bear the full cost of the program.
D ☐ The program will definitely end in three years.

1.7 Ben Struhl …

A ☐ doubts that the program will pay off.
B ☐ thinks that more research needs to be done.
C ☐ has introduced the College Bound Dorchester scheme.
D ☐ wants to end the debates on criminal justice.

2 Short Answer Questions (paragraphs B – D) (3)

Answer the questions with words from the text.

2.1 Which metaphorical expression is used to describe a person that is required to make people change their lives completely? (1)

___

2.2 Which phrase means the same as "comprehensive help"? (1)

___

2.3 Which noun does the author use to describe the most successful and leading project of College Bound Dorchester? (1)

___

3 Mediation Englisch – Deutsch (4)

Bearbeiten Sie die folgenden Aufgaben auf Deutsch.

3.1 Erläutern Sie den Begriff "ripple effect" (l. 35) im Zusammenhang des Textes. (2)

___

___

___

3.2 Nennen und erläutern Sie die Metapher aus Tupac Shakurs Lied, mit der Franklin seine Situation beschreibt (Abschnitt J). (2)

Metapher im Lied	
Bedeutung	

WRITING

Task IV: Descriptive Writing (9)

Choose <u>one</u> of the following tasks (1 or 2) and write <u>about 100 words</u>.

1 Describing a cartoon

Describe and interpret the cartoon.

© *Chappatte,* The New York Times, *www.chappatte.com*

2 Describing statistics

Describe and interpret the following chart.

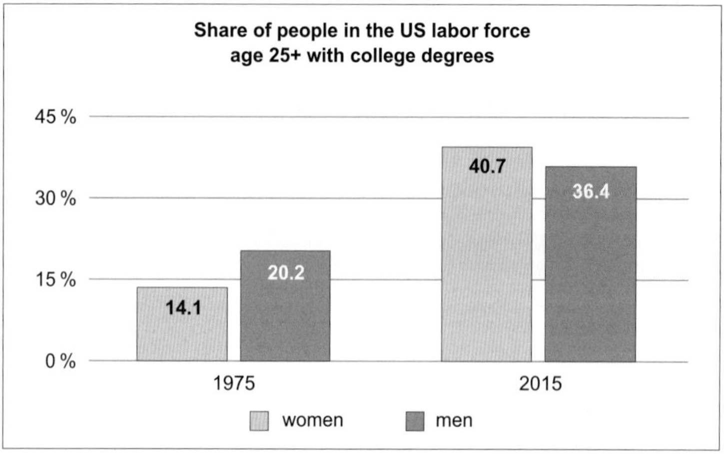

Source: U.S. Bureau of Labor Statistics

Task V: Argumentative Writing (21)

Choose one of the following topics. Write at least 200 words.

1 Composition Topic 1

So-called "vloggers" – people who upload films onto the Internet about themselves or their activities – are often more well-known among young people than other celebrities such as film stars. In your opinion, what are the reasons for their popularity?

2 Composition Topic 2

Donald Trump has claimed that "global warming is a hoax". Present arguments why we should take global warming seriously and express your point of view on Mr. Trump's statement.

READING

Task I: Multiple Matching (Why It's Becoming Cool to Live in Your Car …)

TIPP

Es empfiehlt sich, jeden der neun Namen im Text zu markieren. Lesen Sie dann die Aussagen dieser Personen einzeln nacheinander und versuchen Sie, sie den Statements zuzuordnen. Beißen Sie sich nicht an einem Statement fest, wenn Ihnen auf Anhieb keine Zuordnung gelingt. Stattdessen sollten Sie einfach mit dem nächsten Statement weitermachen und damit die Antwortmöglichkeiten eingrenzen. Neun der zwölf Statements sind Paraphrasierungen von Aussagen, die im Text zitiert werden.

- **Shawna Nelson: Statement 4**
  Siehe Z. 6/7: "I still strive to have some sort of routine"
- **John Infranca: Statement 11**
  Siehe Z. 23/24: "And by virtue of technology, we are able to live with a lot less."
- **Sofia Borges: Statement 2**
  Siehe Z. 25–28: "the recession changed the playing field for a lot of people. […] When a change like that happens, you have to change your ideas a little bit too."
- **Kim Henderson: Statement 1**
  Siehe Z. 40/41: "There's an energy you get from purging. […] You don't need six towels. You don't need a ton of dishes."
- **David Neiman: Statement 9**
  Siehe Z. 43–46: "It's a value proposition, […] I could live for the same price in a central location […]. Or I can live farther away"
- **Alexis Stephens: Statement 7**
  Siehe Z. 55/56: "People are empowering themselves to build housing options that work for them that are not available in the market"
- **Bratt McLean: Statement 5**
  Siehe Anmerkung 3 (Wortlaut der Fachabiturprüfung): "the movement to live smaller may not be as extensive as social media makes it seem"
- **Rita Sanchez: Statement 12**
  Siehe Anmerkung 4 (Wortlaut der Fachabiturprüfung): "she had to contend with engine trouble, the cold and the heat, and unpleasant public restrooms."

- **Christian Parsons: Statement 8**
  Siehe Anmerkung 5 (Wortlaut der Fachabiturprüfung): "In crisscrossing the country, Parsons and his partner opened themselves up to the kindness of strangers.[…] 'We also spend more time connecting with others'"
- Drei der Statements (**3**, **6** und **10**) passen zu keiner der genannten Personen.

Person	Statement
Shawna Nelson	**4**
John Infranca	**11**
Sofia Borges	**2**
Kim Henderson	**1**
David Neiman	**9**

Person	Statement
Alexis Stephens	**7**
Bratt McLean	**5**
Rita Sanchez	**12**
Christian Parsons	**8**

Task II: Gapped Summary (Mo' Money, Mo' Problems …)

1 **TIPP**

Wie in der Arbeitsanweisung angegeben, sollen die Antworten wörtlich übernommen werden (ein Wort pro Lücke). Zudem wird erwartet, dass Sie die Zeile mit angeben. Beachten Sie, dass die Zusammenfassung nicht unbedingt der Reihenfolge im Text folgt. Schlagen Sie unbekannte Wörter nach, wenn Sie diese für das Sinnverständnis benötigen.
Worterklärungen zum Ausgangstext:
Z. 7: *annuity* – lebenslange Rente
Z. 14: *littered with* – hier: voll von, gespickt mit
Z. 14: *cautionary tales* – abschreckende Beispiele
Z. 15: *sprees* – Orgien
Z. 18: *perks* – Vergünstigungen, Vorteile
Z. 21/22: *gawkers* – Gaffer
Z. 29: *harassed (= troubled, molested)* – belästigt
Z. 34: *palpable* – greifbar

For Mavis Wanczyk, becoming a lottery multi-millionaire definitely has its **perks** (**l. 18**), above all the chance to **retire** (**l. 19**) in her mid-fifties as well as the millions of dollars that will turn her into one of the wealthiest women in the US. Of course, the sum will not be paid out entirely, and public authorities are going to impose high **taxes** (**l. 8**), too.

In addition, there are many **cautionary** (**l. 14**) stories of lottery winners that have been unable to cope with their sudden wealth. According to **research** (**l. 15**) done in the past, winning the lottery does not necessarily lead to more happiness.

In some cases, lottery winners even have to be put under police protection to ensure that they are not **harassed** (**l. 29**) by nosy people. In the case of Ms. Wanczyk, the authorities have also called on local residents to watch out for **suspicious** (**l. 27**) occurrences.

Task III: Mixed Reading Tasks (From Gang Life to College …)

1 **TIPP**

1.1 Siehe Z. 2: "he was 'down and out'"

1.2 Drei der Aussagen lassen sich mit dem Text belegen:
- Zu A siehe Z. 16/17: "The program recruits the most influential gang members"
- Zu B siehe Z. 18/19: „mentors and assists them, guiding them through the maze of financial aid applications"
- Zu C siehe Z. 17: „gives them a $ 400 per week stipend"
- Aussage D findet sich nicht im Text.

1.3 Siehe Z. 24–26: "it demands a major shift in thinking: moving from seeing the most disruptive gang members – 'core influencers' – as the central problem, to seeing them as part of the solution."

1.4 Siehe Anmerkung (Wortlaut der Fachabiturprüfung): "I have not seen a program as comprehensive as Boston Uncornered"

1.5 Siehe Z. 47/48: "he had reached the point where he was no longer blaming all his bad actions on his childhood"

1.6 Siehe Z. 61–63: Hier müssen Sie rechnen. Das Programm kostet 18 Millionen Dollar, bisher wurden jedoch lediglich 4,8 Millionen gesammelt. Das ist weniger als ein Drittel – zwei Drittel der Summe fehlen also noch.

1.7 Siehe Z. 64–71: "Calculating costs can be 'tricky,' according to Ben Struhl […]. 'We know in general things like these can work, but we don't have a great sort of mapping of what specific types of programmes are most impactful, and which ones are the most cost effective,' Struhl says."

1.1 When Tony Franklin was released from jail he was …

B ☒ broke.

1.2 What is <u>not</u> true for the Boston Uncornered program? (paragraph D)

D ☒ It pays all the participants' living expenses.

1.3 According to paragraph E, the main idea of the Boston Uncornered program is that …

C ☒ prominent gang members are treated as a force for good.

1.4 Ms. Taylor-Austin regards Boston Uncornered as …

A ☒ an all-embracing approach.

1.5 According to paragraphs H and J, Franklin …

D ☒ was ready to make a U-turn in his life.

1.6 Which problem is mentioned in paragraph K?

A ☒ The program still lacks over two thirds of the funds needed.

1.7 Ben Struhl …

B ☒ thinks that more research needs to be done.

2 **TIPP**

Zur Beantwortung der Fragen sollen Ausdrücke aus den Absätzen B, C und D entnommen werden. Daher ist es sinnvoll, sich zunächst alle unbekannten Wörter in den entsprechenden Textpassagen zu markieren. Diese können für die Lösung relevant sein.

Worterklärungen zum Ausgangstext:

Z. 8: *circuit breaker* – wörtlich: Ausschalter, Stromkreisunterbrecher

Z. 11: *wraparound (support)* – Rundum-(Unterstützung)

Z. 14: *flagship* – Flaggschiff, Aushängeschild

2.1 circuit breaker (l. 8).

2.2 wraparound supports (l. 11)

2.3 flagship (l. 14)

3 **TIPP**

Zu 3.1:
Für die Erläuterung des Begriffs „ripple effect“ (Z. 35), was so viel wie Dominoeffekt bedeutet, sind die Zeilen 35–37 heranzuziehen: “former gang members reach out to their communities, especialy gang involved and at-risk youth.”

Zu 3.2:
Hier ist Abschnitt J heranzuziehen.
- Die Metapher steht in den Zeilen 55/56: “the rose that grew from the concrete.”
- Der Bezug zu Franklins Leben findet sich in den Zeilen 53/54: “We're not supposed to make it, we're going against all odds, but a lot of us, given the right opportunity we'll grow”

3.1 Damit ist gemeint, dass ehemalige Gangmitglieder, die erfolgreich ihre Ausbildung durchlaufen haben, als positive Vorbilder für gefährdete Jugendliche dienen und diese dazu veranlassen können, aus dem Gangmilieu auszusteigen.

3.2

Metapher im Lied	Rose, die aus dem Beton herauswächst
Bedeutung	Für viele junge Menschen aus dem Gangmilieu sind die Zukunftsprognosen schlecht, aber sie können es schaffen, erfolgreich zu sein, wenn ihnen entsprechende Möglichkeiten geboten werden.

WRITING

Task IV: Descriptive Writing

1 **TIPP**

Bei dieser Aufgabe sollten Sie erkennen, dass es um die Allgegenwart von US-Präsident Donald Trump in den Medien geht.

- **Beschreibung:** Ein Paar sitzt im Wohnzimmer, umgeben von einem Fernseher, einem Computer, einem Tablet, einem Smartphone sowie einer Zeitung und einer Zeitschrift. All diese Medien zeigen fast identische Bilder von Donald Trump. Das Paar ist der Situation überdrüssig, der Mann schwitzt sogar. Die Frau wünscht sich einen Filter, der solche Bilder blockiert. Selbst die Katze verkriecht sich erschreckt.
- **Kernaussage:** Die Menschen sind die exzessive Medienpräsenz von Donald Trump in den Medien leid.

The subject of this cartoon is the omnipresence of US President Donald Trump in the media.
A couple is sitting in their living room, surrounded by a TV, a computer, a tablet, a smartphone as well as a newspaper and a magazine. All these media forms show almost identical images of Donald Trump. The couple obviously feels overwhelmed by the flood of images. The man is sweating, while the woman wishes that someone would invent a filter to block images of Trump. Even the cat seems to want to hide itself.
The message of this cartoon is that people are tired of the excessive media coverage of Donald Trump. *(109 words)*

2 **TIPP**

Die Statistik zeigt den prozentualen Anteil der Erwerbstätigen mit Hochschulabschluss in den USA in den Jahren 1975 und 2015 (nach Geschlecht).

- **Beschreibung:** 1975 hatten 14,1 % der erwerbstätigen Frauen und 20,2 % der erwerbstätigen Männer in den USA einen akademischen Abschluss. 2015 dagegen hatten 40,7 % der weiblichen und 36,4 % der männlichen Arbeitskräfte einen Hochschulabschluss.
- **Kernaussage:** Es wird eine allgemeine Tendenz sichtbar, dass mehr Menschen in den USA einen Hochschulabschluss haben. Während Frauen mit Hochschulabschluss 1975 noch in der Unterzahl waren, haben sie mittlerweile aufgeholt und sind jetzt sogar in der Mehrheit.

The chart shows the percentage of people (by gender) with college degrees in the US workforce in 1975 and forty years later.
In 1975 14.1 percent of women and 20.2 percent of men in the US labour force had a college diploma. Four decades later, in 2015, 40.7 percent of the working population were women with college degrees, surpassing male degree-holders by 4.3 percent.
These statistics demonstrate that there is a general tendency for more people in the USA to graduate from college. It is, moreover, remarkable that there are more highly qualified women than men in the American workforce today. *(101 words)*

Task V: Argumentative Writing

1 **TIPP**

Topic 1 fragt nach den Gründen für die Beliebtheit von Vloggern, ist also steigernd abzuhandeln, wobei das wichtigste Argument zuletzt genannt werden sollte.

Vloggers like Bibi or Julien Bam have turned into celebrities, particularly among young people. Some of them have thousands or even millions of followers. But how can their popularity be explained?
To begin with, nearly everyone of the age of, say, ten to thirty uses social media a great deal. Watching videos on YouTube is generally very popular, not least because the clips are accessible at any time and for free. Thus, vloggers reach a relatively large audience.
Many vloggers are about the same age as their viewers. They use similar language and have similar interests and hobbies to their fans. This is why young people can easily identify with them. In addition, they often let their viewers be part of their private lives and offer advice on problems other young people might also be facing. Hence, many young people regard vloggers as good friends. What is more, vloggers give their viewers the opportunity to get in touch with them and enter into a virtual dialogue. Fans can post comments on the videos or ask questions, which a vlogger might then react to either in the comment section or in their next videos.
Summing up, I believe that vloggers are so popular because they are more approachable than other celebrities, such as film stars, who are usually far removed from the lives of most "normal" young people and tend to protect their privacy very carefully.
(235 words)

2 **TIPP**

Topic 2 ist steigernd zu behandeln – die eigene Beurteilung von Trumps Aussage sollte dabei am Schluss stehen. Da Sie darlegen sollen, warum man die Klimaerwärmung ernst nehmen sollte, ist es hier nicht möglich, zu argumentieren, dass man nicht an die Klimaerwärmung glaubt.

According to Donald Trump, global warming does not exist but is a mere invention. However, there are several arguments that negate this claim and show that climate change is indeed a serious problem.

Firstly, extreme weather events such as heat waves and heavy rainfall have become more common in recent years. Weather data recorded over a long period of time shows that the climate on the earth is indeed changing, and that average temperatures are rising. Most scientists agree that this is due to the so-called greenhouse effect, which means that carbon dioxide (which is emitted when burning fossil fuels, for example) prevents the sun's radiation from escaping into the atmosphere. The consequences of global warming can already be felt: Millions of people are losing their livelihood every year due to floods, droughts, or other catastrophes. Moreover, entire islands are in danger of being flooded due to rising sea levels. All this leads to a global stream of refugees who flee to countries that have, so far, been less affected by extreme climate conditions.

I believe that, in denying global warming, Donald Trump is merely trying to satisfy the economic interests of the fossil energy industry. To support his "hoax" argument, he frequently points to the short-term variation in temperatures (such as that some parts of the US have experienced cooler than normal temperatures) rather than focus on long-term developments. In my opinion, his view is extremely short-sighted and irresponsible, both for people in other parts of the world and for future generations.

(252 words)

Berufliche Oberschulen Bayern ▪ Englisch 12. Klasse
Fachabiturprüfung 2019

READING

Text I Cutting Adolescents' Use of Social Media Will Not Solve Their Problems

(A) First they went for tobacco, coal and sugar. Now they are targeting smartphones and social media. On January 6th two large investors in Apple demanded that the technology company must help parents curtail their children's iPhone use, citing research into the links between adolescent social-media habits and risk factors for suicide, such as depression. Old and new media abound with reports about phones' addictive, mind-warping properties. On the school run, parents compare tactics for limiting screen time.

(B) Something has made today's teenagers different from teenagers in the past. As well as being far better behaved and more temperate, they seem more anxious and unhappy. School surveys by the OECD, a club of mostly rich countries, suggest that 15-year-olds find it harder to make friends. In America – though, phone-bashers should note, not in the rich world as a whole – suicides of young people are up.

(C) Before stampeding for the off switch, parents and others should ask two questions. First, are iPhones, Instagram and so on actually to blame for adolescents' problems? Second, will curtailing their use do much good? On the available evidence, the answers are, respectively, maybe and no.

(D) Some studies of Britain and America, which conduct large surveys of young people, have found correlations between heavy technology use and unhappiness. Correlation is not causation, however: it could be that unhappy people seek refuge online. And the correlations are very weak. Only about 1 % of the variability in young people's mental wellbeing can be explained by social-media or smartphone use. One British study suggests that eating breakfast regularly is more than three times as important.

(E) Perhaps technology has messed up all young people, even those who abstain from it. Maybe it makes everyone feel left out, or thwarts all intimate connections: if your friend is always looking at her phone, it may not matter much whether you are. But if the effects are so amorphous it is hard to know what to do. Should parents gang up on teenagers as a group and enforce a universal crackdown? Should they deal with the inevitable charge of unfairness by applying the same restrictions to themselves? Good luck with that.

(F) Parents who worry about their teenage offspring (which is to say, all parents) can do something, however. Prod them out of the house, and worry a bit less about what they get up to. There is plenty of evidence for the cheering effects of hanging out with friends. Yet youngsters are doing less of this. Over-protective parents are probably one reason. Social pressure is another. It is revealing of broader attitudes that, in Britain, "teenagers hanging out on the streets" is a standard measure of anti-social behavior. The authoritative Crime Survey of England and Wales asks people whether it is a problem where they live, alongside things such as drug dealing and burnt-out cars. That the rate of adolescent hanging-out has dropped from 33 % to 16 % in ten years may please criminologists, but is unlikely to signal happier teenagers.

(G) A last cause of teenage angst is the economy and the job market. Financially, the great recession hit young people harder than others. On top of that, some teenagers believe they face crushing competition, not only from their peers but from foreigners and robots. All the more reason for governments to work on improving schools and to get rid of job protection for older workers. Teenagers, for their part, could probably handle a bit more work. Even though homework is associated with higher test scores, it declined by an hour a week across the OECD between 2003 and 2012, from six hours to five. Some put in that much time on their phones in a single day. *(623 words)*

https://www.economist.com/leaders/2018/01/11/cutting-adolescents-use-of-social-media-will-not-solve-their-problems

Task I: Mixed Reading Tasks (Cutting Adolescents' Use of Social Media …) (8)

1 Gapped Summary (paragraphs A–F) (6)

Fill the gaps in the summary with appropriate words or expressions (one word per line) from the corresponding sections of the text. Do not make any changes. Please also provide the number of the line in which you have found the word/expression.

The youth of today is a far cry from the youth in the past. Being distinctly more polite and ____________________ (l.) on the one hand, they are also more uneasy and sadder, on the other.

The media are currently teeming with articles blaming the smartphone for this alarming development. In addition to causing dependence, people ascribe ____________________ (l.) qualities to it. As a result, concerned parents and some businessmen alike are seeking to ____________________ (l.) the time teenagers spend in front of their smartphones.

Yet, neither a ______________ ______________ (l.) imposed on the youths by their parents nor parental self-restriction for reasons of fairness appear to be an adequate solution to the problem. ____________________ (l.) moms and dads may even add to the problem, being too concerned about what their kids might do outside. However, the whole discussion about adolescents' use of social media might be pointless since research in the UK and overseas has revealed that there are few links and ____________________ (l.) between time spent with digital devices and a person's happiness.

2 Short Answer Question (paragraph G) (2)

Answer the following question by providing the required information from the text. You may use words from the text.

What measures should policymakers take to tackle the problem of teenage angst according to the author?

- ____
- ____

Text II The Swedish 15-Year-Old Who's Cutting Class to Fight the Climate Crisis

(A) Why bother to learn anything in school if politicians won't pay attention to the facts? This simple realisation prompted Greta Thunberg, 15, to protest in the most effective way she knew. She is on strike, refusing to go to school until Sweden's general election on 9 September to draw attention to the climate crisis. **Her protest has captured the imagination of a country** that has been struck by heatwaves and wildfires in its hottest summer since records began 262 years ago.

(B) Every day for two weeks, Thunberg has been sitting quietly on the cobblestones outside parliament in central Stockholm, handing out leaflets that declare: "I am doing this because you adults are shitting on my future." She is a diminutive girl with pigtails and a fleeting smile – not the stereotypical leader of a climate revolution. "I am doing this because nobody else is doing anything. It is my moral responsibility to do what I can," she says. "I want the politicians to prioritise the climate question, focus on the climate and treat it like a crisis."

(C) Thunberg's protest might come as a surprise to anyone seduced by Sweden's reputation as a climate pioneer and champion of the environment. This year the country enacted "the most ambitious climate law in the world", aiming to become carbon neutral by 2045 and comfortably beating the 2015 Paris climate targets along the way. "This is too little too late, it needs to come much faster," Thunberg says. "Sweden is not a green paradise, it has one of the biggest carbon footprints."

(D) Her parents want her to give up her protest and go back to school. "My teachers are divided," Thunberg says. "As people they think what I am doing is good, but as teachers they say I should stop." One teacher to have downed tools to join her protest is Benjamin Wagner, 26. He expects to lose three weeks' wages – and his job as a biology teacher – as a result of his strike. "Our inability to stop climate change is like the efforts to stop World War One – we knew for years it was coming, they arranged all sorts of conferences, but still they didn't prevent it," Wagner says. "Greta is a troublemaker, she is not listening to adults. But we are heading full speed for a catastrophe, and in this situation the only reasonable thing is to be unreasonable."

(E) There are signs that more Swedes are listening. The Green Party, a partner in the centre-left coalition government, was languishing in the polls before the country was hit by more than 60 forest fires, which raged for weeks through a **rural tinderbox** created by the unprecedented drought. Now the party's support is up by half to about 6 %. "I am very impressed by Greta's courage and determination," says Janine Alm Ericson, a Green member of parliament. "But I am also sad that she feels she has to be there – the political parties in Sweden have not done enough. Thanks to the hot summer it has become easier for people to imagine what climate change can mean for us and others in Europe if we continue to ignore what is happening."

(F) Thunberg's own awakening to the climate crisis a few years ago caused upheaval in her family. Her mother, the well-known opera singer Malena Ernman, has given up her international career because of the climate effects of aviation. "Greta forced us to change our lives," says her father Svante. "I didn't have a clue about the climate. We started looking into it, reading all the books – she has read them too." Her teachers were telling her to turn off the lights and save paper, then flying off to New York for a holiday. For Greta, this was just not good enough: "Everyone believes that we can solve the crisis without effort, without sacrifice," she wrote in an article widely circulated on social media and translated into English.

(G) While on strike, she has done a lot of homework and read three books, her father says. Greta has Asperger's syndrome, which in the past has affected her health, he says. She sees her condition not as a disability but as a gift which has helped open her eyes to the climate crisis. "The best thing about my protest has been to see how more and more people have been coming and getting involved," Greta says. "I don't care if I get into trouble at school. I believe that one person can make a difference."

(744 words)

Adapted from: David Crouch: The Swedish 15-Year-Old Who's Cutting Class to Fight the Climate Crisis, The Guardian, *September 1, 2018, https://www.theguardian.com/science/2018/sep/01/swedish-15-year-old-cutting-class-to-fight-the-climate-crisis.*

Task II: Multiple Choice (The Swedish 15-Year-Old …) **(7)**

Mark the most suitable option by crossing (✗) the appropriate letter.

1 The introductory question expresses Greta's …

- **A** ☐ realisation that all her efforts have been in vain.
- **B** ☐ resignation when it comes to personal involvement.
- **C** ☐ disillusionment with the education system.
- **D** ☐ frustration in the face of indifferent decision-makers.

2 "Her protest has captured the imagination of a country" in paragraph A means that the Swedish people find her protest …

- **A** ☐ impeccable.
- **B** ☐ inspiring.
- **C** ☐ irrelevant.
- **D** ☐ inappropriate.

3 Which of the following was <u>not</u> a motive for Greta to become active?

- **A** ☐ She is an inconspicuous person.
- **B** ☐ She wants priorities to be reconsidered.
- **C** ☐ She felt obliged to do so.
- **D** ☐ She felt betrayed.

4 According to paragraph D, Greta's …

A ☐ parents feel ambivalent about her playing truant.
B ☐ protest meets unanimous approval.
C ☐ biology teacher thinks that the end justifies the means.
D ☐ protest won't go unpunished.

5 The expression "rural tinderbox" in paragraph E refers to …

A ☐ the fire hazard due to the exceptionally hot summer.
B ☐ the burning issue of climate change in rural areas.
C ☐ the explosive atmosphere in the country.
D ☐ the unprecedented success of the Green party.

6 Which of the following is <u>not</u> true according to paragraph F?

A ☐ Her call for action went viral on social media.
B ☐ Her ideas have had an enormous impact on her family life.
C ☐ Her commitment was sparked by her teachers' inconsistent behaviour.
D ☐ Her activism is deeply rooted in her conviction that you can have it all.

7 Greta's special condition …

A ☐ has no influence on her protest.
B ☐ is yet another obstacle to overcome.
C ☐ has contributed to her environmental awakening.
D ☐ prevents her from becoming more active.

Text III Little Fires Everywhere

In the following you will read an excerpt from the novel "Little Fires Everywhere". In Shaker Heights, a placid, progressive suburb of Cleveland, everything is planned – from the colors of the houses to the successful lives its residents will go on to lead. And no one embodies this spirit more than the picture-perfect Richardson family, whose guiding principle is playing by the rules. However, Izzy, the family's daughter, is different ...

(A) The orchestra teacher, Mrs. Peters, was widely disliked by everyone. She was a tall, painfully thin woman with hair dyed an unnatural flaxen and cropped in a manner reminiscent of Dorothy Hamill. According to Izzy, she was useless as a conductor and everyone knew to just watch Kerri Schulman, the first-chair violin, for the tempo. A persistent rumor – after some years, calcified as fact – insisted that Mrs. Peters had a drinking problem. Izzy hadn't entirely believed it, until Mrs. Peters had borrowed her violin one morning to demonstrate a bowing; when she'd handed it back, the chin rest **[GAP 1]**, it had smelled unmistakably of whiskey. When she brought her big camping thermos of coffee, people said, you knew Mrs. Peters had been on a bender the night before. Moreover, she was often bitingly sarcastic, especially to the second violins, especially the ones who – as one of the cellos put it drily – were "pigmentally blessed."

(B) Izzy, who had been playing violin since she was four, and had been assigned second chair even though she was a freshman, should have had nothing to fear. "You'll be fine," the cello had told her, eyeing Izzy's frizzy golden hair – the dandelion fro, Lexie liked to call it. Had Izzy kept her head down, **[GAP 2]**. But Izzy was not the type to keep her head down.

(C) The morning of her suspension, Izzy had been in her seat, practicing a tricky fingering on the E string for the Saint-Saëns piece she'd been working on in her private lessons. Around her the hum of violas and cellos tuning up grew quiet as Mrs. Peters stormed in, her infamous **[GAP 3]**. It was clear from the start that she was in an extraordinarily foul mood. "Hangover," Kerri Schulman mouthed to Izzy, who nodded gravely. She had only a general sense of what this meant.

(D) At the podium, Mrs. Peters took a long swig from her mug of coffee. "Offenbach," she barked, raising her right hand. Around the room students riffled through their sheet music. Twelve bars into *Orpheus,* **[GAP 4]**. "Someone's off." She pointed her bow at Deja Johnson, who was at the back of the second violins. "Deja. Play from measure six." Deja, who everyone knew was painfully shy, glanced up with the look of a frightened rabbit. She began to play, and everyone could hear the slight tremor from her shaking hand. Mrs. Peters shook her head and rapped her bow on her stand. "Wrong bowing. Down, up-up, down, up. Again." Deja stumbled through the piece again. The room simmered with resentment, but no one said anything.

(E) Mrs. Peters took a long slurp of coffee. "Stand up, Deja. Nice and loud now, so everyone can hear what they're not supposed to be doing." The edges of Deja's mouth wobbled, as if she were going to cry, but she set her bow to string and began once more. Mrs. Peters shook her head again, her voice shrill over the single violin. "Deja.

Down, up-up, down, up. Did you not understand me? You need me to speak in Ebonics?" It was at this point that **[GAP 5]**.

(F) She could not say why she had reacted so strongly. It was partly that Deja Johnson always had the anxious face of someone expecting the worst. Everyone knew that her mother was a nurse; in fact, she worked with Serena Wong's mother down at the Cleveland Clinic, and her father managed a warehouse on the West Side. There weren't many black kids in the orchestra, though, and when her parents showed up for concerts, they sat in the last row, by themselves; they never chitchatted with the other parents about skiing or remodeling or plans for spring break. They had lived all of Deja's life in a comfortable little house at the south end of Shaker, and she had gone from kindergarten all the way up to high school without – **[GAP 6]** – saying more than ten words a year.

(G) But unlike many of the other violinists – who resented Izzy for making second chair her first year – Deja never joined in the snide comments, or called her "the freshman". In the first week of school, Deja, as they'd filed out of the orchestra room, had leaned over to zip an unfastened pocket on Izzy's bookbag, concealing her exposed gym clothes. A few weeks later, Izzy had been digging through her bag, desperately looking for a tampon, when Deja had discreetly leaned across the aisle and **[GAP 7]**. "Here," she'd said, and Izzy had known what it was before she even felt the crinkle of the plastic wrapper in her palm.

(H) Watching Mrs. Peters pick on Deja, in front of everyone, had been like watching someone drag a kitten into the street and club it with a brick, and something inside Izzy had snapped. Before she knew it, she had cracked Mrs. Peters' bow over her knee and flung the broken pieces at her. There had been a sudden squawk from Mrs. Peters as the jagged halves of the bow – still joined by the horsehair – had whipped her across the face and a shrill squeal as the mug of steaming coffee in her hand tipped down her front. The practice room had erupted in a babble of laughter and shrieking and hooting, and Mrs. Peters, coffee dripping down the tendons of her neck, had grabbed Izzy by the elbow and dragged her from the room. In the principal's office, waiting for her mother to arrive, **[GAP 8]**, and she wished she'd had a chance to see Deja's face.

Adapted from: Celeste Ng, Little Fires Everywhere, *London, 2017, pp. 75–78.* *(940 words)*

Task III: Mixed Reading Tasks (Little Fires Everywhere) (9)

1 Multiple Matching (8)

There are eight gaps in the text. In the grid below, match each **gap (1–8)** with the most suitable **sentence part (A–L)**. There are three more options than you need.

Gap	Sentence Part
1	
2	
3	
4	
5	
6	
7	
8	

Sentence Parts:	
A	extended a folded hand
B	damp with sweat
C	Izzy had jumped from her seat and grabbed Mrs. Peters' bow
D	thermos in hand
E	what it's like to be different
F	Izzy had wondered if Deja had been pleased or embarrassed
G	as people joked
H	life will be divided into a before and an after
I	people decide what you're like before they even get to know you
K	Mrs. Peters would likely have ignored her
L	Mrs. Peters waved her arms

2 Mediation (1)

Beantworten Sie die folgende Frage auf Deutsch.

Welches tieferliegende Motiv ist ursächlich für das Verhalten der Lehrerin gegenüber Deja?

MATERIAL-BASED WRITING

Choose ONE of the following tasks (1 or 2) and write at least 300 words.

Task 1 (24)

As an intern working for an international student magazine it is part of your responsibilities to report on current trends and events. The next issue of the magazine will focus on the **future of work**.
Your task is to write an article in which you discuss **opportunities and challenges of automation**.

Write at least 300 words. Include information from all the material provided.

Material 1

"I designed a program that allows me to run the entire plant from my computer. By the way, how's the weather back there?"

© *https://www.automation.com/library/resources/automation-cartoons-february-4-2009*

Material 2

"Automation is great for profits, but it's a real potential trouble area for society."

Chieh Huang (CEO of boxed.com)

Material 3

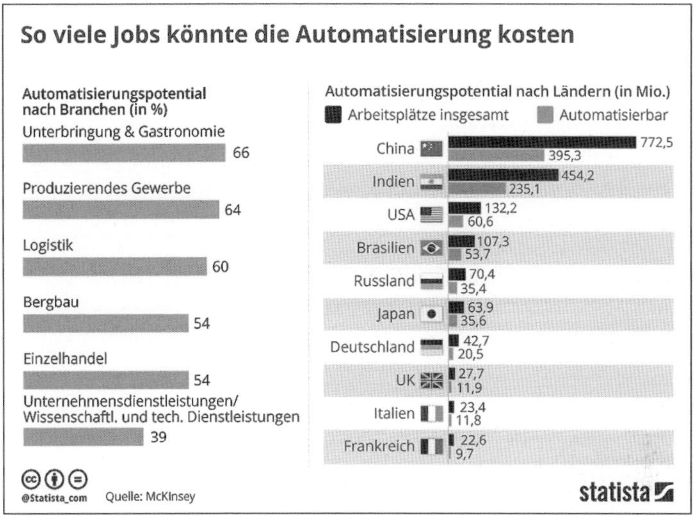
So viele Jobs könnte die Automatisierung kosten
Automatisierungspotential nach Branchen (in %)
Unterbringung & Gastronomie
66
Produzierendes Gewerbe
64
Logistik
60
Bergbau
54
Einzelhandel
54
Unternehmensdienstleistungen/ Wissenschaftl. und tech. Dienstleistungen
39
Automatisierungspotential nach Ländern (in Mio.)
Arbeitsplätze insgesamt
Automatisierbar
China
772,5
395,3
Indien
454,2
235,1
USA
132,2
60,6
Brasilien
107,3
53,7
Russland
70,4
35,4
Japan
63,9
35,6
Deutschland
42,7
20,5
UK
27,7
11,9
Italien
23,4
11,8
Frankreich
22,6
9,7
@Statista_com
Quelle: McKinsey
statista

Task 2 (24)

As an intern working for an international student magazine it is part of your responsibilities to report on current trends and events. The next issue of the magazine will focus on **travelling**.
Your task is to write an article in which you <u>comment on</u> the new trend "**staycation**".

Write <u>at least 300 words</u>. Include information from <u>all</u> the material provided.

Material 1

© Chris Madden/cartoonstock.com

Material 2

"The world is a book and those who do not travel read only one page."

St. Augustine, (Christian philosopher, 354–430 AD)

Material 3

Ferien auf Balkonien sind jetzt Trend

„Urlaub auf Balkonien" nannte man es früher, wenn jemand den Urlaub zu Hause verbrachte. In dem Ausdruck schwang immer eine Spur von Mitleid mit. Urlaub in der Ferne war schließlich mehr als eine Reise. Für manche Menschen war es ein Statussymbol, für andere eine Selbstverständlichkeit und für den Rest ein großes Abenteuer. „Urlaub auf Balkonien" heißt jetzt „Staycation" – und ist angesagt.

Maren Keller: Ferien in Balkonien sind jetzt Trend, https://www.spiegel.de/spiegel/unispiegel/staycation-urlaub-zuhause-ist-jetzt-trend-a-1210549.html, 15. 06. 2018

Lösungsvorschläge

READING

Task I: Mixed Reading Tasks (Cutting Adolescents' Use of Social Media …)

1 **TIPP**

Lesen Sie sich den Ausgangstext zunächst einmal vollständig durch, damit Sie wissen, worum es darin geht. Gehen Sie anschließend das *Gapped Summary* Satz für Satz durch und scannen Sie die Abschnitte A–F nach Wörtern, die in die Lücken passen könnten.

Beachten Sie, dass Sie die Form der Wörter nicht verändern dürfen – die Begriffe müssen also so wie sie im Text vorkommen in die Lücken passen. Oft können Sie bestimmte Wörter daher von vornherein ausschließen: In der dritten Lücke muss z. B. eine Verbform im Infinitiv stehen (kein Gerund); in der letzten Lücke ist die Pluralform eines Nomens (statt Singular) erforderlich. In Lücke 2 würden grammatikalisch sowohl „addictive" als auch „mind-warping" passen. Durch die Formulierung „In addition to causing dependence" im selben Satz ist „addictive" jedoch inhaltlich schon im *Summary* enthalten, sodass hier „mind-warping" die richtige Lösung sein muss.

Sie sollen pro Schreiblinie ein Wort einfügen und dahinter die Zeile angeben, in der das Wort im Ausgangstext zu finden ist. Zusammengesetzte Wörter mit Bindestrich (wie „mind-warping") zählen als ein Wort.

- Worterklärungen zum Ausgangstext:
  - Z. 1: *to target (= to aim at)* – abzielen auf, ins Visier nehmen
  - Z. 3: *to curtail (= to reduce, to decrease)* – beschränken, einschränken
  - Z. 5/6: *mind-warping (= mind-twisting)* – bewusstseinsverändernd
  - Z. 8: *temperate (= moderate)* – gemäßigt
  - Z. 10: *phone-bashers (to bash = to hit very hard)* – Smartphone-Gegner; Menschen, die auf Smartphones schimpfen
  - Z. 17: *correlation* – Korrelation (Zusammenhang zwischen zwei Variablen)
  - Z. 23: *to thwart (= to hinder)* – verhindern, behindern
  - Z. 26: *crackdown* – scharfes Vorgehen, hartes Durchgreifen; auch: Razzia
  - Z. 30: *to prod* – stupsen, stoßen
- Worterklärungen zum Lückentext:
  - *to teem with (= to be full of)* – wimmeln von
  - *to ascribe to (to attribute to)* – zuschreiben

The youth of today is a far cry from the youth in the past. Being distinctly more polite and **temperate (l. 8)** on the one hand, they are also more uneasy and sadder, on the other. The media are currently teeming with articles blaming the smartphone for this alarming development. In addition to causing dependence, people ascribe **mind-warping (ll. 5/6)** qualities to it. As a result, concerned parents and some businessmen alike are seeking to **curtail (l. 3)** the time teenagers spend in front of their smartphones.
Yet, neither a **universal crackdown (l. 26)** imposed on the youths by their parents nor parental self-restriction for reasons of fairness appear to be an adequate solution to the problem. **Over-protective (l. 32)** moms and dads may even add to the problem, being too concerned about what their kids might do outside. However, the whole discussion about adolescents' use of social media might be pointless since research in the UK and overseas has revealed that there are few links and **correlations (l. 17)** between time spent with digital devices and a person's happiness.

2 **TIPP**

Für diese Aufgabe ist nur Absatz G relevant. Lesen Sie sich diesen Abschnitt noch einmal genau durch und suchen Sie nach der Stelle, an der Maßnahmen, die Politiker*innen ergreifen könnten, beschrieben werden. Das ist in den Zeilen 42 und 43 der Fall. Sie dürfen für Ihre Antwort Formulierungen aus dem Text verwenden. Die Einschränkung „policymakers" in der Aufgabenstellung sollten Sie auf keinen Fall überlesen, da Sie sonst versucht sein könnten, Informationen aus den Zeilen 44 bis 46 anzugeben.

- they should improve schools
- they should get rid of job protection for older workers

Task II: Multiple Choice (The Swedish 15-Year-Old …)

TIPP

Lesen Sie sich auch hier den Text zunächst einmal ganz durch, bevor Sie mit der Bearbeitung der Aufgaben beginnen. Überprüfen Sie dann für jede Multiple-Choice-Aufgabe, welche der vorgegebenen Auswahlmöglichkeiten Sie am Text belegen könnten. Manchmal wird danach gefragt, welche Information nicht im Text enthalten ist – dann ist die richtige Lösung die, zu der Sie keinen Textbeleg finden können.

1 Siehe Z. 1/2: "politicians won't pay attention to the facts"
2 Der Ausdruck „to capture someone's imagination" bedeutet „jdn. in seinen Bann ziehen" oder „jdn. begeistern" – die richtige Lösung muss also „inspiring" (= inspirierend) lauten. Die anderen Antwortmöglichkeiten – „impeccable" (= makellos), „irrelevant" (= unerheblich, belanglos) und „inappropriate" (= unangemessen) scheiden aus.

3 Bis auf Option A werden alle Motive im Text genannt:
- zu Option B siehe Z. 12: “I want the politicians to prioritise the climate question”
- zu Option C siehe Z. 11/12: “It is my moral responsibility to do what I can”
- zu Option D siehe Z. 8/9: “I am doing this because you adults are shitting on my future.”

4 Siehe Z. 28: “in this situation the only reasonable thing is to be unreasonable.”

5 Siehe Z. 32: “created by the unprecedented drought” (*drought* = Dürre).

6 Nur Option D lässt sich nicht am Text belegen; zu allen anderen Optionen finden sich entsprechende Passagen im Text:
- zu Option A siehe Z. 45/46: “she wrote in an article widely circulated on social media and translated into English”
- zu Option B siehe Z. 38–41: “Thunberg’s own awakening to the climate crisis a few years ago caused upheaval in her family. Her mother […] has given up her international career because of the climate effects of aviation. ‘Greta forced us to change our lives,’ says her father Svante.”
- zu Option C siehe Z. 42–44: “Her teachers were telling her to turn off the lights and save paper, then flying off to New York for a holiday.”

7 Siehe Z. 49/50: “She sees her condition not as a disability but as a gift which has helped open her eyes to the climate crisis.”

1 The introductory question expresses Greta’s …

D ☒ frustration in the face of indifferent decision-makers.

2 “Her protest has captured the imagination of a country” in paragraph A means that the Swedish people find her protest …

B ☒ inspiring.

3 Which of the following was <u>not</u> a motive for Greta to become active?

A ☒ She is an inconspicuous person.

4 According to paragraph D, Greta’s …

C ☒ biology teacher thinks that the end justifies the means.

5 The expression “rural tinderbox” in paragraph E refers to …

A ☒ the fire hazard due to the exceptionally hot summer.

6 Which of the following is <u>not</u> true according to paragraph F?

D ☒ Her activism is deeply rooted in her conviction that you can have it all.

7 Greta’s special condition …

C ☒ has contributed to her environmental awakening.

1 **TIPP**

Lesen Sie sich zunächst den Text einmal ganz durch. Sehen Sie sich anschließend die Stellen vor und nach den Lücken der Reihe nach an, und überlegen Sie, welcher Satzteil inhaltlich und grammatikalisch am besten in die Lücke passt. Gelingt das für die eine oder andere Lücke nicht sofort, machen Sie zunächst mit den anderen Lücken weiter und schränken Sie die Auswahl so immer weiter ein. Drei Satzteile bleiben am Ende übrig.

Gap 1 Sowohl sprachlich als auch inhaltlich kommt hier nur Satzteil B infrage: "the chin rest [was] damp with sweat".

Gap 2 Hier muss K richtig sein. Vor der Lücke steht ein (versteckter) *if*-Satz vom Typ III („Had Lizzy kept her head down" = „If Izzy had kept her head down"), auf den ein *conditional II* („would […] have ignored") folgen muss.

Gap 3 Da vor der Lücke ein Adjektiv („infamous", Z. 20) steht, muss ein Nomen eingefügt werden. Die Thermoskanne wurde bereits vorher erwähnt und passt daher inhaltlich gut in die Lücke.

Gap 4 Vom Sinnzusammenhang kann hier nur Satzteil L richtig sein. Mrs. Peters dirigiert mit den Händen und bricht das Stück nach zwölf Takten ab.

Gap 5 Hier ist inhaltlich nur Satzteil C möglich. Deja wird von Mrs. Peters schikaniert und Izzy kommt ihr zu Hilfe (siehe Z. 32–37).

Gap 6 Für diesen Einschub passt inhaltlich und sprachlich nur Satzteil G: Deja sagte – wie gewitzelt wurde – nicht mehr als zehn Worte pro Jahr.

Gap 7 Hier ist Satzteil A die einzig mögliche Lösung. Deja lehnt sich über den Gang, streckt ihre Hand aus („extended") und reicht Izzy mit geschlossener Faust („folded hand") ein Tampon.

Gap 8 Nach der Lücke wird gesagt, dass Izzy gerne Dejas Gesicht gesehen hätte. Sie würde also gerne wissen, wie Deja die Situation mit dem gebrochenen Bogen empfunden hat – ob sie sich gefreut oder eher geschämt hat (Satzteil F).

Gap	Sentence Part
1	B
2	K
3	D
4	L
5	C
6	G
7	A
8	F

2

TIPP

Bei dieser Aufgabe sollen Sie auf Deutsch zusammenfassen, warum die Lehrerin Deja vor dem versammelten Orchester bloßstellt. Die folgenden Textstellen liefern Ihnen die nötigen Hinweise:

- Z. 10/11: "she was often bitingly sarcastic, especially to the second violins, especially the ones who [...] were 'pigmentally blessed.'"
- Z. 35–37: "Deja. [...] Did you not understand me? You need me to speak in Ebonics?" Der Begriff „Ebonics" steht hier für die Sprache der schwarzen Bevölkerung.
- In den Zeilen 41/42 wird noch einmal explizit gesagt, dass Deja aus einer afroamerikanischen Familie kommt: "There weren't many black kids in the orchestra"

Der Grund für das Verhalten der Lehrerin ist ihre rassistische Einstellung. Da Deja aus einer afroamerikanischen Familie kommt, wird sie zum Opfer von Mrs. Peters Schikane.

MATERIAL-BASED WRITING

Task 1: Automation

TIPP

Bei dieser Aufgabe sollen Sie im Rahmen eines Praktikums bei einer internationalen Schülerzeitung einen Beitrag für die nächste Ausgabe schreiben, die sich mit der „Zukunft der Arbeit" befasst. Genauer gesagt, sollen Sie sich mit den Chancen und Herausforderungen durch die **Automatisierung** auseinandersetzen.

Für einen Artikel brauchen Sie zunächst eine geeignete **Überschrift**. Sie können sich entweder (wie in der Beispiellösung) selbst eine Formulierung überlegen, die informativ ist und auf den Inhalt neugierig macht, oder aber Sie verwenden die durch die Themenstellung nahegelegte Formulierung („The Opportunities and Challenges of Automation"). In Ihrer **Einleitung** sollten Sie kurz zum Thema hinführen, bevor Sie im **Hauptteil** Chancen und Herausforderungen der Automatisierung einander gegenüberstellen. Es empfiehlt sich, die Position, der Sie eher zuneigen, an den Schluss zu stellen, da die zuletzt genannten Argumente der Leserschaft meist besser im Gedächtnis bleiben. In Ihrem **Schlussteil** sollten Sie zusammenfassen, ob für Sie die Chancen oder Risiken der Automatisierung überwiegen, oder einen Ausblick auf die Zukunft geben.

Achten Sie unbedingt darauf, **alle drei Materialien** in Ihre Argumentation miteinzubeziehen. Am besten notieren Sie sich, bevor Sie mit dem Schreiben beginnen, neben jedem Material Stichpunkte, welchen Aspekt Sie daraus in Ihrem Text anführen könnten. Darüber hinaus dürfen Sie natürlich auch eigenes Hintergrundwissen zum Thema in Ihren Artikel einfließen lassen.

In der Beispiellösung wird das Zitat aus **Material 2** als Einstieg verwendet, um zur Kontroverse um die Automatisierung hinzuführen. Im Hauptteil dient **Material 1** als Beleg für die Vorteile, die die Automatisierung mit sich bringt. Dass nicht alle Menschen von der Automatisierung profitieren, wird anhand der Statistiken aus **Material 3** deutlich. Die Beispiellösung endet mit einem Ausblick, welche Voraussetzungen gegeben sein müssen, damit möglichst viele Menschen an den Chancen der Automatisierung teilhaben können.

Automation – Blessing or Curse?

Einleitung: Hinführung zum Thema mithilfe von Material 2

Few topics are discussed as controversially as the question of the impact of automation. Chieh Huang, the CEO of boxed.com, summed up the ambivalence of the phenomenon when he said that automation "is great for profits" but also a "real potential trouble area for society". Let us look at the opportunities and challenges of automation in a bit more detail.

Chancen der Automatisierung: Material 1

First of all, it is true that many companies profit from the use of robots, appliances and artificial intelligence, as this allows them to reduce production costs in the long run. Automation will also lead to the creation of new jobs, such as in software development and robotics. In addition, the use of machines and digital devices can make working life more flexible. For example, a factory boss no longer has to be on site all the time, but can just as easily run his or her plant from somewhere else. And even "ordinary" workers can benefit from automation, e. g. when repetitive chores are done by robots while they can focus on more demanding tasks.

Herausforderungen durch die Automatisierung: Material 3

However, this brings us directly to the flipside of the coin, namely the risk of job losses due to automation. As recent statistics show, machines and robots could replace roughly half of all jobs worldwide. The potential for automation differs from one sector of the economy to the next, ranging from e. g. 39 % in scientific and technical services to 66 % in the accommodation and food sector. In other words, hundreds of millions of workers might become redundant, and it is quite likely that unskilled workers will be the most affected.

Schluss: eigene Ideen / eigenes Hintergrundwissen

Thus, in order for automation not to become a dividing factor and "potential trouble area for society", it is essential for the workforce and especially for young people to prepare for changing job requirements. This can be achieved by means of further education, but also by specialising in areas that are hard to be taken over by machines, such as those that require creativity and social skills. Only then can automation become a blessing from which people from all walks of society can benefit. *(357 words)*

Task 2: "Staycation"

TIPP

Bei dieser Aufgabe sollen Sie als Praktikant*in einer internationalen Schülerzeitung einen Beitrag für die Ausgabe zum Thema „Reisen" schreiben. Sie sollen darin zu dem neuen Trend hin zum „Urlaub auf Balkonien" *(staycation)* Stellung beziehen. Der Operator „**comment**" erfordert, dass die eigene Meinung klar zum Ausdruck gebracht wird. Da Formulierungen wie „in my opinion" in einem Zeitschriftenartikel unpassend wirken könnten, wurde hier ein etwas neutralerer Sprachstil gewählt, der dennoch eine eindeutige Position erkennen lässt.

Vergessen Sie nicht, Ihrem Artikel eine **Überschrift** zu geben. Sie können dazu die Formulierung aus der Aufgabenstellung aufgreifen („The Trend towards Staycation") oder eine eigene, möglichst aussagekräftige Formulierung wählen.

In der Beispiellösung werden nach der Einleitung die **Materialien 2 + 3** angeführt, um das lange vorherrschende positive Image des Reisens und den negativen Ruf des „Urlaubs daheim" zu verdeutlichen. Anhand von **Material 1** und eigenem Hintergrundwissen wird dann auf die negativen Folgen des Massentourismus verwiesen. Vor diesem Hintergrund erscheint der „Urlaub auf Balkonien" nicht mehr als langweilig und spießig, sondern als ökologisch sinnvoll und wichtig. Dass das Reisen dennoch nicht ganz verdammt werden muss, zeigen Beispiele für nachhaltigen Tourismus.

"Staycation": From boring pastime to ecological must-do

"Staycation" – i. e., staying at home for one's vacation rather than going on holiday – has become a recent trend. This development seems quite surprising given the importance that travelling has had for a long time:

Einleitung: Hinführung zum Thema

As far back as four centuries after Christ, St. Augustine had already realised that travelling was necessary in order to broaden one's horizons. Moreover, travelling was associated with adventure, was seen as a sign of social status or just as the "normal thing to do". With time, package tours and cheap charter flights have made it possible for average families to go on "grand tours", which used to be reserved for wealthy people only. As a consequence, people who spent their holiday at home were seen as boring, narrow-minded or social underclass and often received only pitiful glances.

Rückblick: Positive Sicht auf das Reisen, negativer Ruf des „Urlaubs daheim"

Material 2 + 3

However, in the past few years, the negative impacts of travelling and tourism have become increasingly obvious. It turned out that exhaust fumes from cars, coaches and cruise ships can erode ancient buildings and that mindless tourists all too often damage historical sites. Beautiful landscapes are being destroyed in order to build large hotel complexes, and fragile eco-systems are endangered by the vast quantities of waste produced in holiday resorts.

Imagewandel durch negative Auswirkungen des Massentourismus

Material 1

In view of this, staying at home should no longer be regarded as boring or backward, but rather as a sensitive decision. The fact that staycation is now becoming fashionable can thus be seen as a necessary countermovement to the excesses of mass tourism. However, it is not the only possible response and travelling should not be altogether condemned either. For all those who still long to get into contact with foreign cultures and see new places, the World Tourism Organisation has established guidelines for sustainable tourism. They argue that the cultural and environmental heritage of an area can be preserved by means of eco-tourism and "fair trade" holidays. Plenty of young people also spend some time abroad as volunteers, where they help to preserve parks, protect endangered species or restore historical sites.

Eigene Position: „Staycation" als sinnvolle Alternative neben nachhaltigem Tourismus

In sum, the recent trend towards "staycation" should be seen as a positive development alongside sustainable forms of travelling and other forms of critical consumer behaviour. *(368 words)*

Schluss: Fazit

READING

Text I — Pass the tofu: How eating vegan became a billion-dollar business

(A) From a family of chefs and hunters in Sunderland, Ontario, Sam Turnbull grew up in a house decorated with animal heads, where the eggs they ate came from their own chickens. She says she's the last person who thought she'd give up meat or cheese to embrace a 100 percent animal-free diet. But one day in 2012 she wasn't feeling her best and turned on a documentary called "Vegucated," which she thought was going to inspire her to eat more vegetables. Instead it was about veganism – and she says it dispelled all the ideas she held until then that vegans were, as she puts it, "weird and crazy – and lacking in protein."

(B) Driven by equal parts ethics, health, and environmental concerns, she cleared her kitchen of animal food products, and adopted a new lifestyle cold turkey (no pun intended). Today her visibility over social media is part of the reason why veganism is more mainstream than it ever has been. You don't need to store your grill in the garage just yet. Meat consumption continues to grow worldwide – especially in emerging economies like China. And strict vegans still comprise a fraction of the population in rich countries: just 2.3 percent in Canada, and 3 percent in the United States. But the fundamentals of veganism have been promoted by everyone from Beyoncé and Bill Clinton, to environmentalists, doctors, and government officials. The past five years have ushered in a new era for the legume, the pulse, tofu, and tempeh.

(C) "Veganism has transformed from this more fringe and rights movement into a more mainstream lifestyle," says Nina Gheihman, a Canadian sociologist pursuing a Ph.D. in the social aspects of veganism at Harvard University. "Instead of it being seen as a marginal thing like in the '70s, it's seen as aspirational." That runs the gamut from athletes focused on performance, to those who are seeking glowing skin, to environmental scientists warning the world it must reduce consumption of animal products to be able to feed the planet in the future.

(D) While abstaining from animal products was practiced in ancient societies such as Greece and India, the word vegan is traced to 1944, when the U.K. Vegan Society was founded. And what was once a rights-based or hippy movement has become decisively fashionable. One British survey this summer counted 3.5 million British vegans, or 7 percent of the population, up from half a million people in 2016 (although many claim that increase must be exaggerated, reflecting respondents' aspirations more than what is on their plates).

(E) If the real numbers are smaller, the plant business is booming nevertheless. According to market research in June 2018, in the U.S. the plant-based food industry saw dollar sales growth of 20 percent from the year before, worth more than $ 3.3 billion. A telling moment came in 2016, when Tyson Foods, the biggest meat processor in the U.S., bought a 5 percent stake in Beyond Meat, maker of alternative vegan proteins. In many urban metropolises, new vegan restaurants seem to pop up monthly, while chefs ignore vegan options at their own peril.

(F) And while rich countries have adopted veganism with voguish zeal, vegans point out that it's a democratic movement for all – that a bowl of rice and beans costs much less than oven-baked chicken breasts. Ms. Turnbull intentionally uses ingredients in her recipes from her local supermarket – not high priced products only available in urban specialty stores. And despite the stereotype, it's not just a rich, white movement. Vegetarian dishes, many of them vegan, are the staples in many societies from India to the Middle East. There is a thriving black vegan movement from the U.S. to South Africa. The website "Black Vegans Rock" points out that "saying that veganism is white erases all of these incredible, diverse Black voices and contributions." […]

(G) And vegans can also still be seen as hardliners. Marni Ugar leads noisy protests outside of nonvegan restaurants in Toronto whose policies she objects to. One chef was so fed up with them that he carved a deer leg in his restaurant's front window, and she has received angry messages from pro-hunting groups. She doesn't flinch. "This is a social justice movement. There is sexism, there is racism, there is speciesism. They are next to each other, they are all the same," says Ms. Ugar, who was a longtime vegetarian but switched to veganism after learning about inhumane practices in milk production. "You cannot be a feminist, from my perspective, and support dairy."

Still, many of today's vegans don't identify with some of that militancy. *(760 words)*

Sara Miller Llana: Pass the tofu: How eating vegan became a billion-dollar business, The Christian Science Monitor 29/03/2019, https://www.csmonitor.com/World/Americas/2019/0329/Pass-the-tofu-How-eating-vegan-became-a-billion-dollar-business, "From The Christian Science Monitor.

Task I: Mixed Reading Tasks (Pass the tofu …) **(8)**

1 Multiple Choice **(5)**

Mark the most suitable option by crossing (✗) the appropriate letter.

1.1 According to paragraph A, …

- **A** ☐ the documentary made Ms. Turnbull reconsider certain stereotypes.
- **B** ☐ the documentary was about the detrimental effects of veganism.
- **C** ☐ the documentary inspired Ms. Turnbull to eat more vegetarian products.
- **D** ☐ Ms. Turnbull had already given up meat before watching the documentary.

1.2 Which of the following statements is <u>not</u> true according to paragraph B?

- **A** ☐ Ms. Turnbull's social media presence has helped spread veganism.
- **B** ☐ Ms. Turnbull's ecological conscience was not the only trigger for her new lifestyle.
- **C** ☐ Veganism is not just a fad but has also been endorsed by a variety of people.
- **D** ☐ Worldwide veganism is on the rise while meat consumption has been decreasing.

1.3 What would be the most suitable heading for paragraph D?

- **A** ☐ The birth of veganism
- **B** ☐ An old idea gaining ground
- **C** ☐ Ambitious goals
- **D** ☐ 75 years of healthy lifestyle

1.4 Which statement is true according to paragraph E?

- **A** ☐ The food industry increased profits by 20 percent compared to the previous year.
- **B** ☐ The meat processor Tyson Foods has taken over a vegan competitor.
- **C** ☐ Not taking veganism seriously can be considered an economic risk.
- **D** ☐ In big cities vegan restaurants are still struggling to gain ground.

1.5 The intention of paragraph F is to …

A ☐ promote Ms. Turnbull's recipes and the website 'Black Vegans Rock'.

B ☐ prove that vegan dishes have had a long history in many different societies.

C ☐ show that vegans try to spread unrealistic ideas.

D ☐ refute certain stereotypes about veganism.

2 Mediation (E–D) (3)

Bearbeiten Sie die folgenden Aufgaben auf Deutsch.

2.1 Erklären Sie die Verwendung des Begriffs „cold turkey" im Textzusammenhang. (Zeile 10) **(2)**

____

____

____

____

____

2.2 Erläutern Sie, warum der Chefkoch eines Restaurants in Toronto für alle sichtbar eine Hirschkeule zerlegte. (Absatz G) **(1)**

____

____

____

Text II If we want to help migrants, it's time to move from outrage to action

(A) Having grown up just after the Second World War, I've always wondered what I would have done if I'd known that Jews were being herded into (let's call them) mass detention centers. What if I'd been aware that this was happening in my country? Now that people are being herded into mass detention centers in my country, now that children are being kept in cages, I have – like it or not – been given a chance to find out what I would have done.

(B) If there had been Facebook in the early 1940s, I would have posted on Facebook. I would have written opinion pieces from the safe distance of my study. I would have donated to humanitarian and legal aid organizations. I would even have traveled to Texas to hear the stories of asylum seekers and witness a trial in which 40 immigrants, some of whom had lived here for years, were all deported at once. I would have felt haunted, continually. Haunted and obsessed. And none of these things would have stopped the mass incarceration of children.

(C) Of course, it's important to encourage the like-minded, to assure those repelled by our government's cruelty that they are not alone. But every day I read eloquent essays and informative dispatches from the border. Every day I have outraged or heartbroken conversations. Yet children are still locked up and families separated.

(D) Meanwhile the criminal prosecution of people arrested for supplying basic humanitarian aid – food and water for human beings starving or dying of thirst – seems to have had the desired chilling effect on simple, low-tech gestures of decency and protest. What I can't help wondering is how different the situation would be if a million Americans were leaving water bottles and sandwiches in the desert – or if thousands of Americans were camped outside detention centers.

(E) Something is happening – or beginning. This week hundreds of employees of Wayfair, an online home goods company, walked out in protest over their firm's sale of furniture to migrant shelters. As Alexandria Ocasio-Cortez said in a tweet: "This is what solidarity looks like." It's unclear what effect this has had on company policy, though the fact that Donald Trump lashed out at the "left" for "bullying" Wayfair seems like a positive sign. Even he must realize what might happen if this sort of thing grew more widespread. Bank of America has stopped funding the owners of private detention centers and prisons, but it may be a little early to hail the big banks as beacons of moral clarity.

(F) I came of age during the Vietnam war, and though the atrocities of that conflict were much further away than those now being committed in Texas, Arizona and Florida, we took to the streets – by the hundreds of thousands. I know it's still being debated, how much those demonstrations contributed to the ending of the war. And I agree with those who argue that the protests might never have happened if young Americans hadn't felt threatened by the specter of the draft. But they happened, and many of us can look back on that era with a more or less clear conscience. We tried. We did our best. That will not be possible for us to say in the future, if things continue as they are now, and we continue to stay home and discuss new restaurants, read the papers, preach to the choir.

(G) We need activists and organizers to undo the spell of weird enchantment that allows us to look at the sweet faces of children who died under unspeakable conditions, on our watch. Not everyone will agree. If you don't think that brown children are human children, if you believe that they and their families should be punished (with death, if need be) because their home countries were so dangerous that they had no choice but to leave, you won't want to join those who want to save their lives. We have to do something besides talking, writing, lamenting, hoping that the problem will be solved if Donald Trump is defeated in 2020. By then it will be too late for many kids and their families. With every day that passes, more children are cold, hungry, terrified, alone, separated from their parents. Even as I write this, children go on dying, and it is – or should be – harder for us to live with ourselves. *(728 words)*

Francine Prose: If we want to help migrants, it's time to move from outrage to action, The Guardian *03/07/2019, https://www.theguardian.com/commentisfree/2019/jul/03/if-we-want-to-help-migrants-its-time-to-move-from-outrage-to-action, Copyright Guardian News & Media Ltd 2020*

Task II: Mixed Reading Tasks (If we want to help migrants …) **(8)**

1 Gapped Summary **(5)**

Fill the gaps in the summary with appropriate words or expressions (one word per line) from the corresponding sections of the text (paragraphs A–E). Do not make any adjustments and do not change the content of the text. Please also provide the number of the line in which you have found the word/expression.

The author of the text, Francine Prose, is appalled by the Trump administration's ____________________ (l.) towards migrants, especially about the ruthless methods applied to separate children from their families. She ponders on appropriate reactions to people's indifference, for example writing stirring commentaries or attending a ________________________ (l.) on migration issues. However, she is very doubtful that any of these measures will end the ________________ ________________________ (l.) of young kids kept isolated from their parents in detention centers.

According to the author, there are some glimpses of hope, though: "Wayfair" staff __________ __________ (l.) to demonstrate against their company selling equipment for migrant shelters. Moreover, courageous citizens felt morally responsible, ______________________ (l.) hungry migrants with food and beverages in the hostile surroundings of the desert.

Yet, a paralyzed and lethargic society has to wake up before it is too late for so many migrant children.

2 Short Answer Question (3)

2.1 Apart from moral concerns, which personal motivation did young people in the US have to demonstrate against the Vietnam war? **(1)**

____

____

2.2 Which phrase in paragraph G expresses that people are almost paralyzed and do not do enough for migrant children? **(1)**

____

____

2.3 Which term in paragraph G means that someone expresses a feeling of great sadness? **(1)**

____

____

Text III Americanah (excerpt)

When Ifemelu departs for the United States to study, Nigeria is under military dictatorship. She struggles with the experience of racism in American culture and the many varieties of racial distinctions. Upon coming to America, Ifemelu discovers for the first time what it means to be a "Black Person".

Princeton, in the summer, smelled of nothing, and although Ifemelu liked the tranquil greenness of the many trees, the clean streets and stately homes, the delicately overpriced shops, and the quiet, abiding air of earned grace, it was this, the lack of a smell, that most appealed to her, perhaps because the other American cities she knew well had all smelled distinctly. Philadelphia had the musty scent of history. New Haven smelled of neglect and Brooklyn of sun-warmed garbage. But Princeton had no smell. She liked taking deep breaths here. She liked the campus, grave with knowledge, the Gothic buildings with their vine-laced walls, and the way everything transformed, in the half-light of night, into a ghostly scene. She liked, most of all, that in this place of affluent ease, **[GAP 1]**, someone specially admitted into a hallowed American club, someone adorned with certainty.

But she did not like that she had to go to Trenton to braid her hair. It was unreasonable to expect a braiding salon in Princeton – the few black locals she had seen were so light-skinned and lank-haired she could not imagine them wearing braids – and yet as she waited at Princeton Junction station for the train, **[GAP 2]**, she wondered why there was no place where she could braid her hair. A few other people were waiting on the platform, all of them white and lean, in short, flimsy clothes. The man standing closest to her was eating an ice cream cone. He turned to her and said, "About time," when the train finally creaked in, with the familiarity strangers adopt with each other after sharing in the disappointment of a public service. She smiled at him. Before, she would have said, "I know," that peculiar American expression that **[GAP 3]**, and then she would have started a conversation with him, to see if he would say something she could use in her blog. People were flattered to be asked about themselves and if she said nothing after they spoke, it made them say more. They were conditioned to fill silences. If they asked what she did, she would say vaguely, "I write a lifestyle blog," because saying "I write an anonymous blog called Raceteenth or Various Observations About American Blacks (Those Formerly Known as Negroes) by a Non-American Black" would make them uncomfortable. She had said it, though, a few times.

The ice-cream-eating man sat beside her on the train and, **[GAP 4]**, she stared fixedly at a brown stain near her feet, a spilled frozen Frappuccino, until they arrived at Trenton. The platform was crowded with black people, many of them fat, in short, flimsy clothes. It still startled her, what a difference a few minutes of train travel made. During her first year in America, when she took New Jersey Transit to Penn Station and then the subway to visit Aunty Uju in Flatlands, she was struck by how mostly slim white people got off at the stops in Manhattan and, as the train went further into Brooklyn, the people left were mostly black and fat. She had not thought of them as "fat," though. She had thought of them as "big," because one of the first things her friend Ginika told her was that “fat” in America was a bad word, heaving with moral judgment like “stupid” or “bastard,” and not a mere description like “short” or “tall.” So she had banished “fat” from her vocabulary. But “fat” came back to her last winter, after almost thirteen years, when a man in line behind her at the supermarket muttered, “Fat people don’t need to be eating that shit,” as she paid for her giant bag of Tostitos. She glanced at him, surprised, mildly offended, and thought it a perfect blog post, how this stranger had decided she was fat. She would file the post under the tag “race, gender and body size.” But back home, **[GAP 5]**, she realized that she had ignored, for too long, the new tightness of her clothes, the rubbing together of her inner thighs, the softer, rounder parts of her that shook when she moved. She was not curvy or big-boned; she was fat, it was the only word that felt true.

And she had ignored, too, the cement in her soul. Her blog was doing well, with thousands of unique visitors each month, and she was earning good speaking fees, and she had a fellowship at Princeton and a relationship with Blaine and yet there was cement in her soul. It had been there for a while, an early morning disease of fatigue, a bleakness and borderlessness. It brought with it amorphous longings, shapeless desires, brief imaginary glints of other lives she could be living, that over the months melded into a piercing homesickness. She scoured Nigerian websites, Nigerian profiles on Facebook, Nigerian blogs, and each click brought yet another story of a young person who had recently moved back home, clothed in American or British degrees, to start an investment company, a music production business, a fashion label, a magazine, a fast-food franchise. She looked at photographs of these men and women and felt that they were living her life. Nigeria became where she was supposed to be. And, of course, there was also Obinze. Her first love, her first lover, the only person with whom she had never felt the need to explain herself. He was now a husband and father, and **[GAP 6]**, yet she could not pretend that he was not a part of her homesickness, or that she did not often think of him, sifting through their past.

The rude stranger in the supermarket – who knew what problems he was wrestling with, haggard and thin-lipped as he was – had intended to offend her but had instead prodded her awake. She began to plan and to dream, to apply for jobs in Lagos. She did not tell Blaine at first, because she wanted to finish her fellowship at Princeton, and then after her fellowship ended she did not tell him because she wanted to give herself time to be sure. But as the weeks passed, she knew she would never be sure. So she told him that she was moving back home, and she added, “I have to,” knowing he would hear in her words the sound of an ending. *(1 036 words)*

Chimamanda Ngozi Adichie: Americanah, *Knopf Doubleday Publishing Group, New York (2013)*

Task III: Mixed Reading Tasks (Americanah) (8)

1 Multiple Matching (6)

There are six gaps in the text. In the grid below, match each **gap (1–6)** with the most suitable **sentence part (A–I)**. There are three more options than you need.

Gap	Sentence Part
1	
2	
3	
4	
5	
6	

Sentence Parts:	
A	she could pretend to be someone else
B	counting the days until her departure
C	professed agreement rather than knowledge
D	on an afternoon ablaze with heat
E	as she stood and faced the mirror's truth
F	after years of successful blogging
G	to discourage conversation
H	they had not been in touch in years
I	without knowing what had gotten into her

2 Mediation (E–D) (2)

Beantworten Sie folgende Aufgabe auf Deutsch.

Fassen Sie kurz zusammen, welcher innere Konflikt Ifemelus in den Zeilen 49–55 deutlich wird.

MATERIAL-BASED WRITING

Choose ONE of the following tasks (1 or 2) and write at least 300 words.

Task 1 (24)

You are doing research on the impact of technology on modern society. Comment on the **benefits and drawbacks of "wearable technology"** (wearable devices with the ability to collect, send and receive data via the Internet).

Write at least 300 words. Include information from all the material provided.

Material 1

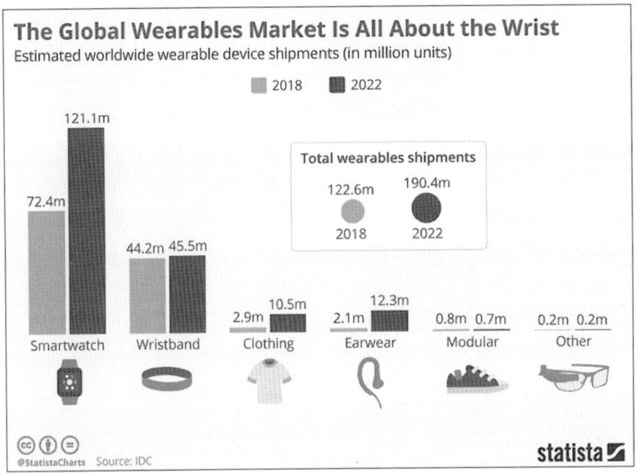

© *Statista 2020, https://www.statista.com/chart/3370/wearable-device-forecast/*

Material 2

Wenn alte Menschen fallen, können sie sich oft nicht selbst fangen. Die Verletzungen sind dann oft viel schlimmer als bei jüngeren Menschen. Moderne Wearables nehmen sich dieses Themas immer mehr an. Gegen Verletzungen beim Fallen stellte ein Hersteller jetzt einen Airbag für die Hüfte vor. Sensoren im Gerät sollen erkennen, wenn eine Person fällt und den Airbag eigenständig öffnen. Tracker senden Kindern oder Enkeln außerdem regelmäßig ein Gesundheitsupdate von Oma oder Opa zu.

Nie mehr Sorgen machen? Wearables für Senioren, AIO vom 11.01.2018, https://aiomag.de/fuer-ein-gutes-gefuehl-wearables-fuer-senioren-4716

Material 3

DON'T TAKE ME! I CAN TELL YOU HIS HOME ADDRESS AND BANK DETAILS
DREW
SMARTWATCH

Task 2 (24)

Nowadays more and more consumers have become critical of the wasteful increase in food packaging. To arouse further awareness of the problem, you decide to comment in an online eco-magazine on the **challenges of the plastic problem and possible solutions**.

Write at least 300 words. Include information from all the material provided.

Material 1

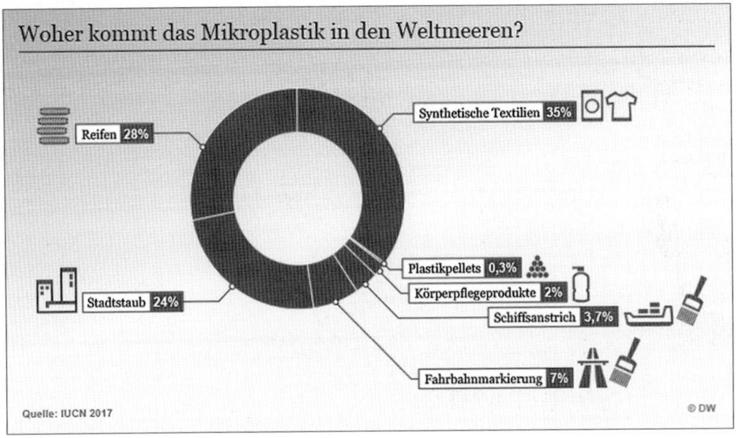

© *Deutsche Welle*

Material 2

© *5PH. Shutterstock*

Material 3

Der Ocean Cleanup

Mit 18 Jahren hatte der Niederländer Boyan Slat seinen riesigen Plastikfangarm entworfen. Er sieht aus wie eine riesige Schwimmnudel. Der Clou: Die U-förmige 600-Meter-Anlage soll sich frei im Meer bewegen – nur gesteuert von der Meeresströmung. Bisher waren alle Tests gescheitert.

Ein großer Unterwasserfallschirm und die Erhöhung der Fangarme über Wasser brachten nun den ersten Erfolg. Das Team sammelte große Plastikteile wie Stühle, Helme, Netze und auch Mikroplastik ein.

Erste Erfolge für „Ocean Cleanup", Tagesschau vom 02. 10. 2019, https://www.tagesschau.de/ausland/ocean-cleanup-107.html

Lösungsvorschläge

READING

Task I: Mixed Reading Tasks (Pass the tofu …)

1 **TIPP**

Folgende Stellen in den Abschnitten A bis F weisen auf die richtige Lösung hin:

1 Siehe Z. 6–8: "[…] and she says it dispelled all the ideas she held until then that vegans were, as she puts it, 'weird and crazy – and lacking in protein.'"; *to dispel* = zerstreuen, verwerfen

2 Siehe Z. 13–15: "Meat consumption continues to grow worldwide […] And strict vegans still comprise a fraction of the population in rich countries […]"

3 Siehe Z. 26–29: "[…] abstaining from animal products was practiced in ancient societies such as Greece and India […] And what was once a rights-based or hippy movement has become decisively fashionable."; *to abstain from sth* = verzichten auf
Siehe Z. 29/30: "[…] survey this summer counted 3.5 million British vegans […] up from half a million people in 2016 […]"

4 Siehe Z. 34–39: "[…] the plant business is booming nevertheless […] Tyson Foods, the biggest meat processor in the U.S., bought a 5 percent stake in Beyond Meat, maker of alternative vegan proteins. […] chefs ignore vegan options at their own peril."

5 Siehe Z. 44–46: "And despite the stereotype, it's not just a rich, white movement. Vegetarian dishes […] are the staples in many societies from India to the Middle East. There is a thriving black vegan movement […]"

1.1 According to paragraph A, …

A [X] the documentary made Ms. Turnbull reconsider certain stereotypes.

1.2 Which of the following statements is not true according to paragraph B?

D [X] Worldwide veganism is on the rise while meat consumption has been decreasing.

1.3 What would be the most suitable heading for paragraph D?

B [X] An old idea gaining ground

1.4 Which statement is true according to paragraph E?

C [X] Not taking veganism seriously can be considered an economic risk.

1.5 The intention of paragraph F is to …

D [X] refute certain stereotypes about veganism.

2 **TIPP**

2.1 „Cold turkey" bedeutet „kalter Entzug" oder „radikale Entziehungskur". Im Zusammenhang mit Ms. Turnbulls Umsteigen auf fleischlose Kost besteht hier die Ironie, dass „turkey" auch „Truthahn" heißt, wobei die Autorin behauptet, dass das Wortspiel (angeblich) keine Absicht war.

2.2 *to be fed up with sth* = von etw. genug haben, etw. satt haben

2.1 Ms. Turnbull verzichtet von einem Tag auf den anderen darauf, Fleisch zu essen. Sie unternimmt sozusagen einen „kalten Entzug".

2.2 Der Koch hatte genug von den Protesten der militanten Veganer*innen.

Task II: Mixed Reading Tasks (If we want to help migrants …)

1 **TIPP**

Für den *Gapped Summary* müssen Sie im Ausgangstext nur die Absätze A–E lesen. Gehen Sie diese gründlich durch und widmen Sie sich danach dem Lückentext. Wie in den Arbeitsanweisungen angegeben, sollen die fehlenden Wörter direkt dem Ausgangstext entnommen werden (pro Leerzeile ein Wort). Beachten Sie, dass der Lückentext nicht immer mit der Reihenfolge im Text übereinstimmt. Vergessen Sie auch nicht die entsprechende Zeilenangabe.

Worterklärungen zum Lückentext:
appalled – entsetzt; *ruthless* – unbarmherzig, mitleidslos, gnadenlos;
to ponder on sth – sich über etw. Gedanken machen

The author of the text, Francine Prose, is appalled by the Trump administration's **cruelty (l. 15)** towards migrants, especially about the ruthless methods applied to separate children from their families. She ponders on appropriate reactions to people's indifference, for example writing stirring commentaries or attending a **trial (l. 10)** on migration issues. However, she is very doubtful that any of these measures will end the **mass incarceration (l. 13)** of young kids kept isolated from their parents in detention centers.
According to the author, there are some glimpses of hope, though: "Wayfair" staff **walked out (l. 25)** to demonstrate against their company selling equipment for migrant shelters. Moreover, courageous citizens felt morally responsible, **supplying (l. 18)** hungry migrants with food and beverages in the hostile surroundings of the desert.
Yet, a paralyzed and lethargic society has to wake up before it is too late for so many migrant children.

2 **TIPP**

Hier müssen Sie sich auf die Abschnitte F und G konzentrieren. Auch wenn es in der Angabe nicht erwähnt wird, können Sie die Antworten direkt dem Text entnehmen.

2.1 *specter (AE)* = (Schreck)gespenst; *draft* = Einberufung zum Militär (Absatz F, Z. 38)

2.2 *spell* = Zauber, Bann; *weird* = bizarr, seltsam; *enchantment* = Verzauberung, Entzücken (Absatz G, Z. 43)

2.3 *to lament* = etw. beklagen, (über etw.) klagen (Absatz G, Z. 49)

2.1 (young Americans felt threatened by) the specter of the draft

2.2 (undo) the spell of weird enchantment

2.3 lamenting

Task III: Mixed Reading Tasks (Americanah)

1 **TIPP**

Bevor Sie die Aufgabe angehen, lesen Sie sich den Text einmal ganz durch, um zu verstehen, worum es darin geht. Sehen Sie sich danach die Sätze mit den Lücken an und überlegen Sie, welcher der angegebenen Satzteile (A–I) inhaltlich und grammatikalisch in die Lücke passt. Drei von den neun Satzteilen passen gar nicht. Finden Sie den jeweils richtigen Satzteil nicht sofort, machen Sie zunächst mit den anderen Lücken weiter und schränken Sie die Auswahl so immer weiter ein.

Gap 1 Sinngemäß passt hier nur **A**. Auch das Wort „someone" gibt einen Hinweis: "[…] in this place of affluent ease, she could pretend to be someone else, someone […]"

Gap 2 "[…] as she waited at Princeton Junction station for the train, on an afternoon ablaze with heat, she wondered […]": **D** ist, was den Textzusammenhang betrifft, die passende Lösung, obwohl grammatikalisch auch B, E, F und I möglich wären.

Gap 3 Hier schließt nur Teilsatz **C** an das Relativpronomen "that" an: "[…] peculiar American expression that professed agreement rather than knowledge […]"

Gap 4 Aus dem Textzusammenhang wird deutlich, dass Ifemelu ein Gespräch vermeiden wollte (**G**): "[…] man sat beside her on the train and, to discourage conversation, she stared fixedly at […]"

Gap 5 Im Rest des Satzes nach der Lücke wird klar, dass Ifemelu ihr Äußeres im Spiegel betrachtet (**E**): "But back home, as she stood and faced the mirror's truth, she realized that she had ignored, for too long, the new tightness of her clothes […]"

Gap 6 Aus dem Kontext wird klar, dass es hier um Ifemelus erste Liebe geht, die sie schon lange nicht mehr gesehen hat (**H**): "He was now a husband and father, and they had not been in touch in years, yet she could not pretend […]"

Gap	Sentence Part
1	A
2	D
3	C
4	G
5	E
6	H

2 **TIPP**

Da keine wörtliche Übersetzung verlangt ist, genügt es, die Hauptaussage der Zeilen 49–55 wiederzugeben, in denen es um Ifemelus inneren Konflikt geht.

Die folgenden Textstellen geben Ihnen die nötigen Hinweise:
- Erfolg: Z. 49–51: „blog was doing well", „good speaking fees", „fellowship at Princeton", „relationship with Blaine"
- Unzufriedenheit: Z. 51–55: „cement in her soul", „fatigue" (= Erschöpfung), „bleakness" (= Trostlosigkeit), „amorphous longings" (= in etwa: undefinierbares Verlangen), „glints of other life" (in etwa: Schimmer eines anderen Lebens), „homesickness"

Ifemelu hat zwar Erfolg im Leben, dennoch empfindet sie eine innere Leere und sie leidet an Heimweh. Manchmal wünscht sie sich, ein anderes Leben zu führen.

MATERIAL-BASED WRITING

Task 1: Wearable technology

TIPP

Lesen Sie zunächst die **Aufgabenstellung** genau durch. In der vorliegenden Aufgabe wird auf Textsorte und Zielgruppe nicht eingegangen bzw. sie lassen sich auch nicht erschließen. Beachten Sie jedoch den Operator ("Comment on ...").

Sehen Sie sich als Nächstes die vorgegebenen **Materialien** an. Prüfen Sie, welche Informationen im Hinblick auf die Aufgabenstellung besonders relevant sind. Zitieren Sie in Ihrem Text die Quellen nicht wörtlich und beschreiben Sie diese nicht im Detail. Es muss allerdings erkennbar sein, an welchen Stellen Sie sich auf welches Material beziehen. Achten Sie auch darauf, **alle drei Materialien** in Ihre Argumentation mit einzubeziehen. Zusätzlich zu den Materialien können Sie für Ihren Text auch auf eigenes **Hintergrundwissen** zum Thema zurückgreifen.

Die **Gliederung** ist insofern schon vorgegeben, als Sie auf die Vor- und Nachteile („benefits and drawbacks") von „Wearables" eingehen sollen. Sie können schrittweise oder blockweise dialektisch vorgehen. Die schrittweise Vorgehensweise (bei jedem Argument gleich das Gegenargument zu bringen) verlangt jedoch größere sprachliche Wendigkeit. Der folgende Lösungsvorschlag bevorzugt die blockweise Variante.

Wearable technology – benefits and drawbacks

Wearables of all kind – smartwatches, wristbands, clothing, earwear etc. – are getting more and more popular worldwide. So what are the benefits of wearables, and are there also serious drawbacks to this technology?

Einleitung: Hinführung zum Thema mithilfe von Material 1

The number of smartwatches in particular is expected to rise considerably by 2022, increasing from 72.4 million products in 2018 to 121.1 million products globally. Other wearables, such as wristbands, garments and earwear equipped with digital technology, are also on the rise.

Wachstum des Marktes: Material 1

For more and more people it seems comfortable and convenient to be digitally connected all the time. They want to know, for example, what their pulse is, what their temperature is, and the number of steps they have taken. Another aid is airbags around the waist. If you fall, it inflates like an airbag in a car. This could prevent elderly people in particular from breaking their hip or thigh bones.

Nutzen der „wearables":

Material 2

On the other hand, there are serious drawbacks to wearable gadgets. Being digitally supervised around the clock can be risky, as your personal data could be misused by digital companies like Google or

Gefahren der Manipulation: Hintergrundwissen

Amazon. They are able to create an individual profile of your personality, your predilections or your buying habits, pursuing you with advertisements and offering merchandise to tempt you to buy.

More dangerous, however, is the fact that such a lot of data – address, bank details, health data, etc. – can be stored in one gadget. If someone gets hold of these sensitive data on a smartwatch, for example, it can be misused. Furthermore, your health insurance company could make health supervision via smartwatch obligatory for you to get a cheaper rate. In a way, when they use wearable gadgets, people give up part of their freedom and privacy, and if you let yourself be constantly supervised, this may also ultimately lead to a lack of independence. The tendency to focus on your personal data is also a form of narcissism which may affect your interaction with other people.

Weitere negative Aspekte: Konzentration sensibler Daten: Material 3, Hintergrundwissen

Auswirkungen auf Freiheit, Privatsphäre und soziales Leben

To conclude, wearable technology can be a great help if you use it wisely without sacrificing your personal freedom or independence.

(346 words)

Schluss: Abrundung, sowohl – als auch

Task 2: The plastic problem

TIPP

Sehen Sie sich zuerst die **Aufgabenstellung** an: hier sollen Sie in einem digitalen Umwelt-Magazin einen Kommentar zum Thema „Plastikmüll" verfassen, in dem Sie das Bewusstsein für die Problematik noch einmal schärfen wollen, auch wenn es sich bei der Leserschaft des Ökomagazins wohl um Menschen handelt, die für Umweltprobleme sensibilisiert sind. Sie können sich daher auch appellierend an die Leser*innen wenden.

Prüfen Sie nun, welche Informationen aus den vorgegebenen **Materialien** im Hinblick auf die Aufgabenstellung besonders relevant sind. Beachten Sie dabei, in Ihrem Text nicht wörtlich aus den Quellen zu zitieren, und beschreiben Sie diese nicht im Detail. Machen Sie allerdings kenntlich, an welchen Stellen Sie sich auf welches Material beziehen. Vergessen Sie nicht, **alle drei Materialien** in Ihre Argumentation mit einzubeziehen. Für Ihre Argumentation können Sie zusätzlich auch auf eigenes **Hintergrundwissen** zum Thema zurückgreifen.

Die **Gliederung** ist Ihnen schon vorgegeben: Probleme – mögliche Lösungen. In Ihrer **Einleitung** sollten Sie kurz zum Thema hinführen, bevor Sie im **Hauptteil** Herausforderungen und Lösungen darstellen. Gehen Sie dabei steigernd vor und stellen Sie die Maßnahme, die Sie am wichtigsten finden, an den Schluss. Vergessen Sie nicht, einen **Schluss** zu verfassen, z. B. in Form eines Appells.

The Challenge of the Plastic Problem and Possible Solutions

Plastic waste has become a global problem. In the oceans, it not only has a lethal effect on wildlife like seabirds, sea turtles or other marine mammals, but it is also transferred up the food chain onto our plates. Therefore, it is high time we got to the root of this maritime tragedy.	**Einleitung:** Lage in den Weltmeeren: Hintergrundwissen
The dangerous plastic micro particles in the oceans come from various sources, such as the rubber abrasion from car tyres, the dust from cities, body care products and, most of all, from synthetic textiles.	**Hauptteil:** Quellen der Verunreinigung: Material 1
A promising idea to help clean the oceans is that of a young Dutchman, who has devised a huge plastic U-shaped noodle, whose improved version collects plastic material like chairs, helmets, fishing nets and even microplastics. However, this project does not get to the root of the problem.	Gegenmaßnahmen: Material 3
As far as rubber abrasion is concerned, it will be a challenge for the rubber industry to develop tyres that are more resistant. Additionally, what each of us can do is to reduce our use of cars and to take public transport instead or ride a bicycle or just walk, which is healthier anyway. Furthermore, we should avoid synthetic clothing, look at the trademark labels and make an environmentally friendly choice.	Hintergrundwissen
Last but not least, each of us could avoid plastic litter by using endurable and recyclable packaging when we go shopping, i. e. buying eggs in boxes that disintegrate naturally and using cloth bags and glass jars, which can be re-used and recycled.	Material 2 + Hintergrundwissen
Reducing dust levels – not only in cities – and using environmentally friendly products should also be promoted by the state. It is therefore most important that we urge our governments and parliaments to enact laws which lead to the reduction of plastic waste and plastic micro particles.	Material 1 + 2, Hintergrundwissen
Summing up, however, not only governments but also industry and every one of us should be conscious of the plastic problem and act in an environmentally friendly way. *(322 words)*	**Schluss:** Appell an alle

READING

Text I **Let It Snow** By David Sedaris

Winters were frustratingly mild in North Carolina, but the year I was in the fifth grade we got lucky. Snow fell, and, for the first time in years, **[GAP 1]**. School was cancelled, and two days later we got lucky again. There were eight inches on the ground, and, rather than melting, it froze. On the fifth day of our vacation, my mother had a little breakdown. Our presence had disrupted the secret life she led while we were at school, and when she could no longer take it she threw us out. It wasn't a gentle request but something closer to an eviction. "Get the hell out of my house," she said.

We reminded her that it was our house, too, and she opened the front door and shoved us into the carport. "And stay out!" she shouted.

My sisters and I went down the hill and sledded with other children from the neighborhood. A few hours later, we returned home, surprised to find that the door was locked. "Oh, come on," we said. I rang the bell, and when no one answered we went to the window and saw our mother in the kitchen, watching television. Normally she waited until five o'clock to have a drink, **[GAP 2]**. Drinking didn't count if you followed a glass of wine with a cup of coffee, and so she had a goblet and a mug positioned before her on the countertop.

"Hey!" we yelled. "Open the door. It's us." We knocked on the pane and, without looking in our direction, she refilled her goblet and left the room.

"That bitch," my sister Lisa said. We pounded again and again, and when our mother failed to answer we went around back and threw snowballs at her bedroom window. "You are going to be in so much trouble when Dad gets home!" we shouted, and in response my mother pulled the drapes. Dusk approached, and as it grew colder it occurred to us that we could possibly die. It happened, surely. Selfish mothers wanted the house to themselves and their children were discovered years later, **[GAP 3]**.

My sister Gretchen suggested that we call our father, but none of us knew his number, and he probably wouldn't have done anything anyway. He'd gone to work specifically to escape our mother, and between the weather and her mood it could be hours, or even days, before he returned home.

"One of us should get hit by a car," I said. "That would teach the both of them." I pictured Gretchen, her life hanging by a thread as my parents paced the halls of Rex Hospital, **[GAP 4]**. It was really the perfect solution. With her out of the way, the rest of us would be more valuable and have a bit more room to spread out. "Gretchen, go lie in the street."

"Make Amy do it," she said.

Amy, in turn, pushed it off on Tiffany, who was the youngest and had no concept of death. "It's like sleeping," we told her. "Only you get a canopy bed."

Poor Tiffany. She'd do just about anything in return for a little affection. All you had to do was call her Tiff, and whatever you wanted was yours: her allowance, her dinner, the contents of her Easter basket. Her eagerness to please was absolute and naked. When we asked her to lie in the middle of the street, her only question was "Where?"

We chose a quiet dip between two hills, a spot where drivers were almost required to skid out of control. She took her place, this six-year-old in a butter-colored coat, **[GAP 5]**. The first car to come along belonged to a neighbor, a fellow-Yankee who had outfitted his tires with chains and stopped a few feet from our sister's body. "Is that a person?" he asked.

"Well, sort of," Lisa said. She explained that we'd been locked out of our house, and, while the man **[GAP 6]**, I'm pretty sure he was the one who told on us. Another car passed, and then we saw our mother, this puffy figure awkwardly negotiating the crest of the hill. She did not own a pair of pants, and her legs were buried to the calf in snow. We wanted to send her home, to kick her out of nature just as she had kicked us out of the house, but it was hard to stay angry at someone that pitiful-looking.

"Are you wearing your loafers?" Lisa asked, and in response our mother raised a bare foot.

"I was wearing loafers," she said. "I mean, really, it was there a second ago."

This was how things went. One moment she was locking us out of our own house and the next we were rooting around in the snow, looking for her left shoe. "Oh, forget about it," she said. "It'll turn up in a few days." Gretchen fitted her cap over my mother's foot. Lisa secured it with her scarf, and, surrounding her tightly on all sides, we made our way home. *(852 words)*

David Sedaris: Let It Snow, The New Yorker December 14, 2003, https://www.newyorker.com/magazine/2003/12/22/let-it-snow

Task I: Mixed Reading Tasks (Let it snow) (8)

1 Multiple Matching: Gapped text (6)

There are six gaps in the text. In the grid below, match each **gap (1–6)** with the most suitable **sentence part (A–I)**. There are three more options than you need.

Gap	Sentence Part
1	
2	
3	
4	
5	
6	

Sentence Parts:	
A	regardless of whether it was allowed or not
B	and we gathered on the curb to watch
C	while we were running back to the house
D	relatively unscathed
E	frozen like mammoths in blocks of ice
F	it accumulated
G	appeared to accept it as a reasonable explanation
H	wishing they had been more attentive
I	but the past few days had been an exception

2 Mediation (E–D) (2)

Bitte beantworten Sie die folgende Frage auf Deutsch.

Erklären Sie im Textzusammenhang, was der Satz "This was how things went." (Z. 55) über die Beziehung zwischen der Mutter und ihren Kindern aussagt.

____

____

____

Text II **Having the Last Laugh? Meet the Preppers** By Graeme Lennox

Graeme Lennox talks to Irish survivalists about how they prepare for disaster – and whether they think society will learn lessons from the Covid-19 pandemic.

(A) Well, you can't say they didn't warn us. For years, preppers have been readying themselves for the sort of situation we find ourselves in now. Mocked for obsessing over doomsday scenarios portrayed in disaster films, building bunkers and talking of "bugging out"[1] at the first signs of societal collapse, they are the ones having the last laugh.

(B) County Wicklow-based survivalist Shayne Phelan looks as if he has crawled off the pages of a post-apocalyptic novel, but he is in no rush to say "I told you so". "I'm more worried about people than I am about the virus because there's no empathy," he says. "I've seen someone taking shopping from an elderly person's trolley in the supermarket and there are videos of people in fist fights over toilet paper. Panic is the paralysis of intellect. When we start panicking, we stop thinking and become lemmings. If the shops run out of supplies, things could get messy very quickly."

(C) Preppers have a mantra that says at any given time we are only nine meals from anarchy. The heavily tattooed man reckons our best chance of survival in any doomsday scenario is arming ourselves with knowledge rather than food. Phelan started learning bushcraft in his teens, after reading John "Lofty" Wiseman's SAS Survival Handbook in a single sitting. He runs Eagle Ridge Survival, a survival-skills firm with courses from € 60 that teach beginners how to make a fire and build a shelter. "The first thing we need for survival is to maintain our body temperature. Within three hours we require some sort of shelter; within three days we need water or we are in trouble. People panic about food because it's hardwired into us, but we can all go three weeks without it and there are a few people who'd benefit from it."

(D) While the coronavirus has taught us to treasure the things we previously took for granted, the post-Covid era is likely to see a resurgence in self-sustainability. Dr Bradley Garrett from University College Dublin's faculty of geography spent four years observing preppers while researching his book *Bunker: Building for the End Times.* He says the image of gun-toting hillbillies is well wide of the mark. "I've seen the entire spectrum, from the guy who has a 'bug-out bag' stashed in the boot of his car, to the € 30 million missile silo someone has turned into a subterranean condo complex," he says. "These are some of the coolest, calmest, most rational people I've ever met. For most of them it's just an insurance policy they hope never to use."

(E) Frank Deegan, 52, from Co Kilkenny, is a co-founder of the Irish Survivalist Group. He started prepping during the early 1990s while in the Merchant Navy. "In 1991 we were delivering a 350,000-ton ship from Southampton to Yugoslavia when war broke out," he says. "We were at anchor for three months off Yugoslavia and quickly ran out of food. It took another three months to get back to England, but we made sure we stockpiled long-life food at every port on the way."

(F) Deegan continues to work as an engineer for a multimedia company. He says alarm bells started ringing when he saw his brother and sister-in-law return from China in

February. "They were in Hong Kong and mainland China for six weeks and I was gobsmacked they could travel freely from Hong Kong to London and Dublin without any checks," he says. "Preppers are always on the lookout for trouble. I got a feeling something big was coming in October last year. The boys took the piss out of me, calling me paranoid, but they are now saying they should have paid attention."

(G) Preppers use the expression "**72 hours to animal**" to denote the fragile peace between functioning society and all-out anarchy. "Preppers consider our current circumstances a mid-level situation. The next level arrives when the trucks stop coming or the grocery-store workers decide it's not worth the risk going into work. When the social fabric disintegrates, we're in trouble – because that's when people start snapping or giving up. "I met one prepper who told me he'd gone around to all of the neighbours' houses in the middle of the night, figured out access points into their properties and taken stock of all of their supplies. That was one of those moments in the project where I started to feel uncomfortable," says Garrett.

(H) Isolated incidents aside, he's confident society will learn lessons from the coronavirus. "For years preppers have been telling me **disaster is a great moment for recalibration**," he says. For those of us who have been able to work remotely it has been a kind of blessing. "When I had my plane tickets and lectures cancelled, I felt the stress drop out of my body. For a lot of people it has been an amazing opportunity to reconnect with people and to think about whether the things we were doing before the disaster actually mattered." *(864 words)*

The Sunday Times/News Licensing

1 to bug out – to leave very quickly

Task II: Mixed Reading Tasks (Having the last laugh? Meet the preppers) **(8)**

1 Multiple Choice **(6)**

Mark the most suitable option by crossing (✗) the appropriate letter.

1.1 According to paragraph A, preppers have …

- **A** ☐ been ridiculed for being too concerned about disastrous situations.
- **B** ☐ long warned us about the disastrous effects of the Covid-19 pandemic.
- **C** ☐ retreated from society well ahead of the global spread of the coronavirus.
- **D** ☐ become aware of potential pandemics through various disaster movies.

1.2 In paragraph B survivalist Shayne Phelan …

- **A** ☐ admits that he became a prepper after reading doomsday literature.
- **B** ☐ is very satisfied that his warnings about a coming disaster proved right.
- **C** ☐ welcomes the fact that the pandemic strengthens solidarity in society.
- **D** ☐ fears that in a crisis people easily lose control and become selfish.

1.3 Which of the following tips on how to prepare for disaster cannot be found in paragraph C?

- **A** ☐ A food stock sufficient for several weeks is indispensable.
- **B** ☐ It is important to acquire the appropriate survival skills.
- **C** ☐ Hoarding food is overrated in a survival situation.
- **D** ☐ Basic needs have to be satisfied in a given order.

1.4 According to Dr Bradley Garret, preppers …

- **A** ☐ are a community that will soon disappear after the corona pandemic is over.
- **B** ☐ are rather uneducated people in rural areas ready to defend themselves.
- **C** ☐ act unemotionally and sensibly when preparing for potential disasters.
- **D** ☐ promote the idea of more self-responsibility on an international scale.

1.5 Which of the following does <u>not</u> describe Frank Deegan? He …

- **A** ☐ had a dramatic experience that turned him into a prepper.
- **B** ☐ states he had an early premonition that a pandemic was approaching.
- **C** ☐ was upset about people's unrestricted access to the British Isles in early 2020.
- **D** ☐ thinks that preppers like searching for trouble spots to test themselves.

1.6 By using the phrase "disaster is a great moment for recalibration" (paragraph H) Garrett wants to express that catastrophes …

A ☐ cause people to travel by plane less frequently.

B ☐ help to re-evaluate what is important in our lives.

C ☐ make people more socially engaged.

D ☐ contribute to a higher personal stress level.

2 Mediation (E–D) **(2)**

Bitte beantworten Sie die folgende Aufgabe **auf Deutsch**.
Keine wörtliche Übersetzung.

Erläutern Sie, was *Preppers* mit dem Ausdruck "72 hours to animal" (Absatz G) meinen und welches Beispiel dafür in Absatz G gegeben wird.

Text III Why are Millennials and Gen Z Turning to Instagram as a News Source? By Katie Bishop

Young people are getting information about protests, police actions and stay-at-home orders from their social media feeds – but the trend isn't harmless.

(A) For many young people, clicking on to Instagram to get the latest news is now as second nature as picking up a daily newspaper once was to generations before. For a site that has traditionally been a platform for sharing lifestyle content rather than hard news, this is a shift in millennials and Gen Z, at a time when news updates seem more important than ever. Recently published data exploring how people accessed news and information about the coronavirus pandemic found, in the US, for 18- to 24-year-olds (the age group most likely to use social media as a source), over a quarter of respondents used Instagram to access news content within the last week, while 19 % used Snapchat and 6 % turned to TikTok.

(B) This trend isn't necessarily harmless. "The challenge with Instagram is that it's a highly visual space," Jennifer Grygiel, who teaches communications at Syracuse University, tells me, "so people share memes that are more about influencing than informing and people need to exercise caution and be aware of who they're engaging with." The use of social media as a news source is complicated by the ability for anyone to act as a reporter, sparking concerns about factchecking, and an oft-cited claim that social media tilts influence towards those with the largest number of followers, regardless of their credentials. For disenfranchised individuals social media may offer an alternative to media outlets that they have begun to doubt. Yet the very nature of social media leaves users exposed primarily to others with similar views, which research suggests can create vast echo chambers – spaces where our own opinions and biases are reinforced by the voices which are filtered into our social media feed.

(C) Amelia Gibson is an assistant professor and director of the Community Equity Data and Information Lab at the University of North Carolina. She sees the events of recent months as highlighting the ways many young people use social media as a news source. The Covid-19 crisis, combined with renewed interest in the Black Lives Matter movement, increased the desire for instant, first-hand information. Mistrust of main stream media meant that many young people turned to their social media news feeds for information about protests, police actions and stay-at-home orders. But with a web of algorithms serving up content from news organizations, political groups or even influencers aligned to their own political beliefs and social circles, this also provoked a deepening of already opposing views and cultural rifts.

(D) "Social media offers, on the one hand, a medium for filling what feels like a vacuum of trustworthy information sources," Gibson explains. "But on the other hand, our social media environments are still so segmented that some people really do live in different information worlds. In one information ecosystem, people might read this moment and current social justice movements as a hopeful international awakening related to anti-racism, others read it as a time of deep existential threat. We see these different worlds clashing when people meet in real life."

(E) For Gibson, the solution lies in a convergence of interests – as social media brings attention to stories that have previously been overlooked and rebalances the power to share news, traditional media still has a part to play." People have always shared the news that mattered to them and their communities," she explains. "I think that the difference in this moment is that news corporations are paying attention and are amplifying a moment of shared struggle … I think that social media has done a lot to push social justice movements forward in the last decade but that traditional media still has a lot of power to command national and international attention."

(F) For Grygiel, who, as a college professor, sees up close how young people are acting as both content creators and consumers, the relationship between traditional media and social sharing has reached a pivotal point. Although sites such as Instagram currently hold significant sway when it comes to distributing content to an internet-savvy youth, Grygiel hopes that this will push news publications to build better websites, attract advertisers and strive for independence rather than relying on social media shares. In the meantime, the need to exercise caution is of utmost importance.

(G) "It's hard to fully realize the benefits of social media because there's so much harmful content out there," she explains. "Social media platforms have not always acted as good corporate citizens – they've paid a lack of attention to political advertisements that are harmful, and fail to monitor hate speech. It's important to be critical of them, but also aware that without them we wouldn't have seen the kind of documentation that we have of societal harms and transparency around injustices … there's still a lot of opportunity to deliver content without social media, and if social media platforms aren't acting as good corporate citizens then we need to find new and better ways of distributing news." *(843 words)*

Katie Bishop: Why are millennials and Gen Z turning to Instagram as a news source?, The Guardian 27. 07. 2020, https://www.theguardian.com/lifeandstyle/2020/jul/27/instagram-news-source-social-media

Task III: Mixed Reading Tasks (Why are millennials and Gen Z …) **(8)**

1 Gapped Summary (paragraphs A–E) **(6)**

Fill the gaps in the summary with appropriate words or expressions (one word per line) from the corresponding sections of the text. Do not make any changes. Please provide the number of the line in which you have found the word/expression.

Over the last few years more and more young people have turned to Instagram for the news although this online service used to focus on ______________ ______________________ (*two words,* l.). Particularly the traditional media's coverage of racial protests in the US and the Covid-19 pandemic has provoked ______________________ (l.) among the young generation who started to make use of new information channels. Their wish to be provided with authentic news has radically altered the media landscape, but this change comes with strings attached.

There are worries that those vloggers and bloggers who attract the biggest audience exert the largest influence on social media platforms even if there are doubts over their ________________ (l.). And social media users tend to communicate with those who share their opinion, which might lead to ________________________ (*two words,* l.), re-affirming internet spheres of like-minded people. This phenomenon can ultimately result in a ________________ (l.) of the social divide because of polarized beliefs.

On the other hand, experts point out that social media has done a lot to raise awareness about issues that were ____________________ (l.) in the past. Now these issues are also addressed by long-established media, which is still influential enough to attract widespread attention.

2 Short Answer Questions (paragraphs F–G) (2)

Answer the following questions. You may use words from the text.

2.1 Which idiomatic expression shows that social media is highly influential in spreading information among youngsters? **(1)**

____

____

2.2 According to Jennifer Grygiel, what have social media platforms hardly kept an eye on apart from offensive posts? **(1)**

____

____

MATERIAL-BASED WRITING

Choose ONE of the following tasks (1 or 2) and write at least 300 words.

Task 1 (24)

Not only rich regions but also developing countries are hit hard by the coronavirus pandemic. Therefore, more and more charitable organisations ask people to support them, either by **donating money** or by **volunteering**.
Comment on how you can help people in disadvantaged circumstances.

Write a **composition** of **at least 300 words**. Include information from **all** the material provided.

Material 1

ANZAHL DER EHRENAMTLICH TÄTIGEN PERSONEN IN DEUTSCHLAND
17,11 Mio.

HÖHE DER PRIVATEN GELDSPENDEN IN DEUTSCHLAND
5,4 Mrd. €

ANZAHL DER GELDSPENDER IN DEUTSCHLAND
19 Mio.

JJ. Rudnicka: Statistiken zum Thema Soziales Engagement, Statista vom 25. 05. 2021, https://de.statista.com/themen/655/soziales-engagement/#dossierSummary_chapter4

Material 2

"Life's most persistent and urgent question is: What are you doing for others?"
Martin Luther King, Jr.

Martin Luther King, Jr., Discover Corps, 01. 03. 2017, https://discovercorps.com/blog/50-inspirational-quotes-volunteering/

Material 3

Polyp.org.uk

Task 2 (24)

According to *Deutsche Welle*, most footballers are inked. Sixty percent of Manchester City's team and over fifty of Bayern Munich's have a tattoo.

Point out **reasons** why people decide to get tattoos and what **consequences** such a decision might have for their future lives.

Write a **composition** of at least 300 words. Include information from all the material provided.

Material 1

"My body is my journal and my tattoos are my story."

Johnny Depp

Johnny Depp, Template Monster, 27. 07. 2020, https://www.templatemonster.com/blog/best-tattoo-fonts-for-vintage-designs/

Material 2

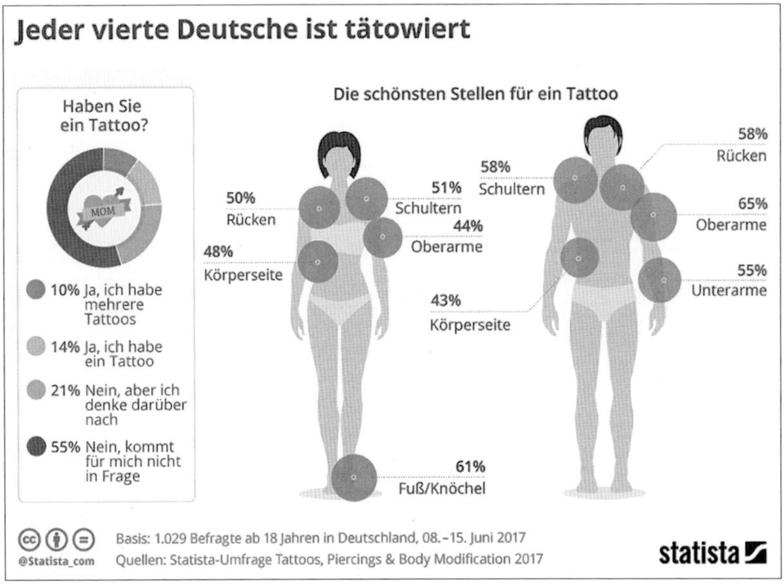

Hedda Nier: Jeder vierte Deutsche ist tätowiert, Statista vom 28. 06. 2017, CC BY-ND 4.0

Hinweis: Für die Bearbeitung der Aufgabe ist nur der linke Kasten („Haben Sie ein Tattoo?") relevant. Aus rechtlichen Gründen muss hier die gesamte Statistik abgedruckt werden.

Material 3

Polizisten in Bayern dürfen keine sichtbaren Tattoos tragen

Tätowierungen an Kopf, Hals, Händen und Unterarmen bleiben bei der Polizei in Bayern verboten. Das entschied 2019 das Bundesverwaltungsgericht in Leipzig.

Polizisten in Bayern dürfen keine sichtbaren Tattoos tragen/Tagesspiegel 14. 05. 2020, https://www.tagesspiegel.de/politik/urteil-des-bundesverwaltungsgerichts-polizisten-in-bayern-duerfen-keine-sichtbaren-tattoos-tragen/25830396.html

READING

Task I: Mixed Reading Tasks (Let it snow)

1 **TIPP**

Lesen Sie sich zunächst den Text einmal ganz durch. Sehen Sie sich anschließend die Stellen vor und nach den Lücken der Reihe nach an, und überlegen Sie, welcher der angegebenen Satzteile inhaltlich und grammatikalisch in die Lücke passt. Gelingt das für die eine oder andere Lücke nicht sofort, machen Sie zunächst mit den anderen Lücken weiter und schränken Sie die Auswahl so immer weiter ein. Drei Satzteile bleiben am Ende übrig.

Worterklärung:
Sentence part B: *curb* – hier: Bordstein

Gap 1 Sowohl sprachlich als auch inhaltlich kommt hier nur Satzteil F infrage: "[…] it [the snow] accumulated."

Gap 2 Vergleichen Sie mit Z. 4 f.: "On the fifth day of our vacation […]" (Zusammenbruch der Mutter, nachdem die Kinder den fünften Tag schulfrei hatten); so ergibt Satzteil I Sinn: "but the past few days had been an exception."

Gap 3 Da die Kinder an einem eiskalten Wintertag in den offenen Carport hinausgeworfen wurden, passt Satzteil E ("frozen like mammoths in blocks of ice") – einschließlich des sarkastischen Untertons.

Gap 4 Hier fügt sich als einzig sinnvolle Ergänzung der Partizipialsatz H an ("wishing they had been more attentive").

Gap 5 Satzteil B "and we gathered on the curb to watch"; vgl. Z. 40: "When we asked her to lie in the middle of the street, […]" und Z. 42: "She took her place, […]"

Gap 6 "[…] while the man […]" kann inhaltlich und grammatikalisch nur mit Satzteil G ("appeared to accept it as a reasonable explanation") weitergeführt werden.

Gap	Sentence Part
1	F
2	I
3	E
4	H

5	**B**
6	**G**

2 **TIPP**

Bei dieser Aufgabe sollen Sie auf Deutsch im Textzusammenhang erklären, was der Satz "This was how things went" (Z. 55) über die Beziehung zwischen der alkoholkranken Mutter und ihren Kindern aussagt. Die folgenden Textstellen liefern Ihnen Hinweise:

Mutter in Bezug auf die Kinder:
- "[…] when she could no longer take it she threw us out. It wasn't a gentle request but something closer to an eviction. 'Get the hell out of my house,' she said." (Z. 6 f.)
- "[…] she opened the front door and shoved us into the carport. 'And stay out!' she shouted" (Z. 8 f.)

Kinder in Bezug auf die Mutter:
- " 'One of us should get hit by a car,' I said. 'That would teach the both [*die Eltern*] of them.' " (Z. 29)
- "We wanted to send her home, to kick her out of nature just as she had kicked us out of the house, but it was hard to stay angry at someone that pitiful-looking." (Z. 50 f.)
- "[…] looking for her left shoe […] Gretchen fitted her cap over my mother's foot. Lisa secured it with her scarf, and, surrounding her tightly on all sides, we made our way home." (Z. 56 ff.)

Die Kinder werden durch die alkoholkranke Mutter vernachlässigt, die nun nicht mehr heimlich trinken kann, weil die Kinder seit Tagen schulfrei haben. Durch den Hinauswurf in den eiskalten Winternachmittag werden sie auch ernsthaft gefährdet. Andererseits haben die Kinder Mitleid mit der Mutter – sie suchen gemeinsam nach dem verlorenen Schuh, nachdem sie es ihr eigentlich heimzahlen wollten, und helfen ihr, wieder nach Hause zu kommen.

1 **TIPP**

Lesen Sie sich auch hier den Text zunächst einmal ganz durch, bevor Sie mit der Bearbeitung der Aufgaben beginnen. Überprüfen Sie dann jeweils, welche der vorgegebenen Auswahlmöglichkeiten Sie am Text belegen könnten. Manchmal wird danach gefragt, welche Information nicht im Text enthalten ist – dann ist die richtige Lösung die, zu der Sie keinen Textbeleg finden können.

Worterklärung:
Preppers: Erklärung in der einleitenden Erläuterung; Wortneuschöpfung ausgehend von *to prepare* = sich (hier: auf Katastrophen) vorbereiten

1.1 Siehe Z. 2–5: "Mocked for obsessing over doomsday scenarios [...] they are the ones having the last laugh." (*to ridicule s.o.* = sich über jmd. lustig machen)

1.2 Siehe Z. 9–11: " 'I've seen someone taking shopping from an elderly person's trolley in the supermarket and there are videos of people in fist fights over toilet paper. Panic is the paralysis of intellect [...]' "

1.3 A ist nicht in Abschnitt C zu finden.

1.4 Siehe Z. 30/31: " 'These are some of the coolest, calmest, most rational people I've ever met. For most of them it's just an insurance policy they hope never to use.' "

1.5 Siehe Z. 42: " 'Preppers are always on the lookout for trouble' " – dies stimmt zwar, aber nicht, um sich auf die Probe zu stellen („to test themselves").

1.6 Siehe Z. 54–56: "[...] he's [Garrett] confident society will learn lessons from the coronavirus." Siehe auch den gesamten Abschnitt H.

1.1 According to paragraph A, preppers have ...

A [X] been ridiculed for being too concerned about disastrous situations.

1.2 In paragraph B survivalist Shayne Phelan ...

D [X] fears that in a crisis people easily lose control and become selfish.

1.3 Which of the following tips on how to prepare for disaster cannot be found in paragraph C?

A [X] A food stock sufficient for several weeks is indispensable.

1.4 According to Dr Bradley Garret, preppers ...

C [X] act unemotionally and sensibly when preparing for potential disasters.

1.5 Which of the following does not describe Fred Deegan? He …

D [X] thinks that preppers like searching for trouble spots to test themselves.

1.6 By using the phrase "disaster is a great moment for recalibration" (paragraph H) Garrett wants to express that catastrophes …

B [X] help to re-evaluate what is important in our lives.

2 **TIPP**

Für diese Aufgabe ist nur Absatz G relevant. Lesen Sie sich diesen Abschnitt noch einmal genau durch, um zu verstehen, was die *Prepper* mit dem Ausdruck (etwa: „drei Tage reichen, um vom Menschen zum Tier zu werden") meinen und welches Beispiel dafür gegeben wird. Folgende Textstellen geben Ihnen die nötigen Hinweise:

- Z. 45/46: "Preppers use the expression '72 hours to animal' to denote the fragile peace between functioning society and all-out anarchy."
- Z. 50–52: " 'I met one prepper who told me he'd gone around to all of the neighbours' houses in the middle of the night, figured out access points into their properties and taken stock of all their supplies.' "

Die Prepper verwenden den Begriff, um zu zeigen, wie schnell in einer Krise in einem funktionierenden Gemeinwesen Anarchie ausbrechen und der Mensch zum Tier werden kann. Im Text wird das Beispiel eines Preppers genannt, der die Häuser seiner Nachbarn ausspäht, um im Bedarfsfall deren Vorräte zu plündern.

Task III: Mixed Reading Tasks (Why are Millennials and Gen Z …)

1 **TIPP**

Lesen Sie sich den Ausgangstext zunächst einmal vollständig durch, damit Sie wissen, worum es geht. Gehen Sie anschließend den Lückentext Satz für Satz durch und überfliegen Sie die Abschnitte A–E nach Wörtern, die in die Lücken passen könnten. Beachten Sie, dass Sie pro Lücke, falls nicht anders angegeben, ein Wort einfügen und dahinter die Zeile notieren, in der das Wort im Ausgangstext zu finden ist. Achten Sie auch darauf, die Form der Wörter nicht zu verändern – die Begriffe müssen also so, wie sie im Text vorkommen, in die Lücken passen. Oft können Sie bestimmte Wörter daher von vornherein ausschließen: So muss in die erste Lücke nach der Präposition „on" wahrscheinlich ein zusammengesetztes Nomen kommen, da zwei Wörter verlangt werden. In Lücke 2 ist ein direktes Objekt zu ergänzen (Was hat die Pandemie hervorgerufen?) und in Lücke 3 folgt nach „their" wieder ein Nomen. Bei Lücke 4 werden erneut zwei

Wörter verlangt – auch hier wieder zwei Nomen. Lücke 5 erfordert ein Gerund und Lücke 6 verlangt als Passivsatz ein *Past participle* nach „that were".

Over the last few years more and more young people have turned to Instagram for the news although this online service used to focus on **lifestyle content (l. 3)**. Particularly the traditional media's coverage of racial protests in the US and the Covid-19 pandemic has provoked **mistrust (l. 26)** among the young generation who started to make use of new information channels. Their wish to be provided with authentic news has radically altered the media landscape, but this change comes with strings attached.
There are worries that those vloggers and bloggers who attract the biggest audience exert the largest influence on social media platforms even if there are doubts over their **credentials (l. 17)**. And social media users tend to communicate with those who share their opinion, which might lead to **echo chambers (l. 20)**, re-affirming internet spheres of like-minded people. This phenomenon can ultimately result in a **deepening (l. 31)** of the social divide because of polarized beliefs.
On the other hand, experts point out that social media has done a lot to raise awareness about issues that were **overlooked (l. 40)** in the past. Now these issues are also addressed by long-established media, which is still influential enough to attract widespread attention.

2 **TIPP**

Bei dieser Aufgabe müssen Sie sich nur auf die Absätze F und G konzentrieren. In Aufgabe 2.1 sollen Sie eine idiomatische Wendung finden, die aufzeigt, dass soziale Medien einen großen Einfluss haben, wenn es darum geht, Informationen unter jungen Leuten zu verbreiten. Die Wendung können sie direkt aus dem Text übernehmen.
Bei Aufgabe 2.2 geht es um die Frage, worauf mediale Plattformen laut Jennifer Grygiel bisher kaum ihr Augenmerk gerichtet haben. Auch hier können Sie die Formulierung dem Text entnehmen.

2.1 hold significant sway (l. 50)

2.2 political advertisements that are harmful (ll. 56/57)

MATERIAL-BASED WRITING

Task 1

TIPP

Bei dieser Aufgabe sollen Sie einen Kommentar verfassen, wie man den Menschen, die z. B. durch die Corona-Pandemie hart getroffen worden sind, helfen kann. Immer mehr Wohltätigkeitsorganisationen bitten die Menschen, Unterstützung zu leisten, entweder indem sie Geld spenden oder ehrenamtlich tätig werden. Beachten Sie dabei, dass hierbei nicht nur Entwicklungsländer gemeint sind, sondern auch die reicheren Länder. Damit ergibt sich schon eine mögliche Gliederung: in den reichen westlichen Ländern kann man v. a. mit ehrenamtlichem Engagement helfen, während man die Menschen in Entwicklungsländern eher durch Geldspenden unterstützen kann – wobei zwar auch die unentgeltliche Hilfestellung möglich ist, dort meist aber professionelle Helfer*innen vor Ort sind.
In der **Einleitung** führen Sie kurz zum Thema hin und leiten mit der in der Aufgabe geforderten Fragestellung zum Hauptteil über. Im **Hauptteil** ordnen Sie Ihre Positionen nach Wichtigkeit, sodass die für Sie wichtigsten am Schluss stehen, da diese der Leserschaft meist besser im Gedächtnis bleiben. Im **Schlussteil** sollten Sie zusammenfassen und zu einem Urteil gelangen, ob und welche Hilfen angemessen sind.
Achten Sie unbedingt darauf, **alle drei Materialien** in Ihre Argumentation miteinzubeziehen. Am besten notieren Sie sich neben jedem Material Stichpunkte zu den Aspekten, die Sie in Ihrem Text anführen könnten. Darüber hinaus dürfen Sie natürlich auch eigenes Hintergrundwissen zum Thema einfließen lassen.
In der Beispiellösung wird zum Einstieg allgemein auf die Konsequenzen der Corona-Pandemie verwiesen. Im Hauptteil wird **Material 1** mit den beiden Aspekten „ehrenamtliche Hilfe" oder „Geldspende" verwendet und kritisch kommentiert, was bei **Material 3** in Anlehnung an **Material 2** drastisch und symbolisch unterstrichen wird.

Donating money or volunteering – how can you help people in disadvantaged circumstances?

There is no doubt that the coronavirus pandemic has shown us the value of things in life we had previously taken for granted. It also caused various economic problems not only in the rich world, but above all in developing countries, where many people had to fight for survival even before the pandemic. This aggravated their plight on top of it all. The question therefore is, how can we help people who have been hit hard in the pandemic, but also people in disadvantaged circumstances in general?

Einleitung: Hinführung zum Thema, Beispiel Corona-Pandemie

As a matter of course you can join the more than 17 million volunteers in Germany. They offer their help without being paid or expecting any other rewards. They lend a hand in vaccination centres by giving information or checking names, for example. Others become members of the Red Cross or the volunteer fire brigade in their town or village. How important their commitment is for society can be seen when their help is needed after natural disasters such as the devastating floods in Germany in the summer of 2021.

Ehrenamtliche Hilfe
Hintergrundwissen mit Bsp.
Material 1

Other support many charitable organisations ask for is donating money to people most hit by, for example, the pandemic. Although there are almost 20 million donors in Germany, the amount of money given could be much more. Isn't this a shame for a rich country like Germany with more than 80 million inhabitants? This appalling situation is impressively depicted in the cartoon, where a rich, well-dressed man, who is sitting amidst loads of banknotes, ostentatiously donates a coin into a piggy bank. He is clearly not aware of the sharp contrast between him and the poor emaciated people in developing countries. This man, who symbolises the rich West, has not really understood what Martin Luther King once asked: "What are you doing for others?"

oder Geldspenden

Material 1; mit kritischer Wertung und Hintergrundwissen

Material 3 mit Deutung

Material 2

To sum up, there are many ways to help people in dismal circumstances, either through volunteer work or by donating money more generously. *(337 words)*

Schluss:
Zusammenfassung, Aufforderung

Task 2

TIPP

Bei dieser Aufgabe sollen Sie **Gründe** darlegen, weswegen sich Menschen Tattoos stechen lassen und welche **Folgen** das in ihrem weiteren Leben haben kann. Im einführenden Satz der Aufgabenstellung wird ein Bericht der Deutschen Welle zu Tattoos bei Fußballspielern zitiert, was Ihnen einen Aufhänger für Ihre Einleitung bieten kann.
In der **Einleitung** sollten Sie kurz zum Thema hinführen. Im **Hauptteil** gliedern Sie Ihre Argumente aufsteigend nach ihrer Wichtigkeit. Im **Schlussteil** sollten Sie zusammenfassen, einen Rat geben oder einen neuen Aspekt aufzeigen.
Achten Sie unbedingt darauf, **alle drei Materialien** in Ihre Argumentation miteinzubeziehen. Am besten notieren Sie sich neben jedem Material Aspekte, die Sie daraus in Ihrem Text anführen könnten. Sie dürfen natürlich auch eigenes Hintergrundwissen zum Thema in Ihren Text einfließen lassen.

In der Beispiellösung werden zum **Einstieg** die häufig tätowierten Fußballer erwähnt. Die Umfrage in **Material 2** weitet im **Hauptteil** diese Beobachtung auf weitere Teile der Bevölkerung mit der Vermutung aus, dass „inking“ als eine Art von Kunst oder Provokation betrachtet wird bis hin zur absoluten Selbstdarstellung (**Material 1**), während z. B. bei der bayerischen Polizei Tattoos an bestimmten Stellen des Körpers grundsätzlich verboten sind (**Material 3**). Anschließend werden einige negative Folgen der Tätowierung besprochen, wie Gefährdung der Gesundheit und hohe Kosten bei einer Entfernung. Im **Schlussteil** erfolgt ein Aufruf, sich eine Tätowierung gut zu überlegen.

The reasons for tattoos and their possible consequences

When you watch professional football games, you see a lot of footballers with tattoos on their arms, legs and sometimes even on their faces. *Deutsche Welle* offers more precise details, concluding that most footballers are inked. As the players of such renowned clubs like Manchester City or Bayern Munich set an example for many, mostly young people, we could ask why people have tattoos and whether they know what consequences such adornments might have for their future lives.

Einleitung: Hinführung zum Thema mit einem Beispiel

Not only football fans but more and more "ordinary" people are getting a tattoo. According to a German survey from 2017, 45 per cent of 1 029 people of over 18 years interviewed are inked or are thinking of it.

Hauptteil: Material 2

So why do people have tattoos? These can be seen as art, as mere decoration, as a way of expressing oneself but also as a means of provocation. Actor Johnny Depp, for example, depicts important moments of his life on his skin.

Material 1

As tattooing is indeed a very personal matter, police officers in Bavaria are not allowed to have one on the visible parts of the body. This, however, seems to be justified as it is their obligation to represent the executive power in a neutral and objective way.

Verbot für Polizei Material 3

The growing number of tattooed people does not diminish the possibly negative consequences of inking, which is a kind of operation on the skin, and which should only be carried out by professionals to avoid inflammation, for example. Moreover, this kind of body art is almost permanent. If you want to get rid of it – because it does not look good any more in old age or because the circumstances of your life have changed – it may cause pain and cost a lot of money.

Konsequenzen: Hintergrundwissen

In conclusion, although tattooing may enable people to express themselves, they should bear the risks in mind. *(304 words)*

Schluss: Warnung

READING

Text I Lego to remove gender bias from its toys

(A) Lego has announced it will work to remove gender bias from its toys after a global survey the company commissioned found that attitudes to playing and future careers remain unequal and restrictive. Researchers found that while girls were becoming more confident and keen to engage in a wide range of activities, the same was not true of boys. Seventy-one per cent of boys surveyed feared they would be made fun of if they played with what they described as "girls' toys" – a fear shared by their parents. "Parents are more worried that their sons will be teased than their daughters for playing with toys associated with the other gender," said Madeline Di Nonno, the chief executive of the Geena Davis Institute on Gender in Media, who conducted the research. "But it's also that behaviours associated with men are valued more highly in society," said Di Nonno. "Until societies recognise that behaviours and activities typically associated with women are as valuable or important, parents and children will be tentative to embrace them."

(B) The study found that parents still encouraged sons to do sports or STEM[1] activities, while daughters were offered dance and dressing up (girls were five times more likely to be encouraged in these activities than boys) or baking (three times more likely to be encouraged). "These insights emphasise just how ingrained gender biases are across the globe," said Geena Davis, the Oscar winner and activist who set up the institute in 2004 to combat negative gender stereotyping and foster inclusion.

(C) "There's asymmetry," said Prof Gina Rippon, a neurobiologist and author of *The Gendered Brain*. "We encourage girls to play with 'boys' stuff' but not the other way around." This was a problem since toys offered training opportunities, she said. "So if girls aren't playing with Lego or other construction toys, they aren't developing the spatial skills that will help them in later life. If dolls are being pushed on girls but not boys, then boys are missing out on nurturing skills."

(D) The Danish toymaker commissioned the report for the UN International Day of the Girl. It surveyed almost 7,000 parents and children aged 6 to 14 from China, the Czech Republic, Japan, Poland, Russia, UK and the US. "We're working hard to make Lego more inclusive," said Julia Goldin, the chief product and marketing officer at the Lego Group, the world's largest toymaker. Since the start of 2021, the Geena Davis Institute has been auditing Lego and consulting to "address the issue of stereotyping", and the company has promised to remove gender bias from its lines.

(E) “Traditionally, Lego has been accessed by more boys, but products like Lego Dots or Lego City Wildlife Rescue Camp have been specifically designed to appeal to boys and girls,” said Goldin. The Lego mandate is now to promote social skills as well as spatial awareness, creative reasoning and problem solving. The Let Toys Be Toys campaign was launched in 2012 in the UK to put pressure on children’s brands to expand their marketing and include both genders, so that no boy or girl thinks they are playing with “the wrong toy”. But progress is slow. A 2020 report by the Fawcett Society showed how “lazy stereotyping” and the segregation of toys by gender was fuelling a mental health crisis among young people and limiting perceived career choices. It is rubbing off on parents, too. The Geena Davis Institute found that parents of both sexes rated men as “more creative”, that they were six times as likely to think of scientists and athletes as being men rather than women, and more than eight times as likely to think of engineers as men.

(F) Goldin said Lego no longer labelled any of its products “for girls” or “for boys”. On Lego.com consumers cannot search for products by gender. Instead, the website offers themes that it calls “passion points”. “We’re testing everything on boys and girls, and we’re including more women and girls as role models,” said Goldin. The recent Lego Con showcased female designers talking about the work they did, while Lego’s Rebuild the World campaign focuses on girls. “Our job now is to encourage boys and girls who want to play with sets that may have traditionally been seen as ‘not for them’,” Goldin added. *(717 words)*

1 STEM – science, technology, engineering and mathematics

Task I: Mixed Reading Tasks (Lego to remove gender bias from its toys) (8)

1 Gapped Summary (paragraphs A–D and F) (6)

Fill the gaps in the summary with appropriate words or expressions (one word per line) from the corresponding sections of the text. Do not make any changes. Please also provide the number of the line in which you have found the word/expression.

According to actress Geena Davis, stereotypes based on the question which sex you belong to are ______________________ (l.) in societies all over the world. In a large-scale study which Lego ______________________ (l.), the Geena Davies Institute has found out that playtime offers are different for boys and girls, which has implications for their professional lives.

Among boys and their parents there is still the widespread concern that boys might get ______________________ (l.) if they play with "girls' toys". According to Professor Rippon, such attitudes have a negative impact on the development of both boys and girls. By preventing them from playing with certain toys, we deprive them of ____________________ ____________________ (l.) which could help them to fully develop necessary skills for their future lives.

The Lego toy company has pledged to tackle the problem and to rid their products of any sort of ____________________ ____________________ (l.). Julia Goldin points out that in addition to not marketing their products solely to boys or girls, they want to introduce an increasing number of female ____________________ ____________________ (l.) in their product lines.

2 Mediation (Englisch–Deutsch) (paragraph E) (2)

Ergänzen Sie die fehlenden Informationen auf Deutsch.

Kompetenzen, die Lego bei Kindern fördern möchte:

- Sozialkompetenz
- Fähigkeit, Probleme zu lösen
- ____ (1)
- ____ (1)

Text II Fashion faces a stark choice: stop flogging cheap clothes or go out of style

(A) Fashion has become a dirty word – and believe me, it hurts. Not long ago, fashion was the VIP room of popular culture and movie stars and politicians flocked to the front row. Now it has come to symbolise everything that is wrong with the modern world – from carbon emissions to global inequality and from crass materialism to unrealistic beauty standards. Fashion is not the only polluting industry, or the only morally dubious one. But even if you love fashion, as I do, it's hard to deny that it tracks in the 99th percentile for pretty much all of the most problematic contemporary issues.

(B) Everyone in fashion knows that they need to get back on the right side of history, and fast. Sustainability is a baseline responsibility that every self-respecting brand must be seen to engage with. The New York brand Collina Strada last week staged one of the first live shows of the first back-to-real-life catwalk season on the rooftop of Brooklyn Grange, an organic city farm that donates 30 % of its produce to community members with limited means. Much of the collection was made out of "**deadstock**" – fabric and products that already exist, rather than being newly produced. Clothes made in 2020, which had been stuck in lockdown and never shipped or sold, were cut up and repurposed into something new. "Old birthday presents" were taken apart and reassembled into beaded bags and rhinestone jewellery, said the designer Hillary Taymour.

(C) There is a powerful business case for fashion to find its conscience: consumers increasingly demand it. Responsible production has become the hallmark of a respectable brand. To the people of Idaho, Washington and Oregon, who recently endured intense heatwaves, the fact that it takes 2,700 litres of water to produce a single cotton T-shirt in a world where droughts are becoming more common probably feels like more of an urgent issue. LVMH, the world's biggest luxury group, faces the prospect of carbon emissions from the fashion industry affecting its lucrative alcohol business. "If climate increases a couple of degrees in the next 25 years, then we simply will not be able to make champagne in Champagne anymore … our economic future depends on the climate change being reduced," wrote Antoine Arnault of LVMH in Womenswear Daily last year.

(D) Sustainability is not a new issue. What does feel very different this time around, as the industry gathers for the first shows and cocktail parties since the olden times, is **fashion's psychological state**. Establishment figures are aware that for the first time in their careers, what they do is seen as a bit, well, uncool. This year has seen a steady exodus of editors from fashion magazines to tech. Netflix recently hired editors of Allure and Them, while TikTok hired Vanessa Craft from the Canadian edition of Elle. Silicon Valley doesn't just have deep pockets: it's also seen as the place to be.

(E) This year's Met Gala was a glitzy showcase of fashion's new progressive bent. Alexandria Ocasio-Cortez's "Tax the rich" dress grabbed the headlines. Versha Sharma, editor of Teen Vogue, carried a clutch bag engraved with the words "Protect Roe/ Kill the Filibuster" in response to the Texas abortion ban. Jonathan Anderson, the British designer of the Spanish luxury house Loewe, collaborated with actor and writer Dan Levy to dress him as "a gay superhero" in a polo shirt embroidered with an artwork of two men kissing, which Levy described as a celebration "of queer love and visibility". In support of the message, Loewe made a donation to an organisation promoting Aids awareness and education.

(F) But although the emotional engagement with social justice and the climate emergency is real, action is not happening at the speed required. (As so often, fashion reflects the rest of the world in this – just in a more exaggerated and exasperating form.) There is still far too much talk of raising awareness around sustainability, which with less than three months to go until Cop26[1] is like **closing the stable doors after the horse has bolted**. A new report on greenwashing, published this week by Eco-Age and the Geneva Centre for Business and Human Rights, reports that while "all major fashion brands claim to be engaged in sustainability efforts [...] many are struggling and indeed failing, because they are using a flawed definition of sustainability, unscientific methods and selective implementation". The report also identifies greenwishing – fancying oneself less environmentally harmful than one is in reality – to be a problem in fashion.

(G) By producing too many clothes, the fashion industry has not just harmed the climate, it has also undermined its own status. A dress in the new season silhouette or a pair of boots in autumn's hot new shade were once aspirational objects. But a two-decade deluge of cheap-as-chips items has left the world disdainful of clothes – and, as a result, tired of fashion. Fashion faces a stark choice: keep flogging cheap clothes, or get back in vogue. *(833 words)*

Fashion faces a stark choice: stop flogging cheap clothes or go out of style by Jess Carter-Morley, The Guardian, September 16, 2021 Copyright Guardian News & Media Ltd 2022

1 Cop26 – 26th UN Climate Change Conference in Glasgow (2021)

Task II: Mixed Reading Tasks (Fashion faces a stark choice ...) (8)

1 Multiple Choice (7)

Mark the most suitable option by crossing (✗) the appropriate letter.

1.1 According to the first paragraph, the fashion industry ...

- **A** ☐ is responsible for 99 % of all 21st century problems.
- **B** ☐ displays an increasing environmental awareness.
- **C** ☐ turns a blind eye on many contemporary challenges.
- **D** ☐ is a showcase for most of today's global issues.

1.2 The word "deadstock" in paragraph B refers to clothes and items that are ...

- **A** ☐ of animal origin.
- **B** ☐ organic.
- **C** ☐ surplus.
- **D** ☐ recycled.

1.3 Which of the following is NOT mentioned as a reason for the fashion industry to become more sustainable in paragraph C?

A ☐ Pressure from environmentalists.

B ☐ Satisfying customers.

C ☐ The more and more tangible effects of climate change.

D ☐ Securing economic success.

1.4 "Fashion's psychological state" (paragraph D) could be best described by:

A ☐ From hero to zero.

B ☐ The show must go on.

C ☐ The winner takes it all.

D ☐ Not all that glitters is gold.

1.5 The Met Gala was NOT used to address …

A ☐ LGBTQ+ issues.

B ☐ the redistribution of wealth.

C ☐ women's reproductive rights.

D ☐ implications of fast fashion.

1.6 The metaphor "**closing the stable doors after the horse has bolted**" (paragraph F) illustrates the fact that the fashion industry …

A ☐ is not just paying lip service.

B ☐ finally lives up to its commitments.

C ☐ acts far too hesitantly.

D ☐ has set itself overly ambitious goals.

1.7 The general tone of the text can best be described as …

A ☐ cautionary.

B ☐ desperate.

C ☐ outraged.

D ☐ satirical.

2 Short-Answer Question (paragraph F) (1)

Which **word** expresses the fact that the fashion industry considers itself more sustainable than it actually is?

___

Text III One of us is lying

'One of us is lying' is the story of what happens when five strangers walk into detention and only four walk out alive. Everyone is a suspect and everyone has something to hide.

1 A sex tape. A pregnancy scare. Two cheating scandals. And that's just this week's update. If all you knew of Bayview High was Simon Kelleher's gossip app, you'd wonder how anyone found time to go to class.

"Old news, Bronwyn," says a voice over my shoulder. "Wait till you see tomorrow's post."

Damn. I hate getting caught reading *About That,* especially by its creator. I lower my phone and slam my locker shut. "Whose lives are you ruining next, Simon?" Simon falls into step beside me as I move against the flow of students heading for the exit. "It's a public service," he says with a dismissive wave. "You tutor Reggie Crawley, don't you? Wouldn't you rather know he has a camera in his bedroom?"

I don't bother answering. Me getting anywhere near the bedroom of perpetual stoner Reggie Crawley is about as likely as Simon growing a conscience.

"Anyway, they bring it on themselves. […]" Simon's cold blue eyes take in my lengthening strides. "Where are you rushing off to? Covering yourself in extracurricular glory?" […]

"Not exactly," I say. As a general rule, and especially lately, I try to give Simon as little information as possible. […] Simon's still on my heels when I reach Mr. Avery's lab on the third floor, and I half turn with my arms crossed. "Don't you have someplace to be?"

"Yeah. Detention," Simon says, and waits for me to keep walking. When I grasp the knob instead, he bursts out laughing. "You're kidding me. You too? What's your crime?"

"I'm wrongfully accused," I mutter, and yank the door open. Three other students are already seated, and I pause to take them in. Not the group I would have predicted. Except one. Nate Macauley tips his chair back and smirks at me. "You make a wrong turn? This is detention, not student council."

He should know. Nate's been in trouble since fifth grade, which is right around the time we last spoke. The gossip mill tells me he's on probation with Bayview's finest for … something. It might be a DUI[1]; it might be drug dealing. He's a notorious supplier, but my knowledge is purely theoretical. […]

I take a seat as Cooper Clay, who's palming a crumpled piece of paper like a baseball, whispers "Heads up, Addy" and tosses it toward the girl across from him. Addy Prentiss blinks, smiles uncertainly, and lets the ball drop to the floor.

The classroom clock inches toward three, and I follow its progress with a helpless feeling of injustice. I shouldn't even be here. […]

Mr. Avery is a give-detention-first, ask-questions-never kind of guy, but maybe there's still time to change his mind. I clear my throat and start to raise my hand until I notice

Nate's smirk broadening. "Mr. Avery, that wasn't my phone you found. I don't know how it got into my bag. This is mine," I say, brandishing my iPhone in its melon-striped case.

Honestly, you'd have to be clueless to bring a phone to Mr. Avery's lab. He has a strict no-phone policy and spends the first ten minutes of every class rooting through backpacks like he's head of airline security and we're all on the watch list. My phone was in my locker, like always.

"You too?" Addy turns to me so quickly, her blond shampoo-ad hair swirls around her shoulders. **She must have been surgically removed from her boyfriend** in order to show up alone. "That wasn't my phone either."

"Me three," Cooper chimes in. His Southern accent makes it sound like 'thray'. He and Addy exchange surprised looks, and I wonder how this is news to them when they're part of the same clique. Maybe überpopular people have better things to talk about than unfair detentions.

"Somebody punked us!" Simon leans forward with his elbows on the desk, looking spring-loaded and ready to pounce on fresh gossip. His gaze darts over all four of us, clustered in the middle of the otherwise empty classroom, before settling on Nate. "Why would anybody want to trap a bunch of students with mostly spotless records in detention? Seems like the sort of thing that, oh, I don't know, a guy who's here all the time might do for fun."

I look at Nate, but can't picture it. Rigging detention sounds like work, and everything about Nate – from his messy dark hair to his ratty leather jacket – screams Can't be bothered. Or yawns it, maybe. He meets my eyes but doesn't say a word, just tips his chair back even farther. Another millimeter and he'll fall right over.

Cooper sits up straighter, a frown crossing his Captain America face. "Hang on. I thought this was just a mix-up, but if the same thing happened to all of us, it's somebody's stupid idea of a prank. And I'm missing baseball practice because of it." He says it like he's a heart surgeon being detained from a lifesaving operation.

Mr. Avery rolls his eyes. "Save the conspiracy theories for another teacher. I'm not buying it. You all know the rules against bringing phones to class, and you broke them." […] *(889 words, abridged and adapted)*

Karen McManus, One of us is lying, Delacorte Press, New York, 2017, pp. 3–7

1 DUI – the crime of driving a vehicle after drinking too much alcohol or taking drugs

Task III: Mixed Reading Tasks (One of us is lying) (8)

1 Multiple Matching (5)

Decide **who** could have made **which statement** based on the information from the text. Choose the most suitable match and complete the grid below – **one number/statement per person**.

Please note: There are two more statements than you need.

Person	Statement
Bronwyn	
Simon	
Cooper	
Nate	
Mr. Avery	

Statements:	
1	Wait until my dad hears about this – he'll teach you a lesson.
2	I won't be fooled by lame excuses.
3	I have never taken any illicit drugs in my life.
4	It's so annoying – this will mess with my performance.
5	I really don't give a damn about any of this.
6	My academic achievements are so underappreciated at this school.
7	If people didn't lie and cheat, I'd be out of business.

2 Mediation (Englisch–Deutsch) (3)

Beantworten Sie die folgenden Fragen auf Deutsch.

2.1 Was sagt der folgende Satz über die Beziehung zwischen Addy und ihrem Freund aus? (Anmerkung: keine wörtliche Übersetzung!) (1)

"She must have been surgically removed from her boyfriend […]." (l. 46)

____

____

2.2 Wie reagiert Mr. Avery auf die Behauptung der Schüler, ihnen seien Mobiltelefone „untergejubelt" worden? (2)

- ____
- ____

MATERIAL-BASED WRITING

Choose ONE of the following tasks (1 or 2) and write at least 300 words.

Task 1 (24)

People's food choices have increasingly become a controversial issue.
How can we make the world a better place by changing our eating habits?

Write a **composition** of **at least 300 words**. Include information from **all** the material provided.

Material 1

"Respect for food is respect for life."

Thomas Keller, American chef and author

Material 2

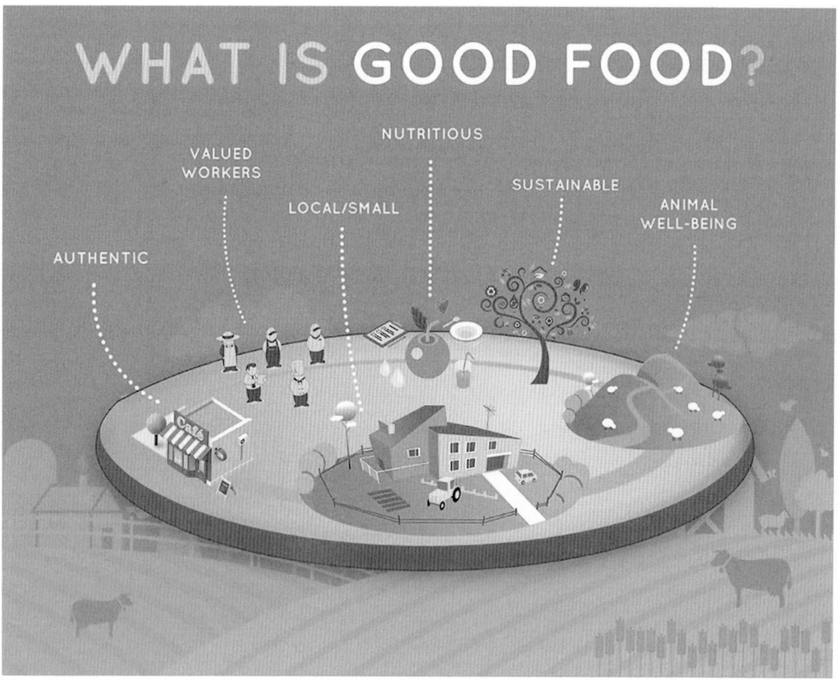

http://lbfresh.org/news/long-beach-fresh-releases-policy-agenda/ (13.12.21)

Material 3

MÖGLICHE FOLGEN DES FLEISCHKONSUMS

Zwar wird nicht jeder Mensch krank, der viel Fleisch isst. Aber zahlreiche Krankheitsbilder werden durch hohen Fleischkonsum mit verursacht oder verschlimmert, z. B. Darmkrebs, Diabetes, Herz-Kreislauf-Erkrankungen und Rheuma.

Eine Verharmlosung des Fleischverzehrs halten Experten für verantwortungslos – zumal der Durchschnittsverzehr in Deutschland mit rund 60 Kilogramm pro Jahr relativ hoch ist. Selbst die sehr konservative Deutsche Gesellschaft für Ernährung empfiehlt maximal 300 Gramm pro Woche, also 15 Kilogramm im Jahr.

Andere Experten raten komplett von Wurst und Schinken ab und empfehlen allenfalls einen geringen Fleischverzehr einmal pro Woche. Dafür sollten jeden Tag 400 Gramm Gemüse auf dem Speiseplan stehen.

https://www.ndr.de/ratgeber/gesundheit/Wie-ungesund-ist-Fleisch,fleisch564.html (07.10.21; gekürzt)

Task 2 **(24)**

The era of a new space race among billionaires is dawning.

Discuss opportunities and downsides associated with commercial space travel.

Write a **composition** of **at least 300 words**. Include information from **all** the material provided.

Material 1

> "We need some of the world's greatest brains and minds fixed on trying to repair this planet, not trying to find the next place to go and live."
>
> *Prince William, Duke of Cambridge*

Material 2

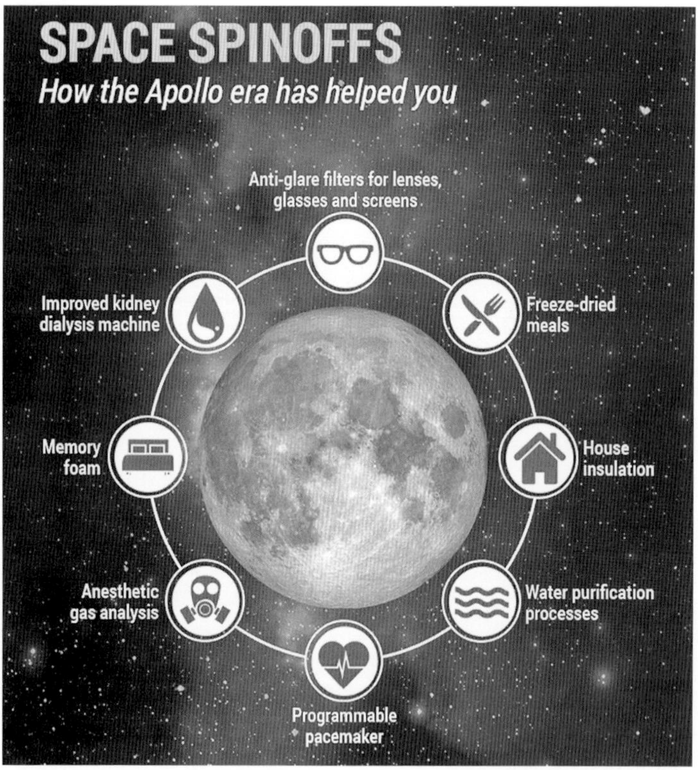

© *Nasa.gov*

The Apollo programme = US space programme to put people on the moon

Material 3

[…] Tatsächlich könnte Weltraumtourismus bei den Reisenden ein neues Bewusstsein für unsere Erde schaffen – und sogar Klimaschutz und internationalen Zusammenhalt fördern.

Das ist zumindest der Effekt, den die Raumfahrt auf Astronauten zu haben scheint. Die Erde aus der „Vogelperspektive" zu sehen, macht offenbar etwas mit einem. Fast alle Astronauten berichten davon, wie sich ihre Einstellung zu ihrem Planeten durch die Sicht auf diesen aus dem Weltall heraus verändert.

Dies nennt man den „Overview-Effekt". Es bezieht sich auf den Effekt, nachdem man zum ersten Mal die Erde vom Weltraum aus sieht. Der Overview-Effekt bezieht sich darauf, dass die Sicht unseres Planeten aus dem All auch unsere Einstellung zur Erde verändert.

Es setzt ein Gefühl der Ehrfurcht ein. Man spürt eine neue Verbundenheit zum Planeten […], ein neues Einheitsgefühl mit allen Menschen. Den Planeten als Ganzes zu sehen, zeigt, dass es kein „uns" und kein „sie" gibt, sondern nur ein „wir".

Marinela Potor, https://www.basicthinking.de/blog/2020/05/26/weltraumtourismus-klima/ (12.11.2021; gekürzt)

Lösungen

READING

Task I: Mixed Reading Tasks (Lego to remove gender bias from its toys)

1 **TIPP**

Für das Aufgabenformat „Gapped Summary“ müssen Sie im Ausgangstest nur die Absätze A–D und F lesen. Lesen Sie diese aufmerksam durch und sehen Sie sich danach den Lückentext an. Wie in der Aufgabestellung angegeben, sollen die fehlenden Wörter direkt dem Ausgangstext entnommen werden (pro Lücke ein Wort). Beachten Sie, dass der Lückentext nicht immer mit der Reihenfolge im Text übereinstimmt. Denke Sie auch daran, die entsprechende Zeile anzugeben.

Worterklärungen:
ingrained – tief sitzend/tief verwurzelt
to commission sth – etw. in Auftrag geben
to tease sb – jmd. hänseln, aufziehen
gender bias – geschlechtsbezogene Vorurteile

According to actress Geena Davis, stereotypes based on the question which sex you belong to are **ingrained (l. 17)** in societies all over the world. In a large-scale study which Lego **commissioned (l. 2)**, the Geena Davies Institute has found out that playtime offers are different for boys and girls, which has implications for their professional lives.
Among boys and their parents there is still the widespread concern that boys might get **teased (l. 7)** if they play with "girls' toys". According to Professor Rippon, such attitudes have a negative impact on the development of both boys and girls. By preventing them from playing with certain toys, we deprive them of **training opportunities (l. 22)** which could help them to fully develop necessary skills for their future lives.
The Lego toy company has pledged to tackle the problem and to rid their products of any sort of **gender bias (ll. 1/32)**. Julia Goldin points out that in addition to not marketing their products solely to boys or girls, they want to introduce an increasing number of female **role models (l. 49)** in their product lines.

2 **TIPP**

Hier ist nur Absatz E heranzuziehen. Die Lösung findet sich in Zeile 35/36: es kommen noch „spatial awareness“ und „creative reasoning“ hinzu.

- **räumliches Vorstellungsvermögen**
- **kreatives Denken**

1 **TIPP**

Lesen Sie den Text zunächst einmal ganz durch, bevor Sie mit der Bearbeitung der Aufgabe beginnen. Überprüfen Sie dann für jede *Multiple Choice*-Aufgabe, welche der vorgegebenen Auswahlmöglichkeiten Sie am Text belegen können. Manchmal wird danach gefragt, welche Information nicht im Text enthalten ist – dann ist die richtige Lösung die, zu der es keinen Textbeleg gibt.

1.1 "[…] [fashion] tracks in the 99th percentile for pretty much all of the most problematic contemporary issues." (Z. 6/7); lassen Sie sich hier nicht von den in Lösung A erwähnten 99 % verunsichern – die Modeindustrie ist nicht für 99 % aller Probleme auf der Welt verantwortlich, sondern in ihr zeigen sich ("is a showcase for") fast alle Probleme, die die Welt gegenwärtig hat: "… has come to symbolise everything that is wrong with the modern world …" (Z. 3/4)

1.2 "Much of the collection was made out of 'deadstock' – fabric and products that already exist, rather than being newly produced. Clothes made in 2020, which had been stuck in lockdown and never shipped or sold, were cut up and repurposed into something new." (Z. 13–16)

1.3 Druck von Seiten von Umweltschützer*innen wird nicht erwähnt, die anderen Punkte jedoch schon: "There is a powerful business case for fashion to find its conscience: consumers increasingly demand it." (Z. 18/19), "… it takes 2,700 litres of water to produce a single cotton T-shirt in a world where droughts are becoming more common …" (Z. 21/22), "'... our economic future depends on the climate change being reduced' …" (Z. 26/27)

1.4 "Establishment figures are aware that for the first time in their careers, what they do is seen as a bit, well, uncool. This year has seen a steady exodus of editors from fashion magazines to tech." (Z. 31–33)

1.5 Die Met Gala wurde nicht als Bühne benutzt, um auf die Folgen von *Fast Fashion* aufmerksam zu machen. Die anderen Punkte werden jedoch erwähnt: "… to dress him as 'a gay superhero' … celebration of 'queer love and visibility'" (Z. 41–43), "Alexandria Ocasio-Cortez's 'Tax the rich' dress grabbed the headlines." (Z. 37), "… carried a clutch bag engraved with the words 'Protect Roe/Kill the Filibuster' in response to the Texas abortion ban." (Z. 38/39)
abortion = Abtreibung; *reproductive rights* = reproduktive Rechte/Rechte im Bereich der Fortpflanzung; das Urteil „Roe vs. Wade", das bis 2022 in den USA bundesweit das Recht auf Abtreibung garantierte, wurde vom Supreme Court aufgehoben.

1.6 "There is still far too much talk of raising awareness around sustainability, which with less than three months to go until Cop26 is like closing the stable doors after the horse has bolted." (Z. 48–50); anstatt zu handeln, wird zu viel geredet, während die Zeit knapp wird – die Modeindustrie ist also zu zögerlich („hesitant"), was die Umsetzung ihrer Umweltziele betrifft (im Deutschen etwa: „Das Kind ist schon in den Brunnen gefallen.").

1.7 Der warnende („cautionary") Ton wird v. a. im letzten Absatz (G) deutlich sowie durch die Gegenüberstellung von Überschrift und letztem Satz, in denen die Modeindustrie davor gewarnt wird, so weiter zu machen wie bisher, da sie sonst bedeutungslos würde: "... stop flogging cheap clothes or go out of style" – "... keep flogging cheap clothes, or get back in vogue"
to flog = hier: verscheuern, verscherbeln

1.1 According to the first paragraph, the fashion industry …

D ☒ is a showcase for most of today's global issues.

1.2 The word "deadstock" in paragraph B refers to clothes and items that are …

C ☒ surplus.

1.3 Which of the following is NOT mentioned as a reason for the fashion industry to become more sustainable in paragraph C?

A ☒ Pressure from environmentalists.

1.4 "Fashion's psychological state" (paragraph D) could be best described by …

A ☒ From hero to zero.

1.5 The Met Gala was NOT used to address …

D ☒ implications of fast fashion.

1.6 The metaphor "closing the stable doors after the horse has bolted" (paragraph F) illustrates the fact that the fashion industry …

C ☒ acts far too hesitatingly.

1.7 The general tone of the text can best described as …

A ☒ cautionary

2 **TIPP**

Das Wort „greenwishing“ ist von „greenwashing“ (sich mit eigentlich unzureichenden Maßnahmen ökologisch reinwaschen) abgeleitet und drückt aus, dass sich die Modeindustrie für nachhaltiger hält, als sie tatsächlich ist: “A new report on greenwashing … reports that while ‘all major fashion brands claim to be engaged in sustainability efforts … many are struggling and indeed failing, because they are using a flawed definition of sustainability, unscientific methods and selective implementation’. The report also identifies greenwishing – fancying oneself less environmentally harmful than one is in reality – to be a problem in fashion.” (Z. 50–55)

Lösung: **greenwishing**

Task III: Mixed Reading Tasks (One of us is lying)

1 **TIPP**

Der Text ist aus der Sicht von Bronwyn verfasst und in unverblümtem Jugendslang geschrieben (z. B. „überpopular“), der evtl. nicht immer leicht zu verstehen ist. Dennoch wird der Sinnzusammenhang verständlich: eine Gruppe Schüler*innen muss nachsitzen („detention“), weil sie (angeblich) verbotenerweise ihre Handys in Mr. Averys Unterricht mitgenommen haben. Es empfiehlt sich, jeden der fünf Namen im Text mit verschiedenen Farben zu markieren und Belege für die einzelnen Statements im Text zu finden. Wenn Ihnen nicht gleich auf Anhieb eine Zuordnung gelingt, versuchen Sie stattdessen mit dem nächsten Statement weiterzumachen und damit die Antwortmöglichkeiten einzugrenzen. Zwei der sieben Statements können nicht zugeordnet werden.

Bronwyn: *I have never taken any illicit drugs in my life.* (**3**): “… it might be drug dealing. [Nate's] a notorious supplier, but my knowledge is purely theoretical.” (Z. 29/30) – man kann hier also indirekt erschließen, dass Bronwyn noch nie Drogen gekauft bzw. genommen hat (“knowlegde is purely theoretical”).

Simon: *If people didn't lie and cheat, I'd be out of business.* (**7**): “… Simon Kelleher's gossip app …” (Z. 2); “… I hate getting caught reading *About That,* especially by its creator …‘Whose lives are you ruining next, Simon?’” (Z. 6/7); Simons Klatsch-App lebt davon, dass andere lügen und betrügen.

Cooper: *It's so annoying – this will mess with my performance.* (**4**): “‘… And I'm missing baseball practice because of it.’ He says it like he's a heart surgeon being detained from a lifesaving operation.” (Z. 64/65)

Nate: *I really don't give a damn about any of this.* (**5**): “… Can't be bothered. Or yawns it, maybe …” (Z. 59/60)

Mr. Avery: *I won't be fooled by lame excuses.* (**2**): “Mr. Avery rolls his eyes. ‘Save the conspiracy theories for another teacher. I'm not buying it …’” (Z. 66/67)

Person	Statement
Bronwyn	3
Simon	7
Cooper	4
Nate	5
Mr. Avery	2

2 **TIPP**

2.1 Sie sollen hier den (sarkastisch gemeinten) Satz nicht einfach übersetzen, sondern erklären, was damit über die Beziehung zwischen Addy und ihrem Freund ausgesagt wird; *surgically removed* = operativ getrennt

2.2 Hier sollen Sie die Reaktion von Mr. Avery auf die Behauptung der Schüler*innen, ihnen seien Mobiltelefone untergeschoben worden, beschreiben, wobei zwei Aspekte zu nennen sind. In den Zeilen 41–44 wird zwar Mr. Averys ablehnende Haltung gegenüber Handys im Unterricht dargestellt, seine Reaktion auf die Behauptung der Schüler aber erst in den Zeilen 66–68.

2.1 Addy und ihr Freund scheinen unzertrennlich zu sein, (sodass es schon besonderer Maßnahmen bedarf, dass Addy einmal irgendwo allein erscheint.)

2.2
- Er glaubt den Schüler*innen ihre „Verschwörungstheorien" nicht.
- Er weist auf das Handyverbot im Unterricht hin, an das sie sich nicht gehalten haben.

MATERIAL-BASED WRITING

Task 1

TIPP

Bei dieser Aufgabe sollen Sie auf die Frage eingehen, inwiefern veränderte Essgewohnheiten die Welt zu einem besseren Ort machen können. Diese Frage ist gerade im Zusammenhang mit der Erderwärmung immer mehr in den Fokus von Diskussionen geraten, berührt aber natürlich auch Fragen der Gesundheit und des Tierwohls angesichts der Massentierhaltung.
Der „Comment" ist in steigernder Form anzugehen, wobei das für Sie wichtigste Argument an das Ende Ihrer Ausführungen rücken sollte, weil es den stärksten Eindruck machen soll.
Achten Sie unbedingt darauf, **alle drei Materialien** in Ihre Argumentation miteinzubeziehen. Am besten notieren Sie sich vor dem Verfassen Ihres Textes neben jedem Material Stichpunkte, welchen Aspekt Sie daraus in Ihrem Text anführen könnten. Darüber hinaus dürfen Sie natürlich auch eigenes Wissen zum Thema einfließen lassen. Denken Sie auch daran, die geforderte **Textlänge** von mindestens 300 Wörtern **einzuhalten**.

How can we make the world a better place by changing our eating habits?

What people eat has become a contentious topic as far as health, the well-being of animals and the environment is concerned. The question is how can we make the world a better place by changing our eating habits?

Einleitung: zu behandelnde Aspekte des Themas

To begin with, discount stores and supermarkets dispose of considerable quantities of foodstuff that have already passed their best before-date, although they would last much longer. In private households, food is thrown away as well, either because too much was bought and therefore surpasses its shelf life, or people do not like it anymore. With regard to food shortage in poorer parts of the world this is a shocking disregard of how precious food is.

Hauptteil: Lebensmittelverschwendung: Hintergrundwissen

Material 1

It is therefore essential that food production becomes more sustainable when it comes to people's health. We should be able to produce food without using chemical fertilizers, for example, which may spoil the groundwater and poison our drinking water.

Material 2 Nachhaltigkeit Hintergrundwissen: Gesundheitsgefahren

Another aspect concerning people's health is too much consumption of any kind of meat, be it beef, bacon or chicken. Nutritionists advise Germans should eat four times less meat per week for health reasons as otherwise they may become susceptible to cancer, diabetes or heart problems. High meat consumption is also connected to factory farming with animals being kept in appalling conditions. Instead of encouraging local and small production, politics promotes intensive livestock farming and farmers believe they would not be able to make ends meet otherwise.

Fleischkonsum
Material 3

Tierwohl
Material 2
Hintergrund-
wissen

Last but not least, if people eat less beef, less cattle would be bred, which – so experts say – would reduce the amount of toxic methane gas the cattle release, which can be even more harmful than CO_2.

Rinderzucht und
Erderwärmung
Hintergrund-
wissen; Material 2

To conclude, people should become more aware of the fact that conscious eating habits will improve their own well-being and that of animals and contribute to the limitation of global warming.

Schluss:
Zusammen-
fassung

(309 words)

Task 2

TIPP

Lesen Sie zunächst die Aufgabenstellung genau durch. In der vorliegenden Aufgabe sollen Sie der Frage nachgehen, ob kommerziell betriebene Weltraumreisen Chancen eröffnen oder aber auch negative Folgen haben können.
Sehen Sie sich als Nächstes die vorgegebenen **Materialien** an. Prüfen Sie, welche Informationen im Hinblick auf die Aufgabenstellung besonders relevant sind. Achten Sie auch darauf, **alle drei Materialien** in ihre Argumentation einzubauen, ohne sie wörtlich zu übernehmen. Zusätzlich zu den Materialien können Sie auch auf eigenes Hintergrundwissen zum Thema zurückgreifen.
Die **Gliederung** ist insofern schon vorgegeben, als Sie auf Chancen und negative Folgen („opportunities and downsides“) der kommerziellen Raumfahrt eingehen sollen. Sie können schrittweise oder blockweise dialektisch vorgehen. Die schrittweise Vorgehensweise (bei jedem Argument gleich das Gegenargument zu bringen) verlangt jedoch größere sprachliche Wendigkeit. Der folgende Lösungsvorschlag bevorzugt die blockweise Variante.

Opportunities and downsides associated with commercial space travel.

It has become a hobby of billionaires, among them Tesla's Elon Musk, to start a private space industry to launch rockets into orbit and further into space. Thus, a new kind of space travel seems to come into sight. The question therefore is if commercial space tourism is just an expensive hobby with downsides or if everyone would be able to profit from it.

Einleitung:
Hinführung zum
Thema: Elon
Musk
Hintergrund-
wissen

Public reactions to this issue have been very controversial indeed. On the one hand, there are comments that urgently advise to concentrate on fighting the global threats we face here on Earth. This is what Prince William's serious warning is about: focusing on the needs of our planet instead of looking for new places to live somewhere else in space. We need to take action here on Earth to slow down global warming, which leads to food and water shortages, flooding and extreme heat, and so threatens the livelihood of millions of people.

Haupteil:
Negative Aspekte
Material 1

Hintergrundwissen

On the other hand, in the past, developing spacecraft and rockets for the Apollo space missions has, for example, also helped to create products that are useful for everyone, like house insulation, which may considerably contribute to saving energy – and in countries with freshwater scarcity systems of water purification can save lives.

Positive Aspekte
Material 2
Hintergrundwissen

What is also important is that commercial space travel could raise awareness about the vulnerability of our precious little blue planet if you look at it from a bird's eye view in outer space.

Material 3

Despite these benefits of space travel, it is not easy to come to a conclusion, because if commercial space travel grows to something like mass-tourism the downsides might prevail – and isn't it enough if professional astronauts provide breathtaking views of our globe to generate a common feeling of responsibility for the planet we all live on and which we should preserve? *(304 words)*

Schluss:
Kritische Abwägung
Anregung

Um Ihnen die Prüfung 2023 schnellstmöglich zur Verfügung stellen zu können, bringen wir sie in digitaler Form heraus.

Sobald die Original-Prüfungsaufgaben 2023 freigegeben sind, können sie als PDF auf der Plattform **MyStark** heruntergeladen werden (Zugangscode vgl. vordere Umschlaginnenseite).

Aktuelle Prüfung

www.stark-verlag.de/mystark